Love
and
Genetic Weaponry

Love

and

Genetic Weaponry

THE BEGINNER'S GUIDE

A Ray O'Brien Mystery

by

Lee Patton

ALYSON*books*

© 2009 by Lee Patton
All Rights Reserved

Manufactured in the United States of America

This trade paperback original is published by Alyson Books
245 West 17th Street, New York, NY 10011
Distribution in the United Kingdom by Turnaround Publisher Services Ltd.
Unit 3, Olympia Trading Estate, Coburg Road, Wood Green
London N22 6TZ England

First Edition: April 2009

09 10 11 12 13 14 15 16 17 a 10 9 8 7 6 5 4 3 2 1

ISBN-10: 1-59350-123-4
ISBN-13: 978-1-59350-123-5

Library of Congress Cataloging-in-Publication data are on file.

Cover design by Victor Mingovits
Interior design by Charles Annis

For Jeremy and Patty

ACKNOWLEDGMENTS

I'm grateful to all readers of the earliest version of this novel, including James T. Kahn, Patricia Mosco Holloway, Mell McDonnell, and Edna Doherty for their comments and guidance, and to Lake Lopez and Chris Kenry for their insights on the next version. I owe an enormous debt to Jeremy Cole for his close reading of the third version. Special thanks to my agent, Alison Picard, and my editor, Leslie Feinberg. Residencies at the MacDowell Colony, Ucross Foundation, and the Anderson Center continue to inspire me.

PROLOGUE

Knotted around the dead driver's throat, a silver scarf flapped in an upstream breeze. The body and the convertible were stuck, stranded in urban white water.

Caught on camera from a bridge ten blocks from my house, the image tantalized Denver's waking eyes. The city sipped Sunday morning coffee to reports the driver had partied at a foothills mansion. In the city's heart, twenty miles from the driver's suburban home, the ancient convertible had leapt from Speer Boulevard into Cherry Creek's artificial rapids.

When the old roadster took flight from the boulevard, it left no tread on the roadway. No brake-slammed tires clawed the creekside lawn. An investigation later discovered a puncture in the brake cylinders, the result, we'd later be told, of a shoddy brake job. The driver, we'd be told, had been under the influence of alcohol.

Denverites would be led to accept these rumors through frenetic news reports. The convertible had landed under creekside headquarters for News7 and NewsChannel 9. Equidistant between them, with Cherry Creek forming the boulevard's median, the old convertible appeared to ride the rapids. Heading to work at dawn on opposite banks, channel 7 and 9 employees first sighted the attractive corpse. The long scarf, struggling like a fallen angel's single wing, was irresistible to cameras.

Yet despite the overblown coverage, the mystery lived so briefly as to be aborted. Almost as soon as questions could be raised, the motorist's identity was established—the "housemate" of a biologist at the party—and the brakes blamed. By evening, the lead story on both channels switched to a college football coach's resignation; a famous homophobe, he planned to direct Jocks for Jesus, Inc.

My curiosity about the driver's fate should have been just as fleeting, my pity as shallow as a local "breaking story." Despite my hangover, I needed to concentrate on the media's spin while appearing to be just another curious neighborhood guy on the banks of Cherry Creek. I knew what I jokingly referred to as my life was about to warp into crisis.

The scarf-trailing corpse was no angel. I wasn't either. In fact, I'd crashed that same foothills company party and behaved so badly that I escaped it with the driver, who gave me a ride to my city duplex in that convertible. After dropping me off, the driver proceeded alone for the final ten blocks to the creek. In all likelihood, after we kissed, I was the last person to see the love of my life alive.

CHAPTER ONE

Though it's not proper for a gay man, I got mixed up with a woman. My misadventure with Lottie Weiss actually began days before that Cherry Creek crash, and by the time I became aware of my ex's death, I was already deeply involved.

I had no idea that Lottie's orbit and mine had intersected years before. All that summer, just before I actually met her, death had begun to stalk my life, driving me to Lottie.

In late May my ex's mother, the woman I still referred to as my "mother-in-law," died with surreal swiftness. Nadia Sanchez barely had the chance to read the card I sent to celebrate her promotion at a research laboratory. It wasn't that the mail was slow. In weeks, as tumors wracked her nervous system, Nadia shrank from triathlete to comatose, wheezing skeleton.

Unable to face her absence, I plunged into self-deceit. I pretended that if I left her name unbothered in my address book, Nadia would still deliver her home-brew plum brandy in time for Dia de los Muertos. If I never deleted her number, I could call Nadia out of the blue and coax her to tell the old joke about how many CEOs it takes to achieve sexual congress with a jackass.

It had been Nadia's financial advice that led me to Lottie in the first place, via a concept almost as inscrutable as death: real estate. A rabid leftist, an environmental justice activist, yet good with money, Nadia became my fiscal mentor and counseled me to invest wisely and shelter my taxes. After my breakup with her son, she urged me to supplement my teacher's salary with rental income. Nadia thought I could afford a government-repossessed house.

Two months after Nadia's funeral, still stunned, delusional in the wake of her rapid decline and death, I believed I could inhabit her wisdom. I decided to sample the repo home market. It would be a tribute to Nadia for all her help rescuing my ex and me from those years of financial snares. Seeing myself as her flesh-and-blood agent, I checked the newspapers' repossessed homes listings and spent the last Sunday morning in July mapping out a tour of open houses.

Each house I visited seemed haunted by some recent evacuation. Brown mysteries stained orange Formica. Disembodied doll's arms wrestled with thistles in dying lawns. Instead of channeling Nadia's business savvy, I felt like what I was, a dope, an impostor, a white guy on the make, blundering into the only squalor I could afford. On one imploding triplex, ABORT ALL EARTHLINGS was sprayed across the roof in neon red.

One block had five repossessed houses squatting in a row. Four were festooned with balloons and streamers to disguise their chintziness. I became drawn to the last, unfestive mini-ranchette, forlorn by itself on the corner. Instead of crepe paper, it had a blonde sitting behind a card table in the driveway. She smiled when I approached, shoving pamphlets closer to the table's edge. She was too engrossed in her book, though, to bother with a verbal pitch.

I picked up a pamphlet and followed her arm's vague gesture to the front door, where I turned to look back at her. This agent was not only uncommonly attractive, but uncommonly careless with her appearance—big, shapeless T-shirt, long denim skirt, running shoes. She turned to catch my stare, peering at me over her sunglasses. "I should warn you," she said. "Hold your nose. It stinks in there."

This shocked a laugh from me. She laughed, too, then shrugged and returned to her book. Inside the house, I was sorry to learn she wasn't joking. Picking my steps over dark spots on lime shag carpet, I glanced at the pamphlet, surprised to see it offered no information about this house or any other. Instead, it was one of the familiar flyers that had littered Denver that summer. A young woman's face, sullen and defiant at once, stared up from the front page over the slogan:

FREE BRANDY MCONNAUGHTY,
AMERICA'S PRISONER OF CONSCIENCE

I stuffed the flyer in my back pocket, toured the four rooms in quick minutes, then passed into the backyard. A crow cackled in a dying sumac tree. Across the roof of an empty rabbit hutch, some entrepreneur had sprayed NEED SPEED? to airborne meth freaks.

Shelter my taxes? What about the family who'd have to take shelter under this hail-pocked roof? I blushed to think of accepting their money. I pictured myself at the courthouse when my tenants' child got falsely accused of running a meth lab in the bunny hutch.

Sweet baby Jesus, I was a bleeding-heart, queer theater teacher who could barely manage a school budget spreadsheet. What made me think, even with the agency of Nadia's ghost, that I was cut out for real estate? I headed out, ready to abandon the afternoon's route of repo houses.

But as I headed back through the little house, Nadia seemed to tug at my sleeve, scolding me—as she often had—for losing heart too easily. Maybe I could improve the place with paint, sod, and some marigolds in the foundation planter. Out front, I forced myself to ask the blonde for sale information.

With a sigh, she put aside her book, *GENETIC WARFARE: A Beginner's Guide*, along with the fudge brownie she was about to devour. She shuffled through the Free Brandy McConnaughty flyers and found a stack of one-page, government-issue repo pamphlets. "We'll take bids at the auction tomorrow. But you don't seem like the type for this place."

"Thanks," I said, taking the sheet, aware that her sly smile had stolen one from me. She offered a brownie from a box full of them. The noon sun invaded her shady spot, dazzling her wild, curly golden hair. I told her, "You don't seem too sold on the place, yourself."

"That's why I'm doing foreclosures. None of the BS is necessary. At these prices, they sell themselves to professional investors. I'm too damn old to go around extolling these shacks. And look"—she gestured around, blonde amidst brownies—"I get to read in the fresh air all afternoon."

And pass out free-the-terrorist propaganda, I thought. From the toppled stack of flyers, several pairs of Brandy McConnaughty's sulky, narrowed eyes stared back at me. I might ask this real estate agent why she was so keen on freeing a convicted felon whose dud bomb had nevertheless paralyzed a janitor and killed a lab monkey in the name of peace. Since Nadia had worked in the same research facility in a different building, I knew how terrified the employees remained even two years after Brandy McConnaughty detonated the explosives.

But I didn't want to talk my-terrorist-versus-your-prisoner-of-conscience right now. From my first sight of Lottie I'd been more personally intrigued. "So," I asked, munching, "what makes you think you're so damn old?"

"I've got more than a few years on you, I'll bet. You can't see the crow's feet under my sunglasses." She tugged at her hair. "I'm only thirty-nine, mind you, but I'm already starting to go gray. You want another brownie?"

I shook my head, patting my waistline.

"Oh, for God's sake, you're lean as a panther." She helped herself to another brownie. "I'm trying," she said, "to get good and fat."

I studied her closely for signs of age. In fact, gray did fleck her golden locks, but she had one of those faces that would hold up past seventy, especially if she went easier on the brownies.

"So . . ." I said, peering closer, "let me see."

"What? My fat? Or my wrinkles?" She laughed and started to lift her sunglasses. Then her smile vanished. She slammed the shades back to her nose. "Wait a minute. Who the hell are you?"

Abashed, I strove to play it cool. I extended my hand and told her my name was Ray O'Brien.

"Where do you work? Who do you work for?"

Since I had a part-time summer job that provided business cards, I handed her one from my wallet. That little paper square had so much more credibility than my real identity, itinerant creative dramatics teacher.

"Estate Liquidators, Inc.?" She studied the fine print, brows scrunched. "Do you know Kurt Weiss?"

"Who?" Actually, the name sounded a little familiar. "No," I said, fudging. "I don't think so."

After a moment of intense scrutiny, she said, "I'm sorry, Mr. O'Brien, I just can't be too cautious." She kept my card and removed her sunglasses, revealing large brown eyes spoked by faint, friendly crinkles. She stood and shook my hand again. Just then, her eyes caught something behind me they didn't like.

I turned to see a bronze Lincoln Navigator go by, its tinted windows pompous on this simple street. A big German shepherd, barking after the Navigator, gave up and stared hungrily at me.

"Shoo!" Lottie cried, wagging the Navigator—or the dog—away. "And I better do the same, excuse me." With unnatural speed, especially compared to her lackadaisical brownie-munching manner, Lottie boxed her leaflets, stuck a few Free Brandy flyers in the house's mailbox, locked the door, and folded the table.

"Call me if you want to make a bid, Mr. O'Brien!" she shouted, refusing my help, and hustled her cargo to a rusty ragtop jeep. Tossing the table and box in the rear seats, she waved and, grinding first gear, took off without a backward glance.

Alone on the exposed concrete, I turned to catch the standard FBI warning pasted in a garage window:

YOU ARE ON FEDERAL PROPERTY
YOU FACE FEDERAL FINES AND FEDERAL PRISON
IF YOU ARE TRESPASSING.

CHAPTER TWO

Monday at my Estate Liquidators computer, I kept wondering about Lottie and that little corner house. Adrift, I stared at the only decor in my cubicle, a blown-up photo of Nadia Sanchez and me atop Colorado's highest peak.

With my ex's shadow crossing the summit rocks as he leaned to snap the picture, it commemorated our ascent of Mount Elbert six years before. Nadia had used the occasion of her fifty-third birthday to begin ascending all fifty-three of Colorado's 14,000-foot peaks for her second time around. I vowed to finish my first round by the time I was thirty. Now, at twenty-eight, Nadia-less, with more than thirty summits unreached, that goal seemed impossible.

Nadia's peaktop image, smiling and triumphant, seemed like a rebuke. Sure that pinko-liberal guilt and inertia would abort my career as a real estate investor, I knew she would scoff at my lack of resolve. So, since I couldn't recall the name of Lottie's realty, I called several agents who specialized in foreclosures. All were pleased to serve me, but none of my inquiries turned up Lottie.

After work, I drove several miles out of my way to find that her FOR SALE sign had vanished from the corner house.

Then I found Lottie's Prisoner of Conscience flyer in the back pocket of my khakis. Flushed with a pleasant sense of Lottie's compassion—no matter how misguided her cause—I had to allow that Brandy McConnaughty's pinched gaze looked pitiable. Underneath this police ID photo of Brandy, beside a logo for the League, I noticed a phone number.

A taped recording told me the number had been disconnected. I called Information for the new number, then got the same recording.

Lottie sure covered her trail. What good was a real estate agent, or human rights activist, who couldn't be reached?

My summer job didn't derail my thoughts from their morbid track, since my very work involved death and property. My task was simple. Upon the death of our clients, I updated data in their estates' inventories. Each file told freshly ended life stories. One woman had set aside her Wyoming ranch as a sanctuary for ailing circus animals; an oilman had assembled the world's greatest display of barbed wire. Despite grieving for Nadia and pondering Lottie's disappearance, I nurtured a tiny flame behind the dead's spreadsheets.

Late the next morning, I scrolled deep into the file of a local born-again preacher whose entire estate seemed more pimp-like than godly, including the Sleepy Rooster Motel on East Colfax Avenue. I was entering data on his used motel beds when Lottie called, bright with repo auction results: "Hey, you didn't bid! That little corner house is gone for good." She explained that a young pregnant couple had won with a bid under the asking price. "It was great. Nice kids like that, getting a fair deal. Makes me feel like less of a creep."

"Do you always speak so highly of your profession?"

"Profession!" She laughed. "A preschooler could sell real estate. I just do it to support my human rights work. And myself, of course."

I didn't mention the disconnected lines, the missing sign, or her sudden bolt from the property on Sunday. I would find out, certain Lottie was about to ask me if I wanted to see more properties. I'd say yes and make Nadia proud.

But she had another plan. "I wanted to ask you a favor, uh, Mr. O'Brien. Want to go to a party with me Saturday night?" Of course, there was a catch. A man was pursuing her, a man whose ardor apparently frightened her.

"A stalker?" I asked.

"Not exactly, but close. Anyway, you seemed so sweet. So low-key, Mr. O'Brien—"

"Ray."

"Uh, Ray. I could use a guy like you right now. Please, come along. We'll have a good time."

Wasn't this what middle-school girls called "being used"? I suppose my honor should've been offended. I should've said, uh, Lottie, I don't do stand-in roles. But I found I had remarkably little honor, which is lucky, since my lack of pride set the whole adventure in motion, a kind of reverse hubris. Or unlucky, maybe, depending on whether this story would play out as tragedy or comedy.

At any rate, when I agreed to be Lottie's stooge, I was rewarded with her address and a meeting time. But before I could get her last name or phone number, she hung up.

* * *

I assumed Lottie's address in north Capitol Hill would be a charming Victorian. Instead, at twilight on Saturday, I found myself in front of a junky old conversion. A harried-looking Asian man let me in, implying no welcome, and withdrew behind a curtain.

Above me, wrapped bare-shouldered in a towel, her hair still wet, Lottie waved from the top of the stairs. "Sorry, I'm running late. Make yourself at home, uh, Ray. There's beer in the refrigerator. I'll be right down."

In the kitchen, the TV blasted a funeral home commercial. A note taped below the fuzzy, jumpy image onscreen warned, DO NOT FINE-TUNE. E. CHOU. E. Chou's cardboard signs decorated the kitchen (DO NOT LET HOT WATER RUN). A balding, skinny guy in red plastic glasses emerged from another doorway, raging to himself. "You can't even die in dignity anymore!" he cried. "Ten thousand bucks for a cheap pine box and a rented Bible thumper!" After the commercials changed to the usual pairings of junk snacks and stomach remedies, the raving man ignored me and kept babbling about the high price of death.

I braved the refrigerator (SHUT TIGHT AFTER USE) to find caches of grocery bags, names claiming them in felt-tip scrawls, including Lottie's six-pack. This took me back to those student shares I had survived to work my way through college—the stingy loneliness of hoarded groceries. What the hell was Lottie, a career woman, doing in a dump like this?

She appeared on the thought in a little red evening dress, her hair a golden mass of blown-dry ringlets. I poured her half my beer. She shook her head but touched the raving man gently, offering the half to him. This subdued his sputtering. "It's never too soon to plan your own funeral . . . Oh, thanks, Lottie." The raver even smiled, toasting her.

"Uh, Ray, you can finish that in my room, if you'd like," Lottie

11

whispered, nudging me through a back doorway to a narrow stair-well. "Once the servants' stairs," Lottie explained, as if we had joined a free tour of Denver's Forgotten Firetraps.

Upstairs, when I asked about her raving housemate, Lottie shrugged. "Mr. Chou is nice enough to take in a few recovering schizophrenics. Special arrangement with City Health. But the rest of us are just quiet working people."

I studied her room: queen-size four-poster, expensive arm-chairs, a gorgeous old oak desk. Still steamy from her shower, the room smelled of perfume and soap. "Sorry it's so sticky in here," Lottie said, raising her voice above the clinking ceiling fan. She led me through French doors to a small balcony. We looked over a panorama of downtown high-rises. "Isn't it wonderful, my little refuge? Right in the guts of the city," Lottie said. "I was so sick of the suburbs."

"But why this place?"

"Don't you like it?"

"Just tell me, please," I asked, "does living here have anything to do with the League?"

"Ah." Lottie turned to the skyline as if to dismiss me. "So you are a detective after all. Kurt Weiss hired you, and I end up taking you to his party. Joke's on me, as usual."

"Hey, I'm not in anyone's hire." I imposed myself beside her at the rail, forcing eye contact. "Like I told you. But who on earth are you, Lottie?"

"OK, OK." She sighed, patting my arm. "You're standing in the League's local headquarters. It begins and ends at my desk. Mostly, lately, it ends. That's my last batch of Brandy McConnaughty flyers under the desk. I've had a few meetings at the Peace and Justice Center, maybe five or six interested volunteers. All we've done is distribute the flyers. And written to Brandy in prison about our ef-forts to obtain her release. Now you know everything."

"You didn't answer my question, though." I smiled despite my irritation, still not sure whom the joke was really on. It seemed pitiful, a League of one. Was it meant to be a parody, some ironic game I was too dense to appreciate? "I asked who you were, and you described the League."

"That's right, though. I am it. It's me."

"Why'd you get your phone disconnected?"

"Oh, you tried to call?" Lottie smiled now. With easy intimacy, she reached to comb back my forelocks with her fingers. "How sweet."

Now all my irritation dissolved, no matter how she'd deflected yet another question. The high-rises ignited, abrupt, a sensual blaze of circuitry. Lottie's perfume mixed with the fragrance drifting from a neighbor's hedge of roses. Her red dress captured the last streaks of sunset outlining Longs Peak. I had admired her bottom when I followed her up the narrow steps; now I sipped my beer and regarded her figure.

She caught my gaze and followed it, regarding herself. "I haven't worn this for decades, seems like. It's too revealing, a bit tight around the middle and bust. I'm half sorry I still fit into it at all."

"Don't be."

"But I've been trying to gain weight. Kurt Weiss hates fat. Sleekness is practically a religion with him. I figured this would show my bulges to the best advantage."

"I see," I said. But I didn't. Weren't women's "bulges" all straight guys ever thought about?

Lottie tugged at loose flesh above her hips. "I meant these. But I just can't gain enough weight. This pudge is three dozen brownies. I gave up jogging, swimming, and aerobics just to be fat for Kurt's party. And, did you notice? No makeup. And the jewelry he hates." She shook dangling, kitschy howlin' coyote earrings, the jangling loops of silver at her wrists. "Maybe he'll decide, once and for all, that I'm just a fat, ugly old broad."

"Sorry, but you're not a very successful fat person. Nor ugly. Nor old."

"Ah, Ray, you're just a kid."

Irksome as it was to be patronized by such a youthful older woman, at least she had exchanged the "uh" before my name for "ah." If she meant to repel Kurt's advances, I asked her, why was she going to his party?

"Kurt's a very useful repulsive person." Lottie's voice lost all humor.

Women this beautiful must find many men useful; I remembered my place as her volunteer escort. I knew I should tell her I was gay, that our flirting was just a game to me as well. But as a former Boy Scout, a public school teacher, a tax-paying, registered voter in loafers, khakis, and a button-down, I also craved to keep what little mystery I possessed.

As we headed off to Lottie's foothills charade, I belted back the last of my beer and let her lead me down the servants' stairs.

Lottie insisted on driving and snatched a gauzy scarf out of the glove box to batten down her curls. In her red evening dress, the long silver scarf trailing, she looked incongruous behind the wheel of her elderly, topless jeep. She forced the rust bucket up to seventy on the freeway, all the while chattering about its history of breakdowns. It occurred to me that she deliberately spewed this smoke screen of car talk. No matter how chatty and natural, it just raised more questions about why she chose this tattered, untenable life in repo real estate and a one-woman human rights crusade.

We rattled beyond the far southwestern suburbs, past Littleton, Columbine, and Deer Creek Canyon, up into the foothills, the dry-grass hogbacks rising behind shopping centers and subdivisions. Lottie finally fell quiet as we began climbing the rocky ridge. In no time we were 2,000 feet above the city, stars blazing in blue-black clarity above, Denver's smoggy firmament below.

After more switchbacks lifted us above the scrub oak and into the pines, we seemed so remote that I was shocked when a well-lit security booth appeared. The guard waved, laughing, when he recognized Lottie. "Kurt must be throwing one hell of a party," he leaned in to tell her. "We sure miss you, honey!"

Lottie bussed the guard on his cheek. "I sure miss you guys, too. You ought to come on up to the house after your shift. For a nightcap."

"If you'll be there, Lottie, I sure will."

"Seen anything of Nicky?" Lottie asked.

The guard's friendly tone flattened. "Yeah. They were the first ones through the gate."

"'They'? Really?"

"Yep. Nicky came with the big bruiser himself." With that, the guard released the cross arm.

As we wended around the bend, Lottie finally responded to one of the hundred question marks hanging in cartoon balloons over my head. "Nicky's my best friend. I'm kind of worried."

"Marriage trouble?"

"You could say that, except they never married. Lived together for the past year or so. The same old story, especially if you grew up in our neighborhood. Waking up from the big infatuation to realize you're sleeping next to a third-rate Prince of Hell."

Now lights from several houses brightened separate, ridgetop acre lots. Lottie aimed for a narrow driveway at the dead end of the sprawling subdivision, past the KEEP-OUT — PRIVATE ROAD — NO TRESPASSING greetings.

"Funny," she said, "I still get knots in my stomach coming up here."

LEE PATTON

"You used to live here?"

"If you wanted to call it living."

"So . . . you worked for this Kurt guy?"

"You might say that. Kurt and I were . . . partners."

Rows of glass canisters lined the road, each ablaze with electric candles. Permanent luminarias, rich folks' upgrade of the paper-bag-and-sand types we peasants prepared for our humble fiestas. They sparkled up the long spiral driveway, which ended at a ridgetop house, huge windows ignited. Tiny white bulbs twinkled in the surrounding pines. All along the loop driveway, we passed Mercedes, Beamers, Jags, and Hummers. Lottie parked behind the house, beside a Lincoln Navigator. I half-expected liveried slaves to hand us down from Lottie's beater.

But we joined the servants, instead. Lottie led me into the kitchen, where she hugged the caterer and howled at some private joke about capers and runny cheese. She helped herself to hors d'oeuvres, opened a bottle of French champagne, and poured us each a glass. She asked the caterer, "What's the mood in there?"

"Tense," he said. "The usual. Don't you hate company parties?"

"Yes, but I've got work to do tonight. Ray's agreed to help. Isn't he a doll?"

You bet, the caterer agreed, I sure was. Why was I enduring this so politely? I wondered if Lottie had been a housekeeper of some kind, if—despite her obvious popularity with the staff—she'd been fired and meant to stage some kind of theatrical labor-management relations stunt.

OK, I was up for it. Improv wasn't my best skill, so I could always use the practice for my teaching, especially to stay in shape during summer break.

As Lottie and I shoved open the double swinging doors into a party I was certain we were crashing, I needed more information, to help me set the scene. "What's the company?"

16

"Oh, Kurt's firm. He's with Dominex. At the Mamie Doud."

Oh. That was short for the Mamie Doud Eisenhower National Laboratory—where Nadia had worked—a research facility named after the only First Lady Denver has yet produced. An old joke claimed the lab was founded as a secret distillery to help poor Mamie stay soused while Ike presided over the tranquilized fifties. But the joke went sour when I tried to digest the fact that Lottie's darling, Brandy McConnaughty, had meant to bomb the Mamie Doud to smithereens. My guts clenched as I asked Lottie, "And what am I helping with?"

"Well, ultimately, if we're lucky, we're going to overthrow the entire military-industrial complex and free Brandy McConnaughty." Lottie laughed, a false hearty chuckle, as if for courage. "But let me take your arm." She swept the wings of the silvery scarf around her neck. "We have dangerous waters to navigate."

Beyond the swinging doors sprawled a great hall wrapped by plate glass on three sides, vast under a transparent dome. The entire party seemed upheld on a stage, under a sky aswirl with galaxies. The room's sole decoration was a massive Mark Rothko triptych along a mezzanine, each panel a huge red-black blob against variations on white. A hundred guests stood around on flagstone floors, clustered around the bar and buffets or lounged on white sofas. A buzz of conversations nearly drowned the fusion jazz ensemble.

"Don't look so impressed," Lottie said, leading me closer to a group standing under the Rothko. "You've plunged into a school of sharks."

"Should I play, like a dolphin? Or masticate, like a barracuda?"

"Play like you're crazy about me. I'll do the rest." Lottie entered the circle, myself in tow, and made introductions all around. She acted gushy among this glum cohort: "Incredible to see you all again! Yes, it was lovely of Kurt to invite me, considering."

Considering what? That she'd leafleted the entire city on behalf of the terrorist who'd bombed their lab? Then why the hugs and kisses all around? The circle even closed tighter around her, as if Lottie were the savior who had rescued them from their halting conversation about a receptionist who'd been dismissed for circulating racy e-mails. A woman eager to join the closing circle inadvertently shouldered me, casting me adrift in an attempt to save my champagne.

A guy, also marooned, steadied me with a friendly hand against my spine. In a voice deeply familiar to me, he spoke to my back: "That e-mail story's so bogus. You can bet she was fired for—"

I turned around. "Nick?"

"Jesus Christ! Ray!"

So, after the gasps and double takes, it really was Nick, Nicholas Ivan Sanchez, my ex. And somewhere was the big bruiser he'd taken up with after we split. So, Nick was Lottie's "Nicky"?

"Yeah," he explained when we'd both returned to earth. "Lottie was my best childhood friend, Ray. I've told you a million stories about her. A year ahead of me in school? Used to babysit my little sister? Charlotte, Charlotte Vjiovinovic, my neighbor from Globeville?"

"This Lottie's that Charlotte? But why didn't I ever meet her?"

"She was overseas, then Utah, the whole time we were . . . together."

I vaguely remembered e-mails and cards Nick received from Germany, Israel, and Saudi Arabia. Yes, I had a foggy recollection of a glamorous friend connected to Nick's childhood in Globeville, one of Denver's poorest neighborhoods. I knew, too, via Nadia, that his new boyfriend also worked at the Mamie Doud Labs, as a biologist. Beyond that, I never wanted to know the details, and Nadia and I maintained our closeness with a strict policy not to discuss Nick and his new love.

"Hey," I said, "that means your mom must have known Lottie."

"Like a daughter."

"Why didn't I meet Lottie at your mom's funeral, then?"

"Charlotte . . . couldn't come. Besides, Ray, you didn't stay long at the wake, yourself."

I searched dim, disused files in my memory for Nadia's any mention of "Charlotte" from the old neighborhood while, simultaneously, I planned to explain why I'd wimped out after Nadia's funeral. Meanwhile, Nick was drawn in to a muttered, intense conversation with a brawny guy who'd appeared from the laughing circle surrounding Lottie.

In a moment, Nick led the guy to me for introductions. "Patrick, you may have heard me mention Ray O'Brien?"

Patrick smiled tightly while gripping my hand, his shake hearty and ironclad. "Yeah. Only three thousand times." Yep, he was Nick's type of dreamboat, bulging biceps straining his sleeves, mountainous shoulders, a linebacker's thick neck. From my seat in the last row at Nadia's funeral, I remembered noting the size of that neck on the big guy seated up front, beside Nick.

So Nick had caught the juicy football player he'd fantasized about while, eyes closed in the sack with a too-lanky schoolteacher, he'd made what passed for love.

"You've sure kept yourself scarce, Ray," Patrick was telling me. "Nice to meet you, man."

I raised my glass to him. "Same here."

"Besides me, Ray must be the only person here from the real world," Nick said. "A precious commodity."

"Why so precious?" I asked.

Like a fifties gentleman, Patrick spoke on his sweetheart's

behalf. "Office parties are bad enough anywhere, but—especially since the terrorist attempt—what's worse than an office party where people can't talk about their work?"

"But isn't shoptalk exactly why office parties are so bad?"

"I guess," Patrick said, "but this would be the most fascinating shoptalk in the world."

"Yeah," Nick put in. "Plus, I could find out what Patrick actually does for a living. Especially since Dominex took over the laboratories."

Everybody in Denver already knew that the Mamie Doud—now contracted to Dominex, Inc.—had massive grants to work on medical applications of genetic engineering. So I asked, "Is it really that secretive?"

"I'd just like to know a little more," Nick said, "about how all these nice biologists and engineers and technicians can get up every day and study their genocides with a smile."

"Genocides!" Patrick cried.

"Oh, I'm sorry, Patrick." Nick smirked. "I meant genetics."

Patrick was not amused. He excused himself and disappeared around Lottie's circle, stalking toward the bar.

Nick glanced after his boyfriend with a look I couldn't read. Frustration? Contempt? They'd been fighting, that much was sure.

The only clear emotion I could read was the pain in Nick's face. I'd always been slain by those bold, pretty brown-black eyes, his long dark lashes, and high, arched eyebrows. Not to mention his fleshy lips, so soft in contrast to the hard, masculine line of his jaw. OK, this was one big reason why I'd avoided Nick since the breakup; my lust always simmered in his presence and it was past time to douse the flame.

Nick nodded toward Lottie. "I'm so glad she came. These parties are worse than funerals, with everybody so bottled up, avoiding the dread topic. Then enter Charlotte, with nerve enough to face the dread with a gutsy laugh. And just unbelievable idealism."

"So, Nick, are you in with Lottie on this League deal?"

"Well, don't tell," Nick said, smiling sideways, "but Lottie and I founded the damn local. It makes Patrick go ballistic. And you, Ray? Are you in with Lottie?"

"I don't really know a thing about it. All I know is, I'm playing her date. I think she's in a labor dispute with somebody named Kurt."

Nick laughed—sweet, surprised. He clutched my hand. "Oh, God, Ray, how wonderful it is to talk with you. And not just because I've never stopped bein' crazy about you. I'm just jazzed to be with someone who's completely outside of this poisonous pond. You're probably not even supposed to be here. I'm a pariah, myself, as you can guess. But Lottie's very brave to sneak a complete outsider into one of these soirees."

"Sneak? Not at all." I sensed trouble. "We came in through the kitchen, Lottie and me. She seems to know the caterer."

Nick beamed at this, suppressing another laugh. He reveled in my cluelessness. Thirty-eight now, ten years my senior, he always loved to play the urbane insider, casting me as the hapless little brother.

When Patrick returned with a fresh drink for Nick and kindly offered me a new flute of champagne, I enjoyed how he treated Nick with the same condescension Nick once reserved for me. "I trust you're behaving, Nicky?"

Nick scowled. "Don't patronize. I was just enjoying a civilian conversation with Ray."

"You mean 'civil,' don't you think? So," Patrick said, turning to me, "what exactly brought you here, Ray?"

"Ray's a great friend of my mom's," Nick said, adding, with a twist of petulance, "and he's Lottie's date."

Lottie had struggled out of the circle and hooked her arm into mine. "Yes, where were you, Ray? I wanted to show you off to everyone."

"Your fans edged me out. So I caught up with my old friend Nick . . ."

At this revelation, Lottie expressed what seemed to be honest astonishment. She turned to confirm it with Nick. Then she and Nick hugged wordlessly, clinging and long.

But as soon as Nick let go their embrace and attempted to straighten the scarf loosely noosed, now, around Lottie's neck, Patrick led him forcefully aside.

"Damn it, I will not be silenced on this one, Patrick," Nick cried as they resumed bickering in a nearby alcove. "It's not the kind of secret I should keep!"

Lottie glanced their way, unable to mask her concern, yet soon got back to work. Her goal was to present me to as many partygoers as possible, nuzzling me or fussing over my collar or laughing too much at my mild jests.

As the party waxed and waned, we waded deeper and deeper into the champagne. Up on the mezzanine, Lottie fell into what was apparently an ongoing Boris-and-Natasha routine with a world-class expert on DNA mutations.

"Ees goodt zaphane, no?" Lottie proclaimed, stuck in Natasha mode even after we bid the geneticist good night. We hovered against a railing just above the Rothko blobs, staring down at dwindling packs of guests. Even the jazz band mellowed into slower tempos, winding down. "Maybe I toss glass on head of host. Vhat you think, Squirrel?"

"Is Kurt really here? You haven't introduced him yet, and the party's almost over."

"He's been aware of you," Lottie said, rolling the glass against her cheek. "That's what matters." She pointed to a tall blond man

LOVE AND GENETIC WEAPONRY

who leaned against the grand piano, talking to two dark-suited men who listened intently, as if the blond guy were giving intricate instructions. "That's Dr. Weiss, there."

On her words, Kurt broke off and turned to peer all the way across the room, then up to Lottie and me. She gasped, "Kiss me, quick!"

I grabbed Lottie around the waist, but, after my hands slipped on the slick fabric, I grasped too hard, causing her to drop her glass. Glass shattered on the flagstone below. Beside the spot it landed, a yell rose, echoing up.

It was Nick who'd yelled. All remaining guests turned to watch Patrick reach for him, as if he meant, seconds too late, to pull Nick to safety. But Nick yanked his hand away. When he stepped carefully around the broken glass, unharmed, Lottie's lungs finally expired, and she cried down: "Nicky! I'm sorry! Are you OK?"

"I'm scratchless, Charlotte," Nick called back, smiling. "Thank God it was you, though. For a second there, I wondered if some assassin were taking aim."

A fraught silence followed, with the multitudes below staring upward. "Speaking of taking aim," Lottie muttered to me, puckering up. "Now!"

I positioned my lips upon Lottie's as she made a moment's show of resistance. "Thanks for helping me, Ray," she whispered, then slipped her lips into alignment with mine. Long and champagne-flavored, our kiss provoked whoops and applause below.

But Kurt had turned his back on us. He continued to instruct the two solemn men with acute jabs into empty space.

The bubbling haze in my brain seemed doubled in Kurt's Jacuzzi. Around midnight, Lottie had led me to this brink, where Kurt's whirlpool perched in a redwood deck. The deck itself perched on the rocky ridgetop. City lights blazed below a clump of ponderosa pines.

Lottie stood across the Jacuzzi from me. In the faint light from the great hall's glass walls, I could detect her wry smile. "Toss a penny in," she told me. "You'll get your wish."

I fished one from my khakis and flipped it into the gurgling pool. "OK, I wish to know what the hell you're trying to prove."

"I've already proven it," Lottie said. "Here's my wish. You'll take off all your clothes, Ray, and hop in."

"You first. It was my penny . . ."

"OK." She stepped into a shadow and turned her back to me, slipping out of her pumps, dress, scarf, and underwear with such speed that her body was submerged under the bubbles before I had the barest glimpse. Laughing, she surged forward to tug at my pant cuffs. "Your turn."

"I see you've practiced this plunge before." I moved into the shadow myself, piling my clothes beside Lottie's on a bench built into the railing. The sight of her panty hose crumpled atop her bra and dress made my stomach jumpy. I hadn't been with a naked female for the seven years since I stopped fooling around—and fooling myself—with college girls. I stripped to my boxer shorts and sat on the edge of the whirlpool. "I assume we're not going to be arrested for public indecency or anything?"

"I assume you're a chicken?" Lottie searched the rim for the flute of champagne she'd set aside. "Who would arrest us?"

"How about those armed rent-a-cops Kurt was giving instructions to? Aren't they here to kick the riffraff out?"

"Kurt's bodyguards? They're here to protect Kurt's God-given right to dance around his property naked. To cavort with who knows how many playmates. Nobody I know is as prone to shimmy out of his clothes as quick, easily, or often as our host. Now, what about you, Ray? You look so cute, shivering in those boxers."

"Good." I sat still, my legs dangled into the hot bubbles. "I'll leave 'em on."

"No way. Cotton shorts are strictly verboten. The fibers screw up the circulation system. Spandex, boy, or nothing at all."

"So," I stalled, "who is Kurt, anyway? I didn't know lab scientists lived like the Great Gatsby. Is he some kind of rip-off artist? Is he running rum, or cocaine? Is that what the big mystery's about?"

"What mystery? Kurt heads a research division contracted to the Mamie Doud. He's with Dominex. They're awash in government-subsidized corporate contracts. It's all legal rip-off artistry."

"Why didn't you just tell me?"

"When did you ask, exactly? And why are you changing the subject?"

"What subject?"

"Your shorts, Mr. O'Brien! Get 'em off and get in. You're going to catch pneumonia like that."

I sighed, unaccountably shy about stripping. It was cool, at this altitude, but the starry night still felt benign. I slipped off my shorts. Lottie wolf-whistled while I slinked into the stinging water.

"You haven't got anything to be ashamed of, Ray," Lottie said. Indulgent, I thought, as if I were a teenager who needed encouragement. "Lots of women don't think size matters at all." She laughed. "They actually go for your sort of thing."

I groaned a laugh, too, then splashed her. Inspired, I slapped chlorinated bubbles in a relentless attack until her hair was saturated. She only laughed harder, then counterattacked.

After we declared a truce, I asked, "What sort of thing?"

"Slender. Nicely proportionate. Sweetly endowed."

"Sweetly!"

"Yes. Now, don't play the innocent, Ray. You know how scrumptious you are. Especially when you're out of those preppie clothes."

"What about you, Lottie? You know damn well how perilous you are in that skimpy red dress. And you shimmied out of it pretty quick, yourself."

"Perilous . . .?" She seemed about to question my choice of words when she turned toward a whooshing noise.

I heard the glass door slide open across the deck, but before I had a chance to turn my head, Lottie took my face in her hands. She rose out of the water, pressing her mouth against mine in a surprise assault, a frontal attack. Her breasts pushed against my chest, her legs locked around mine. I didn't retaliate, flattening myself under her blitzkrieg, helpless as the Polish countryside.

"I wouldn't say 'perilous,'" she whispered, drawing back, then suddenly dove again for my lips, invading my mouth with her tongue while she gripped my shoulders. "I'd say 'imperiled.'"

I hardly noticed that light had flooded the deck. Then an underwater bulb in the Jacuzzi switched on, exposing our naked flesh as if we were boiling in a test tube.

The figure approached the whirlpool slowly, a floodlight on the pumphouse roof throwing his shadow over Lottie and me. I knew it would be Kurt but couldn't see his face, only the bright, back-lit halo of his blond hair. He sipped from a champagne glass, then toasted Lottie. She finally released me and leaned against the rim, facing Kurt.

"How nice of you to have attended, Lottie," he said. "Our paths never crossed during the festivities, so I thought I'd take the initiative before the party's over. But what makes me think of Goldilocks?"

"Because you caught her necking in your hot tub," Lottie said. "It's the naughty, R-rated version, where the sweet girl brings her new boyfriend to the bear's house. Ray, please meet our host. My ex-husband, Dr. Kurt Weiss."

"A pleasure." Kurt crouched down to shake my wet hand.

"But at the risk of quibbling, Ray, I'm not really Lottie's ex-husband. We're still married. She's been pulling your leg."

Lottie had actually pulled more than my leg. I wanted to explode from the tub and run naked into the suburban wilderness. Even though I had agreed to be Lottie's chump, I felt I was in too deep now, naked, exposed. It was my fault for not asking the right questions, for not really wanting the answers, probably because I was infatuated with the night's improvisations. Our hot tub act had a light, Neil Simon velocity before this downshift into scary Edward Albee territory. Abstractions like adultery, betrayal, and jealousy suddenly seemed to cry "blackout!" on our make-believe.

As I began to rise, Kurt pressed my shoulder gently. "Please, let's not break up the party yet," he said. "You don't mind if I join you two? That tub looks so inviting."

"It's yours," Lottie said, uninviting. "Actually, Ray, Kurt really means that he's not yet my ex-husband. A technicality. We've been separated for six months."

Kurt set his glass beside Lottie's, then undid his necktie. "A trial separation."

"A separation separation," Lottie corrected. "Leading to the inevitable divorce." She looked at me with a naked approximation of sincerity. "I'm sorry if I didn't explain thoroughly."

"Lottie," I tried to say, "you didn't explain anyth—"

"I am so sorry," Lottie went on. "But you have to understand that this was my first attempt to set foot in the house since our separation. Kurt's invited me so many times, he finally wore down my resistance." She kicked me under the bubbles. "Plus, I thought it would be the perfect opportunity for Kurt to meet you, Ray."

"How long have you two been going out?" Kurt asked. He unbuttoned his shirt, slowly, revealing a well-toned torso. Pulling off the shirt, he folded it and untied his shoes. "If you don't mind my asking."

"I do," Lottie said. "I don't ask you questions about your love life."

"I don't have one," Kurt said. "My wife left me six months ago."

Kurt's laconic tone seemed to yank a side-splitting laugh from Lottie. She tossed her wet locks against the rim, shaking with hilarity. "Didn't I tell you Kurt was a riot, Ray?"

"You didn't tell me anyth—"

"Kurt has that gift of keeping a straight face no matter how outrageous his little jests," Lottie rattled on, her momentum desperate. "This from a man who has never denied himself a moment's pleasure. With anyone."

"Lottie, you used the term 'love life,'" Kurt said, still teasing her with that laconic sincerity. "And love has been null and void since you left." He unfastened his trousers, pulled off his shoes, socks, and then, slipping out of his shorts, took a moment to pile his clothes neatly on a side table.

Kurt ended his slow striptease by slipping off his gold watch, then sank in, forcing himself between Lottie and me. "I like your hair, Lottie," he remarked, leaning back, and raised his legs so that he could nudge her knee.

"But you hate curls!" Lottie kicked his leg away.

"I like these. They soften you. And those earrings. Didn't I get those for you in Santa Fe?"

"You know damn well I got these at Target. And you hated them."

"You look like a million dollars. It's no wonder you drove all the men crazy tonight." Kurt caught my glance and smiled. Quick, he brushed my outer thigh with the back of his hand.

His other hand clutched the rim behind Lottie's head. She shuffled away. She reached underwater to switch off the light and floated closer to me. On instinct I nearly clasped her hand but decided to rebel against my ridiculous role. Sensing my resistance, Lottie put her arm around my shoulders. "Isn't Ray just adorable?"

"Quite a catch," Kurt said. "A fine specimen. Lottie, are you proposing a ménage?"

"Careful," Lottie said, massaging my arm. "It's about to begin. Kurt's been known to force his charms on all possible genders. And for all I know, species."

"Excuse me," I said, surging out from under Lottie's arm and hoisting myself toward the rim. "I think I'll be going."

Lottie yanked me back. "Ray, despite what I said, Kurt really was just teasing us."

"No I wasn't," Kurt said. "Let me repeat the offer. You're both more than welcome to spend the night. Lottie, you didn't bring this fine young man just for conversation. Do we need to call Ray's mom and ask if he can stay over?"

"Stop it, Kurt. Ray may seem young for me," Lottie said, "but he's actually an investor. A client of mine."

I wiggled from Lottie's grasp and pulled myself entirely out of the water. "I'm twenty-eight," I said. "I don't think my mom would appreciate the call." Clasping my legs, I huddled, cooling and furious on the redwood rim. Annoyed by my relegation to third-person status, petulant and drunk, I studied the steam rising from my arms and legs.

"I'm sorry," Kurt said. "We've lived so long, Lottie and me, in our own sarcastic universe we sometimes forget others' feelings."

"Speak for yourself," Lottie said softly, her head against the rim, the damp ringlets only inches from my toes. "Ray, I'm the one who's sorry about this. I was wrong to involve you in our private squabble."

Kurt smiled up to me, but directed his words to Lottie. "I hope, when your little escapade is over, you'll continue to bring your little friends up to our house. I never had any intention, Lottie, of keeping you all to myself."

"This little escapade is called my life, Kurt. And I'm never coming back to your house. And since when did you ever 'keep' me?"

"An unfortunate figure of speech."

"No, it's revealing. You really do think of everyone in your orbit as captives, whether it's in the lab, kitchen, or bedroom."

"Speaking of captives, Lottie, I haven't ignored your little campaign on behalf of Brandy McConnaughty."

"Stop calling everything I do little."

"Small efforts are bound to come to nothing. I just wonder if you gave a second's thought to how I might feel, spotting one of your flyers around town. After all, I might have been in the lab that night. Just as easily as that poor janitor, working late."

"The night of the bombing? You were screwing in the scrub oak with Bubbles. Or banging in the bubbles with Benny."

"I've already apologized for my midlife indiscretions. You know how much I regret ever hurting you."

"I wish you felt half as regretful about your research," Lottie said. "Then we'll talk about hurting people. Then maybe you could understand what Brandy was trying to do."

"Paralyze a young father and kill a lab monkey?"

"You know she didn't intend to injure anyone. She'd taken every precaution to ensure the lab was empty. You're worse, you know that? It's comparing jaywalking to mass murder."

"Lottie, please don't make me condescend to explain the obvious, not in front of your young man."

"Go on," I babbled, bubble-brained. "I'm fasc . . . fascinated."

"Lottie knows very well that our projects serve the opposite cause, to prevent the very possibility of mass murder. How can anyone compare our work to a heedless act of terror?" Kurt's baroque facetiousness was funny and scary at once, as though he were aware it was all bullshit. But bullshit he somehow believed, like an actor overcommitted to his part. "I am sorry for this charge and countercharge, Ray, but Lottie and I have so much to catch up on tonight."

"OK," I said, "I'll just excuse myself."

"No-no," Lottie said, catapulting herself from the tub to land, steamy and pink beside me. She reached for an oversize towel from a stack on the bench, then stood to cover herself. "Let's just stay for a while longer, Ray. At least until I have a chance to check on Nicky."

Huh? Dumb, losing my steam, shivering now, I watched as Lottie strode toward the darkening house, collecting her clothes as she went, the spotlight having switched off on a timer.

"You look cold, Ray," Kurt said, out of the sudden dark. "I don't want you to catch anything." His hand clasped my ankle. "Come back in."

Good people, those among us who live guided by sobriety and principle, may have trouble understanding why I slid into that hot tub instead of hightailing it inside, joining Lottie and Nick.

Well, Nick had captured his linebacker fantasy, hadn't he? And hadn't I been alone and adrift ever since? Neither sober, principled, nor any good at all, I had a much more twisted fantasy. In some sick backwater of my libido, I'd always craved seduction at the cruel hands of a dominant World War II B-movie Aryan, a cheap but compelling snip of self-porno stuck on replay in my waking dreams.

So I slipped into the pool. Weightless, waterborne, I let Kurt pull me toward him. Earlier, when he'd undressed and slipped into the water, I hadn't been able to take my eyes off his golden, lineless tan, the blond pelt on his wide chest, the seam of darker hair from his navel downward.

Now Kurt smirked at me, his blue eyes at half-mast with self-assurance. Even cooking in the chlorine effervescence, I could detect Kurt's cologne as he pulled me by the hips into a suitable position—me against the rim, him against me as his lips sought mine.

By the time he slipped his hand up the underside of my thigh, I knew any pretense of resistance was limp hypocrisy. And nothing in that pool was limp. Kurt pressed roughly forward, his hands seizing my legs, forcing them back as he thrust. Straight out of my drenched psycho-porn dream, the Aryan commander seized new territory, silent aggression pulsing in every strike.

I came to, alone and prone on the deck, half-covered by an oversize towel. My face planted in another folded towel, I didn't know what time it was, except it had grown cooler, even darker, and quiet. Unfelt, a breeze nickered in the ponderosa pines above me.

I looked up. Across the yard, most lights were out in the great hall. In an upstairs window, two figures moved in crisp shadow against a broad shade. Lottie's silhouette played against the screen, her movements quick, her arms flying for emphasis until she was replaced by Kurt's shadow, just as animated and frantic.

I groaned, aching behind my eyes and sore deep below. Repulsed that I'd surrendered to pure lust with Lottie's husband, I braced myself for hours of ricocheting between self-loathing and dreaming about doing it all over again.

To my deeper disgrace, this degraded condition was familiar. I soaked up my reputation as a grown-up Boy Scout, played it up even to myself, but what troop gave merit badges for Nazi sex acts? When, when was I gonna learn?

There was nothing to do but get into my scattered clothes, drag a comb through my hair, and call a taxi. As I dressed and slunk toward the house, I checked out the silhouettes on the shade above. The couple, blessed in their exclusive heterosexual sacramental union, stood face-to-face now. Calmed, Kurt reached for both of Lottie's hands. I aimed my gaze away. I'd had enough obscenity for one night.

I stumbled across the dimmed great hall, where a large figure hunkered over the piano, playing "Someone to Watch Over Me," in a slow, sorrowful tempo. It was Patrick, who raised a hand to me as I passed.

I hoped to find a phone in the kitchen. Nick stood at the swinging doors as if he'd been expecting me. He clutched Lottie's silver scarf, balled up in his hand. "She left this with me for safekeeping," he told me, "before she went upstairs to engage the devil." Nick dangled car keys in the other hand, asking, "So, you want a ride into town, Suzy Creamcheese?"

"Why Suzy Creamcheese?"

"Under that wholesome surface, there's all kind of nasty additives and sugar substitutes. You're a bad, bad boy, Ray."

"Yeah." So it was unanimous. "And you're an angel, Nick. Let's get out of here."

As we passed through the bright kitchen, one of the black-suited bodyguards, munching on leftover shrimp, raised his chin to us in that straight-guy greeting. The other scrubbed his hands at the sink. Flamboyant, Nick waved to them, then unraveled Lottie's scarf. He had it choked around his neck before he was out the door, a long silver tail trailing behind him.

I was puzzled. Since Nick oozed too much masculinity to be misunderstood, he was never afraid to camp it up. But why tease Kurt's bodyguards? On the way across the parking loop to a vintage Austin-Healey, I asked him how he planned to fit Patrick and me in the two-seater.

"The hell with Patrick. And that's where I told him to go, Ray. We're through."

"I'm sorry."

"Don't be. It's about time I faced up to my mistake. Now I'll really be able to serve the League. I'll be completely outside Dominex's sphere of influence. I'm happy about it. Free, free at last."

We stood face-to-face, each on one side of the roadster. "Hey, you want me to drive?"

"I'm fine, Ray. Just manic. Haven't had a drink for hours."

Despite how ridiculous he looked in the flapping scarf, Nick did seem sober. With smooth precision, he ushered the Austin-Healey slowly down the curvy descent. As if refusing to guide our flight downhill, the subdivisions' streetlights switched off. Just as we reached the first stop sign, the little coupe squealed and skidded. My shoulder knocked against Nick's. Then I was lurched so far forward I pressed my hands against the dashboard.

"Sorry," Nick said. "We just had the brakes rebuilt. I'm not used to their actually working."

As we passed the guard station, the attendant—a female, now—waved us through, then reached for a phone. We began down the mountain's switchbacks, each outward loop serving a view of the city below. Luminous grids stretched to the horizon where the eastern plains lined the darker sky. I hadn't realized how closely this road hugged the canyon in which the Mamie Doud Eisenhower Lab complex huddled, hidden behind foothills. Its high-lit labs and power plants strung a humming strand across the canyon floor.

The sight provoked an impression from childhood, of being driven to a Christmas party way up here. "I thought the Mamie Doud was like some wonderland," I told Nick, recalling my first glimpse of its brilliant webs of light. "An amusement park."

"It's not very amusing anymore," Nick said. "More like a be-musement park. A delusion park. A confusion park. I used to imagine Patrick and Kurt were busy down there curing cancer and disease. Now they seem like funeral directors in a giant crematorium."

I wasn't sure what Nick meant, but it made me think of his mother. Like everyone else who worked at the Mamie Doud labs, Nadia Sanchez had refrained from discussing her job, but I knew she'd been drawn to hers when Dominex opened an environmental office. She'd processed data for a division working on cleanup sites under federal indictment, dismantling urban chemical plants. Environmental restoration had been Nadia's passion as a community activist, and once she was getting paid to help neighborhoods, she said, "in the guts of the goddamn beast!" I knew if she'd had half a chance against those tumors, Nadia would've thrived as a project manager. "You know, Nick," I said, "I'm sorry I didn't stick around longer at your mom's wake. I wasn't snubbing you. I should've given you more support."

"It's OK, Ray," Nick said, patting my knee before he downshifted. "I know how you are about funerals. Hiding out, tissues balled up in your jacket, sunglasses to hide your boo-hoo-hoo."

"That's the best I could do, man. I had to get the hell out of there as soon as I paid my respects to your family."

"What matters is, I know how much you loved my mom. I was so glad you stayed friends with her. But I was kinda jealous; you two were so crazy about each other."

Oh Jesus, now I was tearing up. Amazing how sharp my loss still stung, as if, so long without Nick and now, without Nadia, I could barely navigate my own life.

But I knew I had to snap out of this self-absorption. Jesus, Nick was the one who'd lost his mother. "And how have you been doing?" I asked, inane. "With your grief?"

"I don't think I've reached grief yet. I'm still so damn mad." The Austin-Healey screeched down the last switchback. "Considering what Mom must've found out."

"About what?"

"About . . ." Nick glanced at me, hesitating. "Whatever their real 'cleanup' was. That supposed environmental office was just a front, you know."

I didn't know. A front for what? I knew Dominex from glossy magazine ads: inner-city kids in a playground reclaimed from a cadmium plant; recovered cancer patients, their arms upraised to mountain sunsets. Never much text, just the Dominex logo and slogan, HEALING A WORLD OF HURT. The corporation was also familiar as a sponsor of free park concerts and every good cause from AIDS Walk to Race for the Cure. I'd vaguely understood from Nadia that Dominex had started to take over more and more of the Mamie Doud's operations in biotech and genetics. "Doesn't Dominex develop antidotes for anthrax and serin bomb attacks?"

Nick sighed, exaggeratedly, that way he had of making a show of his amazing patience with my naiveté. He pointed back up the mountain. "Patrick once led work on antidotes for biological weapons, that's true. Kurt pioneered genetics-based cures for the National Labs. But once Dominex took over the Mamie Doud, their mission reversed itself. What they're working on now will make anthrax and serin gas seem like confection sugar."

I could tell Nick was aching to tell me more, in much more graphic terms, in his usual blurted style. He was as rambunctious as always, his legs twittery, his fingers rapping, his head nodding to imagined tunes, but I'd never known him to be so restrained verbally. I figured his time in the Dominex "sphere" had forced him to be more circumspect. Plus the blowout with Patrick just now must've daunted him, coming in the midst of his ongoing struggle with Nadia's death, hardly more than two months past.

I still wanted to give him an opening to talk about her. "Well, no matter what Dominex is doing with anthrax and confection sugar," I said, "I'm sure Nadia would have used her promotion to go on saving the world."

Nick glanced at me. "Ray, you know what? It's better that you stay innocent of all this."

Innocent of what? I considered that Lottie, as Charlotte of Globeville, must have known Nadia all her life, and how Lottie and Nick had passed every milestone of life together. As adults, their lives still seemed twinned. The fight between Nick and Patrick seemed a species of the same hostilities between Lottie and Kurt. Why on earth were Nick and Lottie so devoted to freeing Brandy McConnaughty, to the League, as to take a position so contrary, so hurtful, to their partners? I watched the southwestern suburbs blur by, the cloverleafs stirring all the 2 A.M. traffic from the closing bars and terminated parties and who knew how many finished relationships.

When we reached Washington Park, Nick pulled up in front of my dinky duplex and cut the engine. His sober gravity and self-restraint made him even more attractive, if that were possible. "Well," I said in hopes to lighten the mood, "you've grown up real nice, Nick. From party boy to human rights man."

Nick smiled at our old trope, the youngin' playing father to the grown-up, and reached to cover my hand with his. "But you're just the same, Suzy Creamcheese. I wished I still lived in a world where Dominex was 'wonderland.'"

"So, enlighten me."

"Just think of how quickly my mom went, that's all."

I recalled one of my last hospital visits with Nadia. On arriving, I'd glimpsed Nick crossing the parking lot toward this Austin-Healey, and waited, hunched in my Subaru, until he was gone. I'd ascended onto Nadia's floor expecting to hear her bossing around the nurses, blaming her discomforts on the "corporate-controlled medical system"; her obnoxious, perfectionist personality still undiminished. But that night I'd found her shriveled up, barely able to respond to anything I said. "I think of it," I told Nick, "all the time."

"And there still hasn't been a postmortem that makes any sense, just a bunch of renowned specialists scratching their heads like interns. How's that even possible, Ray, after two months and nine days?" He caught a breath. "OK, I don't want to say more." He squeezed my hand, still measuring his breathing, as if determined to censor—or maybe just calm—himself. "Not right now. Right now, I'd like to exploit your innocence."

I enjoyed his sudden shift to flirting, no matter how un-innocent I still felt after allowing Kurt to exploit me. "You were always so good at seduction," I told him, breathing easier myself. "I wish I learned more from you when we were together. I'm still very bad at being gay."

Nick shrugged. "Not really. You may not have drunk up the club scene, like I did. But you've got that gay dramatic nature. Not that you're a drama queen—you never were—but you're a sucker for sweeping romantic bullshit."

This stung. I knew where it was going, an indictment of my emotionalism when we broke up, so I attacked his mixed metaphor. "I didn't know bullshit could sweep."

"Come on, you know what I mean. When we first met, you went into overdrive. How we would be the big deal, the big, life-long love."

"So, I was wrong." I withdrew my hand from under his. "I was twenty-one, OK?" I crossed my arms. "So kill me." I forced myself not to say the rest of what I wanted to, that our breakup really had almost killed me, that between occasional dates that only seemed to explore two themes, disappointment and disaster, I'd spent the past couple of years numb and mostly alone.

Nick smiled, roughing my hair. "Maybe you weren't wrong. I think we had a damn good chance at the real deal. Maybe you were my only chance."

Hearing that, even knowing it for past-midnight hyperbole, I still wanted to hustle inside alone and lock my door against the possible truth of his words. Exactly as much as I wanted to invite him in, then hold on to him all night long. So, neutrally as possible, I asked Nick where he was going and if he needed a place to stay.

"Thanks, but I'm headed downtown. I have one of Patrick's expense account credit cards. That should put me up in style at the Oxford Hotel." Laughing, he flipped Lottie's long scarf back, campy.

"Hey, before you go, Nick, can you tell me what the hell Lottie was up to, inviting me to Kurt's party?" Crazy as it seemed, I suddenly wondered if it had all been an elaborate delivery of merchandise. Maybe Lottie had to feed male flesh to Kurt, to appease the bisexual beast she loved and loathed in equal measures. "I don't see what she meant to accomplish."

"Ray, I want you to believe me when I tell you this, no questions asked. I love Lottie like a sister. We grew up side by side and have never really lost our closeness. But I don't want you getting mixed up with her. I mean it. I know how you are. Don't be tempted to join in her schemes as a theater exercise, a chance to 'grow as a dramatist,' OK? This is not a situation you can trust or control. Stay away from Lottie. Don't get any more involved."

I smiled. Such vintage Nicholas Ivan Sanchez, treating me like a schoolboy, knowing the best for me, no questions asked. I kissed him good night.

He kissed me back, one hand pressing back the scarf, the other caressing the nape of my neck. "Love you, Ray. Good night."

CHAPTER THREE

It should've freaked me beyond panic, past three in the morning, a prowler in the house. A prowler who dropped his shoes on the entry tiles, loud enough to rouse me from the first tug of sleep. His bare feet on the hallway floor padded straight through my bedroom door.

He was already out of his silk shirt when he eased into the room, tossing it atop mine on the armchair. On the bed's edge, he undid his belt. His slacks slid to the floor, then his boxers. As if positioned for naked push-ups, he stretched above me. That broad, golden-brown chest, fur swirling to define his pecs. The darker swirl down his stomach. Of course, I couldn't detect these details in the dim streetlight glow, but I'd memorized every inch of that body years before.

"You're still hiding that extra key under the potted geranium, Ray. It's so obvious."

"Maybe I was hoping for a naked intruder."

"Maybe that's why I turned around when I got to Speer Boulevard."

"Maybe I'm kind of glad you did."

Nick's hand slipped under the covers, fingers straying below my stomach. "I can tell."

"I miss you."

"I expected to miss you, but not as much as I have. And the life we had together. This duplex. Normality."

"We haven't gone anywhere, Nick, my life and I."

"Thank God. Pray it stays that way."

We kissed, a quick buss to locate our mouths in the dark. A luscious slide of lips locked into desperate pressure. Later, after making love, we relaxed into laughter and jokes in stupid accents and ludicrous endearments almost forgotten from disuse. These morphed into multiple, muffled rings from my home office phone, along with answering machine mutterings.

I awoke alone. Daylight the color of old Crayola Caucasian "flesh" penetrated the bedroom shades. The phone had rung eight or nine times already.

I must've pushed the spread and top sheet away. I lay naked, sprawled diagonally, smelling sour. I groaned to remember my tryst with Kurt in the hot tub. I wondered, too, if Nick and I had really linked in a much sweeter coupling, which I relived upon fully waking. All that in one night seemed vaguely illegal, let alone with more than one man. Were those calls from Denver's vice squad?

Were my crimes mitigated by having drunk so much and waking with such a titanic headache? I wondered if Nick were fixing coffee, though I couldn't smell any aroma wafting from the kitchen. In fact, I couldn't smell anything but Ray O'Brien's bitter sweat, no hint of Nick's light cologne on the sheets, no undersmell of his deodorant or shampoo, no redolence of his natural scent.

I tried to outfox my hangover's insistence on even more sleep. I forced open my eyes and commanded them to focus on the nightstand and the floor beside the bed. I then forced myself up and onto my feet and donned my boxers—my gay apparel, patterned with fig leaves as if arrayed for my expulsion from Eden.

What if Nick, no matter how nightlong amorous, had sneaked off before breakfast?

He wasn't making coffee. The only sign of life in my entire half of the duplex was the blinking red "full" light on my answering machine, winking 15 . . . 15 . . . 15 . . . 15.

Fifteen people desperate to know if I knew that, around three that morning, Nick had been killed in a one-car accident.

Sunday afternoon, I stood on that slope above Cherry Creek, grateful for my anonymity among the onlookers. I hoped a ball cap and sunglasses hid my red-eyed, fixed gaze on Kaneesha Klein-Anderson as she taped her report for Fox News: "This accident may end not as a mystery but merely in a lawsuit against Secure-Brakes, Inc."

The morning's hungover shock had devolved into numb disquiet. Pent and strained, I'd managed the steady phone calls. Now, escaping my airless duplex, here at the scene of the crash, I cast all my stupefaction into detection, into monitoring the reporters' every utterance against whatever body of evidence remained at the site.

Above all I wondered why Ms. Klein-Anderson seemed determined to reverse every aspect of her own bureau's morning reports. Now Nick "had simply been thrown forward with such force that his spine had snapped."

Simply thrown forward. I tried to remember if he'd worn his seat belt when he dropped me off.

But I also realized my speculations were suspect, since I still wasn't absolutely sure whether our night-long lovemaking afterward had been a dream. I mean, my brain knew it was, because all reports continued to verify Nick had died minutes after he kissed me good-bye, but my heart couldn't quite admit it yet.

So I forced my brain to concentrate on how the facts were shifting. In the morning, Denver's news channels had played up "the mystery": Nick's excellent driving records, his apparent speed-up before his brakeless, dead-center crash into the barrier that created the creek's artificial rapids. With morbid delicacy, they'd detailed Nick's odd posture behind the wheel, that gruesome parody of his corpse sitting up as if to drive the little Austin-Healey downstream.

Yet the reporters' exacting, constructed mystery vanished by afternoon, as if that story angle got towed away along with Nick's roadster from the creek's rapids. In Denver, where a brain-damaged kitty up a maple tree could lead the local news, how did a handsome gay socialite's bizarre death lose all traction as a worthy headline?

What had happened to their earlier interest in those muddy brakeless treads in the grassy slope? The mud tracks careening across the bike path? Ms. Klein-Anderson had already explained away the brake failure, including a brief audio confirmation from the brake shop, which transferred the blame to their corporate office.

I waited in vain for any further mention of Nick's "street speed" and how it could be, then, that he'd accelerated enough to crash into the creek with such force? Even without brakes, at boulevard-cruising speed, he could've downshifted to a stop. And failing that, why hadn't Nick leapt out of the open convertible onto this soft knoll?

Already, police dismantled the yellow tape barrier protecting Nick's tire treads in the grass. Down the embankment, under the supervision of police detectives, a city worker swept Nick's caked-mud tracks from the bike path.

Ms. Klein-Anderson took a call from the station, her voice raised in response. "His mother died in May? Really? Do we want to pursue that?"

Apparently the station did not, because Ms. Klein-Anderson nodded, terminated the call, and told her technician, "I think we're done here," sounding a bit bewildered herself.

Along the slope, the other channels' news crews almost simultaneously dismantled their own prowling vantages on the scene. Video equipment disappeared into vans while, in the cottonwoods' shade, Kaneesha Klein-Anderson snuck a few puffs from her technician's cigarette.

As if to speed this immediate collapse of attention, the white vans hustled within half-minutes into the adjacent garages of the news stations. They only had to cross the street from the crime scene, until all the vans swarmed around the fake rapids were swallowed by traps of steel and tinted glass, their buzzing silenced.

My neighbors disappeared almost as fast. Summer Sunday battalions of bicyclists and roller bladers charged through the cleared-up pavement below. With the cops gone, a shuffling guy wheeled his shopping cart, laden with heaped clothes, back under the Logan Street bridge. A pink Frisbee, carried on the stream, got stuck just where Nick's roadster had been. It vacillated gaily among the riffles.

By the time I strolled over to stand beside the tire treads impressed in the mud, I was alone on the grassy knoll.

Straight from the crash scene, I sped past downtown on the interstate, north to Nadia's house. Thunder clouds obliterated the harsh sunlight across the mountain crests and leached all luster from downtown's metallic office towers. My stomach fluttered as a massive cloud shadow stalked eastward across the plains.

I didn't want to be alone, no matter how painful it would be to sit with Nick's assembled family and friends. I should try to be the one who offered consolation, but, selfish, I looked forward to losing myself in Nadia's arms. I craved that contact, even if it were only for a moment. The pain in her brown eyes might sting, but her fierce demeanor might tether me to reality again.

I pulled in front of her Globeville bungalow, amazed to have found a parking space so close.

Despite my nervousness, my fear of being consumed by Nadia's grief, I was still relieved to be here. Nadia's place always made me smile, its newer clapboard additions winging out from the small, squat brick bungalow where she'd single-handedly raised Nick and his sister. She'd installed a walk-out, semi-illegal office in the basement for her activist group, called "BREATHE FREE!"

* * *

I stood at the wrought iron gate, expecting I would recognize graying heads of Nadia's environmental justice colleagues among all the relatives. I was amazed at the quiet, though. No hushed teeming through the screened windows. Maybe it was a smaller group, just the family. Maybe I could steal some time with Nadia to myself.

Maybe silence choked the cramped living room, the Mexican-American and Russian-American and Mexican-Russian-American cousins and uncles and neighbors crowded on folding chairs, unable yet to find a damn thing to say. No matter how awkward it was, though, this time I would outwait everyone, wait out the whole evening until the last little old ladies wrapped the leftover tortillas and collected their casserole plates, so we could be alone together, just Nadia and me. I just had to be patient. More patient than I was in May, the vigil in that very room, after Nadia herself had died.

After Nadia herself had died.

OK. I was delusional, but I finally caught myself. No one would be here, of course. Except that, on the realization, Nick's first cousin, a woman with ghostly, pale blue eyes, appeared on the porch. Clutching some documents, she locked the front door.

"Ray?" She approached, touching my arm. "The family's gathered at my father's. Join us over there?" She kindly explained she was on her way to the hospital, where rotating family members were keeping watch over Nick's sister Natalia, who had collapsed when she'd heard the news and was under sedation.

I told the cousin thanks, I'd be there soon.

But first, there was this Catholic church. A white church, founded by some Slovak or Croatian congregation back in Globeville's Slavic heyday. A little white church where I'd gone once, with Nick and Nadia, for Natalia's daughter's First Communion.

Wind ahead of the oncoming thunderstorm swirled dust devils, gritty at my feet with old street snow sand nobody'd bothered to collect. The city obliterated Nick's tire tracks with breakneck determination from the Cherry Creek bike path, but couldn't remove this Globeville street sand from last winter, when both Nadia and Nick had braved the ice and scraped their windshields and walked the earth.

Clouds massed, so black I took off my sunglasses. Yeah, there it was, the white chapel, facing the rows of concrete piers under the I-70 freeway.

Over the freeway grumble I could hear rhythmic bursts, masculine, measured, indecipherable. Some crazy Catholic Sunday thing, I figured, monks yelling out the Stations of the Cross in Old High Church Slavonic. Up the steps. I'd light a candle to a calm transit for Nick's excitable soul. Not that I believed in souls. But just in case.

No. Church locked. Sign: ENTER ON THE OTHER SIDE FOR ALL TAE KWON DO SESSIONS. Like a fallen, soul-searching Catholic, the little white church had converted to Korean martial arts.

But I remembered the tiny garden out back where Natalia's daughter had posed beside Nick in her white gown, smiling, a gap where her front baby teeth used to be.

Statue of an unknown saint, a Slavic saint, Saint Marko, Saint Milos? Saint Nicholas? Jesus, that was Santa. Couldn't yet ponder everything Nick had given. Or taken. Stalky weeds where the dahlias, the zinnias used to surround the gurgling fountain. Now dry, empty except for a crust of dead algae and a tossed water bottle.

The first drops hit, pelting ice on my cap. I sank on the cracked marble bench, my head lowered against the hail. In synch with ferocious martial chants, my first sobs finally burst.

Monday morning at Estate Liquidators, I tried my best to concentrate on liquidating my summer job.

But I kept waiting for the phone to ring, as I had all the previous evening at home. I prepared myself to face requests for interviews from the news channels and the police. By now, I figured, no matter how cold the story seemed, someone had done enough investigation to trace Nick's death to Kurt's party, where someone else would recall his fatal flight into the night with sex fiend Ray O'Brien. Which would trigger some journalist to juice up the story by indicating Mr. O'Brien's status as the deceased's estranged boyfriend.

I could just hear the buzz back at school: Yes, children, that's how Mr. O'Brien, our mild-mannered itinerant theater teacher, was outed by Kaneesha Klein-Anderson on the statewide evening news. As if anyone assumed a single male theater teacher was straight in the first place, but still. And no matter what the media spun, I was certain the cops would have plenty more questions for me.

Past eleven, I guessed the phone's silence was a tactic; the detectives were messing with my mind so I'd be jumpy and pliable when they finally hustled me into some barren interrogation room.

I tried to concentrate on cataloging my last assignment, which involved the estate of a Bosnian refugee who'd fled the Balkan wars to make his fortune in biotech software. An amateur historian, he'd collected relics of the Spanish Inquisition. So my final task involved updating the rising value of various religious torture instruments.

In a few weeks, I'd be back at my real job, peddling student-scripted drama around the school district, pushing the drug of adolescent angst stage to stage. Originally, I'd hoped to spend my brief free time in August climbing a few peaks, for relaxation, but that was before Nadia and Nick vanished into this Summer of Death. Beyond surviving one more funeral and dreading the eventual police phone call, I didn't know what the hell I was going to do.

Finally, the phone rang.

"Can you meet me right away?" It was Lottie. "I'll apologize in person. It's urgent, Ray."

I looked for Lottie under the clock at the D&F Tower, where despite my better judgment, I'd agreed to meet her at noon.

My nerves jittered in equal measures of grief and guilt. Wasn't I violating one of Nick's last wishes? Actually, a command: Stay away from Lottie. Don't get any more involved.

Yet Lottie had been so distraught on the phone, so anxious for my company and my confidence, that if I'd refused I would violate another taboo, abandoning a damsel in distress. And Nick's life-long friend, at that. I had to believe Lottie's call for help trumped Nick's warning.

Waiting, I visualized Lottie handing out Free Brandy Mc-Connaughty flyers among the 16th Street pedestrian mall's other characters, the ex-con who hit on women with a reality TV scam, or the "undertaker" who offered ten-dollar preburial certificates to passersby.

On this brilliant early August noon hour, downtown's outdoor mall was frenetic. Giving Lottie a chance, I tried to make myself visible in a clearing near the tower, but hungry lines for street vendors obscured me. Then a saxophone player decided to set up shop beside me. He was so good that within minutes, masses mobbed the clearing.

I sidled around the tower into Skyline Park, only to find it thronged as well. Brown baggers assembled around a stage under the banner HEALING A WORLD OF HURT proclaiming the DOMINEX SUMMER FOLK DANCE FESTIVAL. Dancers in traditional Mexican costumes took to the stage as the crowd whooped and clapped. Even when I stood on a concrete planter to survey the plaza, it seemed impossible I'd ever spot Lottie now. The narrow park swelled with ever more fans of free ballet folklorico.

What the hell. Whatever little trust I had for the woman evaporated in the shimmering heat. Stepping down, jostled back into the crowd, I even began to wonder if Lottie might be implicated in Nick's suspicious death. I pictured her silhouette kissing Kurt's upstairs at their manor house. After having fed me to her husband as an appetizer, she was probably providing Kurt the main course just as Nick . . .

"Uh, Ray!"

I turned to find myself face-to-face with a woman in costume, her features half-concealed under a Mexican shawl and sunglasses.

Before I could exclaim, Lottie shushed me. She pulled me by hand to a bench beside a fountain, where backsplash had chased lunchers away.

"Don't think I'm crazy," she muttered. "I'm taking a few sane precautions to protect myself. And you, by the way. I'm so sorry, Ray." Tears slid from under her sunglasses. "I'm so ashamed."

Now I noticed her convincing-looking traditional blouse and long, swirling skirt. Heavy ceramic earrings trembled under her tightly bound shawl. From under its fabric curled newly dark-brown locks. This was serious incognito.

"I didn't have any right to set you up like that. And when I think of what I did . . . what I was doing, when . . ."

She was so upset that she couldn't finish her sentence, blubbering a bit. I couldn't help patting her arm while she composed herself. She dabbed her heavily mascaraed eyes with a tissue, which only made bigger, black-purple blots of her swollen eyes. "I was just afraid," she went on, the words wet and spilling, "if I told you the whole story, you'd never come along. I hoped you'd get to enjoy the party while I made Kurt jealous, nudge him to accept a divorce, and leave me alone. But it all backfired. It's so much worse than I ever dreamed."

On the bench, we were lightly spritzed by the fountain but completely concealed by people standing to see the stage. "Did you know I was Nick's ex, Lottie, all along?"

"No. No! Maybe I should've had a flicker of recognition, though, from pictures Nicky sent me when I was overseas. If you'd said you were a teacher, I might have made the connection. But at the open house, when you gave me that business card, I didn't give that another thought."

"But why did you lie about the League? You told me it 'begins and ends at my desk.'"

"I said I had volunteers."

"But Nick was involved, wasn't he?"

"I didn't know that you knew Nicky, so why would I mention him?"

"If you knew Nick, you knew he was not exactly an activist. Nothing like Nadia. Most of his life he was dedicated to closing sales, cruising Neiman-Marcus, and finding the hottest party. So how on earth did you push him into the League?"

"Ray, I didn't push him anywhere. It was the other way around. Nicky became the catalyst. Last spring, just before Nadia got sick, Nicky started attending her presentations."

I knew Nadia would deliver her BREATHE FREE! contamination-in-poor-neighborhoods slide show free to any audience, from the Denver Greens to the Rotary Club, but never dreamed Slick Nick would ever sit through any of them. "Really? I thought that whole scene exasperated him."

"Nick changed, Ray. He helped Nadia improve her speaking style, for one thing. You know, she didn't suffer fools lightly."

"That's putting it nicely." Blunt and often accusatory, Nadia probably alienated more Rotarians than she ever recruited. "So what did Nick do?"

"He smoothed over Nadia's edginess. After she had the audience riled with facts, Nicky'd seduce them, appealing to their hearts. They actually made a great team. So, after Nadia got sick, Nicky pushed me to do more, too, especially about what was really going on at the Mamie Doud. So much of Nicky's nerve, his fire, came from his mother. I was never a timid person, but I wasn't nearly as committed, as bold, as they became. Then, after Nadia was killed, I promised myself to follow Nicky's lead and live up to Nadia's passion."

Killed? "Wait. Nadia died of a brain tumor."

"But so quickly?"

"It happens," I said.

"To a perfectly healthy woman? An athlete who was climbing mountains at fifty-eight? Ray, you still don't understand."

I didn't, huh? This pissed me off. I'd seen Nadia's rapid decline with my own eyes. I'd stood helpless as, crippled and paralyzed by pain, she shrank to an agonized sack of bones. Lottie's extreme paranoia had the perverse effect of dousing my own doubts about Nick's death, now, too, making me wonder if I'd made too much of those discrepancies at the accident scene. "Tell me, Lottie. How do these killers induce a brain tumor?"

"It was Nicky himself who said it best. If they're devoting their careers to design weapons to kill the greatest number of people cheaper and faster, then what aren't they capable of inducing? Ray, wasn't Nicky fairly sober when he left the party?"

"Stone cold."

"That's what I thought. OK. Now I know they won't stop at anything to silence all of us."

"Who's this all-powerful 'they'?"

"Whoever is behind Kurt and Patrick's research. Dominex. The military-industrial complex. OPEC. Opus Dei. Them."

I sighed, clasping my hands and leaning forward as the crowd cheered the dancers' whooping, swirling virtuosity.

"You think I'm nuts, right?"

"No," I answered, a white lie. Lottie had a right to hysterical paranoia. She'd lost her lifelong friend to an inexplicable accident. "I think you're distraught."

"That's nice of you. But I can tell you're humoring me. The crazy lady in Mexican drag. But there was logic, cold calculation, under what I tried to do Saturday night. That would've been my corpse in Cherry Creek if Kurt hadn't decided to fall back in love with me."

"Has he?" Even though he acted so solicitous of her, so deadly sincere, moments after his protestations of love for Lottie, how could he have seduced me like that? "Are you sure?"

"No. It could be just another of his useful deceptions. That's one thing I wanted to find out, by bringing you along as my new boyfriend. But I was playing the wrong game. I played, in fact, right into his hands."

Lottie's candor and self-castigation moved me to more sympathy. "Well, I was a free agent that night, no matter how clueless. Nobody has talked to me, by the way, about my ride down the mountain with Nick. Maybe I should call the investigators."

Lottie bolted to her feet. She stood directly above me, blocking out the sun. "Don't you dare, Ray! No one, including the police, can be trusted. And if you get further tangled up in this, God knows what they might do to you."

They again. And God knew what I was implicated in now, suddenly cast as the only ally of this beleaguered, delusional, erratic near-stranger. Yet I felt the smallest sliver of credulity shiver down my spine. Maybe it was only the fountain's backsplash against my shirt, but the realization chilled me for a moment, the vast and merciless power that might lie behind Lottie's *they*.

In between acts, a spokeswoman pitched her corporation's underwriting and "Dominex's long love affair with all of Denver's arts" to cheers and ardent applause.

"OK," I said, standing to face Lottie. "I'll wait for the police to come to me."

"They won't, believe me. Ray, you're truly the only person I have to turn to. I never meant to put you in this position, but now that I know you're grieving for Nicky and Nadia, too, we're bound. Aren't we?"

How could I argue with that? I nodded.

"I'm going to ask you to help me. But I'll understand if you refuse."

It all started as a small request. Lottie wanted to stay at my place, just until the day of Nick's burial. Then while everyone was preoccupied with the funeral, she would drive to Wyoming, to the federal juvenile women's prison in Sweetwater.

Lottie "explained." They had manipulated Brandy McConnaughty's trial. Now, with Brandy demonized as the country's newest captive terrorist, Dominex had been able to continue its secret weapons work at the Mamie Doud with impunity. "Meanwhile, they haven't even let her answer my letters or respond to my appeals. But I'm sure if I can talk with her, she'll help me galvanize the League's campaign for her release. Once I've gained her trust, she'll help expose Kurt's research for what it really is. Brandy's no terrorist, Ray. She was just trying to call attention to the truth."

So, Lottie would stake herself out in my very bed (for I only had one bed) while under delusions about the possible murders of two people we'd each loved. Meanwhile, Lottie nursed deeper illusions about her own possible murder, my possible murder, all the while preoccupied by a teenaged terrorist in a remote prison—you know, the one who'd bombed the alleged murderer's evil, murderous science lab.

And I was supposed to welcome her?

Following the dancers' last number, the crowd dispersed quickly in a post-lunch rush. It seemed as if the human screen that had protected our conversation unraveled according to cosmic stage directions. But I didn't know what we'd been protected from, exactly, except the excesses of Lottie's imagination.

Exposed amid the litter of the emptied plaza, I suggested we move on. I needed to join everyone else heading back to their offices for my last afternoon in my Estate Liquidators cubicle.

Instead, Lottie pulled me under the shadows of a locust tree beside the D&F Tower. "Look at that!"

A bronze Lincoln Navigator floated by on Lawrence Street.

"So what?"

"Notice the extra-dark tinting? It's got to be Kurt. Ray, if we make it to that mall bus, he can't follow us."

The free mall shuttle, the only vehicles allowed on the pedestrian corridor, overflowed with lunchers heading uptown. As we crammed aboard, Lottie's shawl got pulled off her head, revealing her dark brown hair, soft waves down to her shoulders. In the heavy makeup she looked exotic, a refugee from some tropical coup d'etat. I felt like a refugee myself, shuttled farther away from my office and deeper into downtown's overheated heart.

Not for long, though. At a standstill on Stout Street, other shuttles lined up behind us. Police on mountain bikes made a jaunty barrier, sealing off the mall. The driver announced into the intercom mike, "There's a demonstration we've got to stop for." He opened the side doors. "Be my guest if you wanna walk, folks."

Outside, among the clamorous crowd emptied from the shuttles, we could hear an unintelligible, feminine chant coming up the cross street. An orderly parade of young women, most in ordinary college student clothes, but many in full scarves and long, loose dresses, marched behind a huge banner: STOP SAUDI VIO-LENCE AGAINST WOMEN!

Hidden completely among the onlookers at the intersection, Lottie and I pieced together the point of the protest from the previous week's news. Ambushed by self-appointed Islamist "morality police," four Saudi Arabian girls had been found wearing uncovered hair and Western-style jeans. Following their public arrest, in an outbreak of mob violence, religious extremists stoned the twelve-year-olds to death. Saudi authorities, looking on, had done nothing to protect them.

Now, passing protesters, mostly Middle Eastern students and supporters from college women's groups, handed out flyers detailing their demands: that the United States officially condemn the Saudi government's timidity—or complicity—with the Saudi fundamentalists. They were marching on the federal Customs House and meant to encircle it. Every few paces, each of the young women raised a fist bearing a rock and cried, "Stop Saudi violence NOW!"

A few rowdy souls among the women implored the onlookers to join them. "It's only a few blocks, and we need more people to circle the building! Come on! Help us," one girl cried, her plea joining with the next chant, "Stop Saudi violence NOW!"

"Come on, Ray, this is perfect!" Lottie called, pulling me by the hand into the thick of the marchers. Letting go of me to cover her head with the shawl, she transmogrified into a vaguely Middle Eastern type. She fell into step immediately and raised her empty fist with the best of them.

When we reached the Customs House, a smiling student handed out rocks to the unarmed. "Wonderful, thanks," Lottie cried. "I was beginning to feel so defenseless." She scooped up another for me as we were swept into the locked-arm circle enclosing the great white neoclassical building.

Closer to the human chain's rear, Lottie and I were shaken into a crack-the-whip. Ever faster, we at the tip of this whip snapped onto the sidewalk along 20th Street, thick with hostile traffic.

"Oh damn, Ray, not again!" There it was, the bronze Navigator, waiting at a red light. Luckily Lottie and I were hustled around the corner, our backs to the enormous SUV as we passed the intersection. From there, we broke from the chain and ran down a side street, then ducked through foundation shrubbery across a small plaza. We joined hands again, plunged back through the chain's very tail end, and sprinted across the street and up the steps of Holy Ghost Church.

Because a glassy bank tower had long enveloped the church on three sides, it appeared to be no more than a chapel. Inside, amid a cavernous hush, though, it had a cathedral's scale, its brooding dim lighted with stained glass and candles.

Lottie seemed to know her way around. Right away she reached for the holy water, made the sign of the cross, and genuflected. I imitated her moves and followed her to a pew in the back. She bowed her head, then fixed a pious gaze on the altar. Slipping her hand aside, she gently set her rock on the pew. As if surrendering her brief Muslim incarnation, sunglasses removed, she now became a devout Catholic lady, an old believer who still covered her head in the house of God.

Still catching my breath, I set my rock beside hers. My gaze roved to the floodlit marble crucifix. "Impressive, huh?" I whispered to Lottie.

"Vicarious atonement disgusts me," Lottie whispered back, harshly. Then, softer, she added, "Sorry. I get peevish whenever I come back here."

"This was your parish?"

"Kurt and I were married here. Nuptial mass, the whole spectacle." Leaning against the pew in front of us, Lottie rested her head on the back of her hand. She seemed sincerely upset now, not posing.

I sat back, reluctant to engage her attention and wondering if, now that I'd delivered her to this hiding-place sanctuary, I could head back to work. A sudden light illuminated the side chapels. I glanced back to see a priest operating switches in the vestibule, then studied the huge blown-up photo portraits the floodlights revealed. Like secular Stations of the Cross, grainy black-and-white faces lined the inner archways.

A soggy whimper rose from Lottie. She fumbled in her purse for a tissue to dry her eyes. "The last thing I need is to get weepy," she whispered. "I was just thinking how Nicky and I were baptized here. Then, when I got married, instead of having a maid of honor, I chose Nicky to be my best man."

"Yeah. He told me about that."

"Now, they'll have his funeral here, Ray." She put her head against my arm, unable to control her tears. I put my arm around her, pulling her face against my chest as she struggled to suppress her sobs. Her tears inspired mine, which trickled steadily until I sensed a presence behind us, in the aisle—breathing, a sigh, a shrug—something as subtle as a sport coat's crinkle, a pair of glasses getting wiped. When I glanced, wet-faced, over my shoulder, I spotted two backs in suits, exiting through the vestibule. Two businessmen ducking into church for a few quick Stations of the Cross or the photographic display?

I didn't mention them to Lottie, though, not wanting to inspire more agitation. Soon, Lottie calmed. She sighed heavily and sat back, so I did the urging this time, nodding my head toward the vestibule and urging her up and out.

We passed the photo portraits as we went, which stared back, ordinary, soulful, imploring, silent. Amnestia, a Catholic, Latino human rights organization, commemorated their anniversary.

They had helped win release of these political prisoners in Latin American dirty wars in the 1970s and '80s, citizens whose democratic convictions had led them to be "disappeared" in ditches or detained in rancid cells. Lottie and I stopped to read the caption for a girl of fifteen, smiling in her school uniform for her class picture. Daughter of a labor leader, she'd been tortured because she refused to reveal her father's hiding place.

All right then. I would slink back to my cubicle to terminate my summer job itemizing the torturous plunder of a rich refugee. What could I ever do to test my fortitude, my courage, against this girl's, here in our free-for-all of getting and spending?

Were Americans just as merciless, only more subtle in our methods? Had Nicky actually been "disappeared" in a Denver ditch? Lottie, absorbed by the schoolgirl's portrait, leaned against my shoulder.

"I wonder," I whispered, "if this could ever happen here."

"It already has," Lottie said, hushed. "Brandy McConnaughty's only seventeen, hardly older than this girl. Two weeks ago, when Amnestia installed this display, I asked the archdiocese if I could include a portrait of Brandy, our very own prisoner of conscience. They said no thanks." She took my arm. "They said America doesn't have political prisoners."

I looked at the sun pouring into the vestibule. "Shall we go back to reality?" I asked, wondering what the hell that could possibly mean.

CHAPTER FOUR

In the cramped courtyard behind my duplex, liberated from the shawl, Lottie's dark curls still surprised me above the Mexican blouse. Her disguise, though, reminded me I harbored an inter-urban fugitive on my brick patio.

After slipping out of Holy Ghost Church, I'd called my boss, begging to finish my Inquisition-torture-instruments account the following day. I drove Lottie to my place, where high fences, two maples, and a wall of lilac hid us from any but airborne scrutiny.

"Why are your planters empty?" Lottie asked when I served a pitcher of gin and tonic.

"Didn't get around to it this season. Again." I shrugged. "Nick used to take care of that . . ."

"I'm sure he did. Nicky had one hell of a green thumb. Even as a little kid. My dad let him tend several rows in our garden when he was still in grade school."

It kept jolting me, how Nick and Lottie had been bonded since early childhood. But thinking of Nick also made me wonder how false our sense of security was. By now, someone would have connected the dots between Nick, Lottie, and me. Her insistence on hiding at my place made little sense.

Unless I was the one being set up for some nasty ambush.

Lottie seemed more relaxed now, sipping her cocktail, chatting about gardening. "It's my one big regret, living at Mr. Chou's. I can't really thrive without turning soil and seeing what comes up. Kurt and I were once maniacs in the garden. Once we got the hang of what would grow above seven thousand feet."

So there was more to their marriage than Jacuzzi sarcasm and sex? I encouraged her to tell me the history of Lottie and Kurt, if only to listen for discrepancies that would support my thesis that Lottie, however amiable she seemed, was a femme fatale. Or maybe nothing so exotic, just a dangerous maniac.

The basic story was suspiciously conventional. She claimed her ticket out of Globeville had been a scholarship for a science education program at Metropolitan State College. As a fledgling biology teacher, Lottie met Kurt when volunteering at a regional conference. Assigned to host the keynote speaker in the hotel auditorium, Charlotte Vjiovinovic led Dr. Kurt Weiss to the podium to introduce his presentation, "The Cure Is in Our Genes." Lottie's introductory charms inspired the young scientist to invite her for dinner that evening.

The dinner stretched into a whole weekend, during which Lottie skipped conference sessions for one-on-one tutorials with the keynote in his suite. Kurt kept the young teacher up past two in the morning with his extravagant dreams. Bound for a prestigious research team, he'd develop gene therapies to cure cancer; he'd dedicate his career "to eradicate disease itself."

For the rest of that school year, Lottie and Kurt bounced back and forth between her Denver apartment and his in Boulder. "When I should have been grading lab reports on the weekends," Lottie told me, "we were exploring each other's reproductive equipment. He boinked my brains out. I mean literally, which is the only explanation for why it took me so many years to figure out what kind of man I married."

I didn't need to use my imagination to understand Kurt's attraction, but couldn't bring myself to admit this to Lottie. Still, would she be surprised to know her husband had screwed me? He'd blatantly hustled me while Lottie was still in the Jacuzzi. "Tell me the truth," I started. "Do you two have some kind of 'arrangement'?"

"I'm a Catholic girl from Globeville, Ray," Lottie said simply. "I've never done a three-way. I don't know why Kurt implied that was the norm, except to get a rise out of you."

I couldn't buy that, as one intimate with how easily Kurt rose to our hot-tub quickie Saturday night. Recalling it, though, in Lottie's presence, I felt my face redden. To deflect my embarrassment,

I asked her when she finally realized what "kind of man she'd married."

"I still wonder, Ray. Before Kurt started becoming a star on the international genetics circuit, we lived together here in Denver through our late twenties, commuting to our jobs. Just going through the usual hassles of establishing careers. I admired Kurt. I adored him. But I wasn't so big on marriage."

As Lottie's mother's diabetic neuropathies worsened, threatening amputation, Kurt became a patron saint in Globeville when he arranged her experimental therapy at University Hospital. Eventually, though, Lottie's mother declined beyond any hope of further treatment. "My mother told me it was her dying wish to see her only daughter married. Preferably in Holy Ghost Church. Despite Kurt's failure to be Catholic, he was practically God."

Mrs. Vjiovinovic lived long enough to witness her daughter become Mrs. Dr. Weiss. Alas, the wedding meats also served the funeral. Nick Sanchez wore his best man suit to serve as one of Mrs. Vjiovinovic's pallbearers only a few months before I was to meet him.

"After that, Kurt and I started traveling," Lottie said. "The research scientist gypsy life. That's when Nicky started sending me letters and e-mails about his new love." Lottie smiled. "He'd fallen for this young teacher who was so strangely normal."

"Normal." I cringed. "What a horrible word."

"Considering Nicky's love life before you came along," Lottie said, winking, "take it as the highest compliment."

Overseas, Kurt Weiss accepted positions with military-subsidized genetic research teams in Germany, then Saudi Arabia.

"So when you jumped into that Islamic women's protest march downtown," I said, "that was more than a distraction."

Lottie agreed. Having lived in a "cloistered bubble" in Saudi Arabia, she was glad when Kurt's next opportunity turned out to be in Utah. "Compared to anything Saudi, Utah's a bastion of liberalism."

At the National Proving Ground in the western Utah desert, Kurt's team would be under the Pentagon's influence. "We had long earnest talks about the morality of it all," Lottie continued. "Kurt insisted the best research was where the money was, and he'd be guaranteed freedom from military considerations. Kurt claimed he hadn't forgotten anything he'd told me on our first night together; that he was closer than anyone dreamed to developing gene therapy for cancer, diabetes, AIDS." Lottie paused, finishing her drink. "I gave in, mostly because I was only one state away from my father, Nicky, and Nadia."

While I ordered early dinner, a thunderstorm massed overhead, booming closer. On hold for a pizza delivery, I studied Lottie through the kitchen window. She'd vacillated between grief and mania all afternoon, and I wondered how much was real. Why had Nick warned me against the very thing I was doing, getting involved with her? Had I just heard the true Lottie, minus her self-presentation as a beleaguered do-gooder, in that calm exposition of her passive life as a scientist's wife? She might be Kurt's perfect match, a fellow opportunist. While Nick had proclaimed his love and attachment to Lottie, I had few signs, besides a few tearful performances, that Lottie returned the sentiments.

I considered Kurt's party's stagy, engineered quality. Maybe Lottie's playacting had nothing to do with making Kurt jealous. In a plotline that led to Nick's unlikely one-car crash, what role had Charlotte Vjiovinovic played?

By the time I hung up the phone, huge raindrops splattered the patio. Lottie rose from the table, but instead of running inside, she opened her arms, arching her neck to catch the rain on her face. Slowly, eyes closed, palms outstretched, she spun until her hair was drenched.

When I hustled out to urge her inside, she put her arms around me, shivering, her blouse soaking my shirt. Hard, cold drops ricocheted off the maples until I was as saturated as Lottie. She clung to me, her mass of dark ringlets trickling against my shoulder.

Then, as suddenly as it struck, the rain ceased. Lottie tried to smile as she leaned back to face me. "Nicky was always wild about thunderstorms."

"Yeah." Sliding into another bout of grief, my defenses low, I wanted to share the feeling with Lottie. Or maybe just punish her with the force of his vivid life. I told her a little memory of Nick at a gay club one summer. Though dressed to the nines and hair moussed to the last spike, he'd hurried out to the deck, at the first thunder rumble, into a midnight downpour. "All the other fairies ran inside after the first drop," I told her. "But Nick danced alone on the deck, drenched to his toes."

"Yeah. As a kid, he'd dash into a storm and hop around in the puddles. Nadia always yelled down the block, 'Nic-oh-las! Get your butt in here now!' We all grew up thinking Nadia's cries were the thunder's echo. 'Nic-oh-las, if you get struck by lightning, don't come crying to me!'"

The clouds growled again in a long, rolling series. "We might get struck, too," I said, imploring her inside, where, after wine and pizza, Lottie fell asleep in my bathrobe on the bed.

On the evening news, I caught Kaneesha Klein-Anderson's brief postscript on the Cherry Creek crash: "The victim, a Denver real estate agent, attended a party late into the night Saturday. He may have driven with his judgment compromised." The police had determined that Nick's brakes had been compromised, as well, "to the point of complete failure."

Odd that local news failed to exploit Nick's reputation as a homo high-society party boy. Even though he had settled down the past two years with Patrick, how could they dismiss Nicholas Sanchez as a mere "Denver real estate agent"? Who had the power to deflect media scrutiny of sexual identity gossip and a solitary death past midnight? It was as if some magic had lured piranha away from a hunk of floating, bloody flesh.

Just after dark, I checked on Lottie, who rose wild-eyed from a nightmare. "These workmen were removing all the planks from under my floor, at Mr. Chou's," she explained, her voice still shaky from the dream. "So that when I tried to run, I fell . . ."

"Run from what?"

"Spies, cops? Criminals? Kurt?" She pulled me toward her. "Thank God you're here, Ray, to tell my nightmares to. Thanks for letting me sleep."

"You need more."

"Yes. But I need dry clothes, too, and my toothbrush. Plus my glasses. But I'm not sure I should brave a trip back to Mr. Chou's. I'm sure I'm under surveillance."

I urged Lottie to get more rest, then volunteered to brave Mr. Chou's all by myself to raid her room for toothbrush, glasses, and dry panties. Alone in the very belly of Lottie's League, I might also conduct a little surveillance of my own.

E. Chou led me upstairs in peevish silence. Ahead of my arrival, Lottie had called to tell him she'd left town on business for a few days and had sent me to retrieve some papers from her desk. So I couldn't understand Chou's obvious reluctance and suspicion. At the top of the stairs he announced, "You're not the man who was here last night."

"No. But I was here Saturday night, remember?"

"Were you? This man was older. Taller." Chou touched his own graying hair. "And blond. Last night."

"What did he want?"

Chou huffed and led me down the dim hall. "I don't discuss my tenants' personal lives."

You started it, old bastard, I muttered to myself, staring down his withering glare as we approached Lottie's door. Chou made a production of searching through his key ring, sighing as he tried three or four old skeleton keys before the lock clicked.

Even in the moment before Chou switched on the light, I had a fleeting reprise of Saturday night, Lottie's essence amid the gauzy sway of drapes. How the crescent moon's light filtered against the open French doors. Instead of wondering why they were open, I wished Chou would vanish so I could ransack the room for my own secret mission. I meant to uncover any evidence of Lottie's duplicity—journals, League mementos, maybe even a file on a certain useful chump, Ray O'Brien.

But as Chou switched on the light, my plan got reversed. Free Brandy McConnaughty flyers were strewn everywhere, as if sprung from all the open drawers in Lottie's old oak desk. No, they'd been kicked out from a stack beside it. Once again Brandy's weaselly visage, that face born for police mug shots, multiplied everywhere underfoot, staring up in defiance.

Chou caught his breath, stricken, his hand on his chest. "Thieves!" he hissed. "Burglars in my house! I have vulnerable people here!" He trampled the flyers on his way to the French doors, where he investigated a broken latch.

I resisted my urge to put back the drawers, hang the clothes yanked from Lottie's closet, and rack the shoes that had been kicked and scattered around the room. In the bathroom, a perfume bottle had been hurled into the tub. Under the wide-open medicine cabinet, a fingernail polish bottle lay shattered. Its red streaked along the flesh-pink linoleum like an exposed artery.

As I ducked back into the bedroom, "Oh my God! Oh my God!" arose from the hallway. The funeral babbler appeared in

LEE PATTON

the doorway. Chou tried to restrain him, urging him not to touch anything, so the babbler continued his ravings standing behind the desk chair, clutching its back rail: "I knew this was going to happen. I warned Lottie about it all the time, and all she ever did was smile. Death can come for you just like that, right over the balcony. Just like a prowler in the night. And where is she now? Does she have a prepaid end-of-life account? Where is she now?"

Chou, livid with indignation and impatience, hooked his hand onto the babbler's arm and just as the doorbell rang, led him out.

Aware that all of Lottie's possessions were now reduced to evidence and clues once Chou called the police, I looked around for her glasses, thinking I might smuggle them out in my pocket. I did locate the case, tossed to the floor beside her nightstand and landed atop a book. That book. *GENETIC WARFARE: A Beginner's Guide.* I reached for it and the case, but as shards rattled, I realized Lottie's eyeglasses had been smashed.

Hearing Chou's voice in the hall, rattled myself, I set the case back on the floor and kept the book pressed under my arm.

Kurt Weiss entered ahead of Chou, as jolted by my presence as I was by his. In polo shirt, jeans, and cowboy boots, he scanned the room with a pained, shocked expression, then shook my hand. He glanced back to Chou, who hovered in the doorway. "So," Kurt asked, "when was the last time either of you saw Lottie?"

"I have not seen her since we spoke yesterday," Chou said. He cocked his head in my direction. "Ask this young man."

Kurt just looked at me, asking nothing—thank God—then began to rove the room, stepping over the flyers. He leaned out to the balcony and ducked into the bathroom. "I hope you've called the police," Kurt said to Chou. "That nail polish is still fairly fresh. We ought to get an investigator here as soon as possible." I half-expected him to add, "Chop chop!"

Chou just nodded before he disappeared into the hall.

Kurt roamed behind Lottie's desk, hands on the chair back, taking the babbler's exact position. "This is what I wanted to protect her from," he said, his head lowered, his voice quavering. "How can she stay safe in this neighborhood? Considering the kind of fanatics she's keeping company with."

"Should I take that personally?"

Kurt turned to face me. "I'm sorry." He pointed toward the flyers. "I mean these fringe groups. These terrorist apologists she's been flirting with."

"It's hardly flirting," I declared with a proprietary air. "Lottie helped found the local League chapter herself."

"Well, I mean the whole network—" He stopped, glancing at the book under my arm. "So, are you in the League, too?"

"Yes," I lied, my voice thin, starved for breath. In the thrall of two separate impulses, to maintain the privacy I'd promised Lottie (no matter how suspicious I was she might double-cross me) and to fight off the shock of my attraction for her not-yet-ex husband. At least my feelings now transcended that hot tub Aryan-master fantasy. Tonight, in the harsher light, Kurt looked older, more vulnerable, more down-to-earth.

My nerve endings went raw in his presence. I liked his soft, tousled blond forelocks. I liked his deep-voiced, articulate tone, and the compelling urgency and concern in his voice tonight. "I've just gotten involved . . ." I said, "in the Brandy McConnaughty campaign."

"Didn't Lottie say you were a client?"

"Yes. I am. See, that's how I found out she was in real estate."

Kurt stared at me, not dubious, but steady and expectant. "How?"

"How? Oh, we were passing out flyers together. On the downtown mall."

"I see. But Patrick told me you were Nicky's ex."

LEE PATTON

"I was. But I never knew Nick was connected to Lottie." I sighed, wondering if this unlikely truth sounded false among my stream of lies. "How is Patrick?"

"In seclusion. Grieving." Kurt turned back to the desk, pushing the chair in. "And how are you doing, Ray?"

"I'm horrified . . . " Abashed by the sympathy in his question, I couldn't tell him more.

"I'm very worried about how Lottie is taking it. She tends to take any death hard, but Nicky was her alter ego since childhood. I'm afraid she might slip into irrational action." Kurt sighed heavily, then stared into me. "So you haven't seen Lottie since the party, either?"

Grateful for his assumption, and that Chou was out of the room, I breathed easier. "I was just . . . returning this book."

"Right." Kurt raised his brows, then smiled faintly. So he assumed I was bisexual, like he was, and had popped by for a tryst with his not-yet-ex? He nodded toward the book. "Old buddy of mine wrote that, you know. Ex-buddy. Larry Lucas thinks I've lost my idealism. But that's OK, because despite how much I admire the guy, I think Larry's lost his marbles." Kurt shook his head.

Then, glancing back at the desk, Kurt's face opened in surprise. "I'll be damned. Look!" He motioned for me to join him.

A note, printed in block letters on League stationery, sat atop a disrupted pile of envelopes, bills, and paper clips dumped from an overturned desk drawer:

DEAR MRS. WEISS (TRAITOR):
    THIS INVESTIGATION COURTESY OF CITIZENS AGAINST TERROR. HOW WOULD YOU LIKE TO BE BEHIND BARS YOURSELF (TRAITOR)? THATS THE PENALTY FOR TREASON. IN THE GOOD OLD DAYS, WE HANGED YOUR KIND (NOT TO MENTION

68

YOUR SEDITIOUS LITTLE PRECIOUS UP IN
WYOMING. WHO SHOULD BE

    P.S. WE FOUND WHAT WE WERE LOOKING FOR.

    SINCERELY, THE TRUTH SQUAD OF C.A.T.

"For Christ's sake," Kurt said, holding his hands in midair to avoid the impulse to lift the note. "What the hell were they looking for? God knows I kept warning Lottie about all these vigilantes."

I reread the note, peering over Kurt's shoulder. "This can't be for real. It sounds too—"

"Too puerile?" Kurt smiled. "C.A.T.'s never been accused of being sophisticated." Then, his smile vanishing, he pointed around. "But they get the job done."

"You know this group?"

"Sure. Just the opposite end of the lunatic spectrum from Lottie's. They go after judges, the ACLU, parole boards, commentators. Scientists called in as expert witnesses. Anybody they think is promoting defendants' rights."

"They're like a right-wing militia, then?"

"Yeah. They stalked a friend of mine, a lawyer, last year, after he reduced this retarded kid's sentence for manslaughter. But I didn't know Citizens Against Terror had taken up burglary."

I stepped back, surveying the damage, the extent of it—and the danger to Lottie—finally sinking in. "This is terrorism. At least, it's terrorizing."

"Yeah, they meant to violate her sense of security." Kurt shoved himself from the desk to prowl the room again, noting the seemingly untouched jewelry box, the torn nightgown. "It's a form of material rape, isn't it?"

Suddenly it hit me. If these antiterror terrorists were capable of this, why wouldn't Citizens Against Terror have had similar fun terrorizing Nicky, the League's new local honcho? Wouldn't that explain the brake failure, the chase into Cherry Creek? A nasty prank that had gone deadly.

Kurt's thoughts regarding Lottie seemed headed to the same conclusion. He retrieved a gold-fringed scarf from the floor, then wrapped it through his fingers. "I'm afraid they meant to do more than scare her with this infantile note."

"I just hope these nuts don't know where Lottie's hiding out."

"So, Ray, you actually think she's hiding somewhere?"

Damn. "Don't you? I mean, what did she say after she left you on Sunday?"

Kurt kinked an eyebrow. I'd really blown it now. How would I know she'd left Sunday?

Gazing at me through an excruciating pause, he asked, "What do you mean?"

"I'm sorry," I said, stalling, straying out to the balcony for inspiration. "I just assumed that Lottie stayed over with you on Sunday, after you and I . . . you know."

"Fucked." Kurt joined me at the terrace rail.

"Yeah. After I woke up, I saw you two together in the upstairs window. See, I was pissed off that she left me stranded there. She made such a big deal out of our date at your party, then made an idiot out of me. That's really why I dropped by tonight. I haven't even read this damn book. I just wanted to unload it and let her know that I was quitting the League. And tell her off."

"Honestly, I'm sorry you got mixed up in our little marital melodrama. Lottie and I both had too much strong drink. But I'm not sorry about what happened between me and you, Ray. I admit, I acted childishly. Resentfully. It started out as tit for tat, if you'll forgive the expression, like, 'if Lottie gets to fool with a boy toy, why can't I?'"

"I'm not—"

"I know. Neither a boy, nor a toy. That's part of your charm. That you'd insist on being a grown man."

"I am a grown man."

Kurt smiled, nodding. "I think my feelings have evolved since Saturday night, Ray. I'd like to have a fresh chance with you." In the balcony's darkness, edged by a hard glow from the room's overhead light, the lines under Kurt's eyes creased. Lines cut his cheeks, all the way to the corners of his large, thick lips. More aging cowboy than mad scientist, he seemed too proud of his own mischief to be quite as seductive as he supposed.

Nevertheless, when he kissed me, slow but urgent, and his lips lingered, his tongue tracing my lower lip, I found Kurt Weiss seductive enough. His hand slipped down my back, then grasped my belt to tug me into another kiss.

I gasped, pulling away, and, like a B-movie librarian, wrapped my arms in front of me, using the *Beginner's Guide* as a shield. "Aren't you still hoping to get back together with Lottie?"

"Yes. Hell yes." Kurt let go of my waist and leaned back so we were side by side now, against the balcony railing. "And I think she's gradually waking up to the truth. Which is that she and I are still in love. We're in crisis now; she doesn't have the mental focus to admit it to herself." He slapped my shoulder with the back of his hand. "So, Ray, how'd you get home, yourself, Saturday night?"

"Oh, I finagled a ride back to town."

"After we heard of Nick's accident Sunday morning, Lottie took off. Just flew down the mountain without telling me where she was headed."

"Did she take that old jeep?"

"Yeah. And I did find it, with a little police help, this morning. Illegally parked near the mall. I spent all afternoon patrolling downtown. Even dodged some damn demonstration. No trace of Lottie, though."

Mr. Chou called to us, then appeared on the balcony. The police, he said, would be here in minutes. I asked Kurt to give Lottie my regards and made for the door, praying Chou would fail to mention anything about Lottie's call and my original mission.

My prayer worked. Chou fingered the French doors, still crestfallen over the broken latches. Kurt remained at the rail, raising his hand in farewell.

Realizing I still had the book, I concealed it behind me, back-stepping from the room as Kurt called, "I'd love to see you again, Ray. And give my regards to Lottie, too, if you ever see her?"

Framed in my rearview mirror, the police pulled in front of E. Chou's. Now I was more baffled than ever. Whose side was Kurt on? And what exactly were the sides? I tried to convince myself he was only a privileged research scientist who wanted to recover his flaky, do-gooder wife. In his horror at C.A.T.'s assault on Lottie's possessions, Kurt had seemed so sincere. So sober, so amiable. Despite his teasing and the pro forma sexual innuendo, I was sure he really had reached out to me, not as a plaything but as a peer. You know, a man.

But Nicky really had been killed in a one-car accident that seemed to have inspired a cover-up. So who was placing the cover?

After all, what forces could Kurt command? They couldn't include the Denver police or the entire local news media. Kurt didn't even seem capable of intimidating C.A.T., considering their brazen harassment of the good doctor's wife.

I wondered, too, if Kurt were truly unaware that I'd hitched a ride with Nick. Maybe that balcony kiss, just like the hot-tub quickie, was designed to addle a perceived adversary, to mess up my perceived loyalty to Lottie.

But it was C.A.T.'s terrorizing of Lottie's room that provoked the paranoiac route I took home. I drove my aging Subaru north through Five Points on obscure, diagonal back streets, then east across City Park, where the zoo's creatures screeched, cackled, and keened, as if ready to pounce from overhung branches into my open sunroof. South through Mayfair, I wound down dark, quiet blocks before zigging west to Congress Park. Zagging across Cherry Creek on deserted bridges, I got spooked by a solitary, undefended sensation.

In the crosshairs of unseen pursuers, Nick must've intuited something, a hollow tug in the guts. That might have been Nick's final feeling before the jolt into brakeless panic, right here. But I crossed the creek without incident, releasing caught breaths as my headlights scanned my neighborhood's sleeping side streets.

As I parked in the alley and meant to slink in silence through my back patio, I heard a rustle nearby. Then a gate creaking. Damn. In a harsh whisper, my semidemented duplex neighbor cried out my name.

In her seventies now, Myna had spent most of her life prowling her narrow quarters, tormenting decades of duplexmates. She scurried across the carport now, tiny, bow-backed, leading with her head like a scavenging hen.

I groaned inside. Better an hour distended on a medieval torture rack than a minute in Myna's company. Her suspicion and self-important schadenfreude seemed to whack ever deeper into solitary madness. I had long stopped believing her cautionary tales of neighbors running prostitution rings, prowlers caught with gonads impaled on wrought iron window spikes, gangs using her half of the backyard for ritual initiations, and "illegals" smoking crack in her basement.

Usually I made a nonverbal show of having to hurry inside for imaginary phone calls or urgent errands. But she hardly ever bothered me after dark like this. "Ray!" she cried again. "That woman who's staying with you. I saw her in that police lineup. When the city detectives wanted me to identify the con artists."

"What con artists?"

"The ones who were peddling miracle cures, till I chased them away, remember?"

"No, Myna. I don't."

"Tried to act as if they were gonna help the poor sick people, when they were actually doing more harm. Making 'em sicker! The police knew I was their only hope."

"Good, Myna." I pulled my back gate open. "I'm glad you could be of service."

"Yes." Myna stood on the concrete pad, rocking forward on her slippers as if daring herself to follow me through the gate. "Even though the cops won't return the favor. Never come when I call them, no sir."

"Good night." I let the gate slap shut.

"Good night, Ray," she called over the fence. "You be careful, now. God knows what that woman's been mixed up in, trust me."

Inside, finding Lottie asleep on my bed, I realized I'd failed in my simple mission to E. Chou's. Except for *GENETIC WEAPONS: A Beginner's Guide*, I'd returned empty-handed: no toothbrush, no glasses, no panties.

I set the book down, then studied Lottie from the bedroom doorway. Her darkened hair, massed in soft curls, spilled over the pillow. She held her bare shoulders hunched as if, even in her dreams, she expected a surprise attack. A box of Kleenex lay toppled, at arm's reach, with balled-up tissues scattered across the bedspread.

I sat as gently as I could into a scoop of space between her bent knees and elbows. I half-feared, half-hoped my weight on the bed would rouse her. After a moment's struggle with the pillow she reached toward me, murmuring, eyes still closed, "Kurt?"

"No. It's me, Ray."

Lottie opened her eyes without alarm, as if calmly letting my face focus in her sights. "Oh. Ray. I was still half-asleep. Thought I smelled Kurt's cologne."

"Huh. Well, I don't use cologne."

"Must've been dreaming. Can't control my subconscious, you know, not after having been married all these years."

"You OK, Lottie?"

She shifted, looking at the mess of tissues. "I'm sorry. After you left, I fell into this . . . crying jag. You know. Nicky."

"I'm glad you got some sleep." I thought better of asking her if she'd ever been in a police lineup, but I did want to warn Lottie not to get caught up in Myna's imaginings. "You know, I should have told you I have my own crazy ranter, right next door."

Drowsy, Lottie shrugged. "It's the sane people I'm scared of." She hugged the pillow, then nuzzled her face into it, slipping back into shallow, defensive sleep.

My fingers reached to caress her arm, to connect with her apparent grief over Nick, to offer, to share in whatever solace I could muster. But I forced my hands off, clutching the mattress edge and grappling with contradictory impulses. Lottie seemed so trusting of me—never a doubt since those brief flashes of suspicion when she thought I was one of Kurt's lackeys—even now, when she could smell Kurt's scent on me.

Still, Lottie was ready to accuse Kurt of vast, nebulous crimes while all he wanted to do, it seemed, was to protect her from her real enemies. At the right time, tomorrow, I would have to tell her about the break-in at E. Chou's, to help her realize her real pursuers were the crackpots at C.A.T., and not Kurt, Dominex, and Opus Dei.

Yet maybe Kurt's party had been an audition that had cast me as clueless understudy to a drama written in indecipherable code. Maybe I'd invited my antagonist into my very bed. Maybe for once I ought to heed Myna's ravings.

Exhausted, I meant to grab a pillow and sink onto the couch, but I found myself curving against Lottie's hunched slumber. The rhythms of my breaths matched hers, and I wondered at my strange, intimate transit between these two married strangers.

Now, as I pressed into Lottie's warmth, Kurt's seductions induced a childlike guilt. At E. Chou's, like a kid, I'd insisted on being a "grown man," but what kind of man was I, really? Obviously, a sexual opportunist. I dreamed about Kurt's kiss and where it might have evolved if Chou and the cops hadn't interrupted. But when I stood face-to-face with Kurt, back on Lottie's balcony, he disappeared to allow space to another intruder.

His hand gently cradling the back of my head, Nick pressed his lips to mine. Then he whispered, "Good-bye."

But Nick's dream farewell was premature. The next afternoon, just home from my final shift at Estate Liquidators, I detected forgotten, almost spectral cooking smells. A meal, actually being prepared in my kitchen. From the foyer, with spicy scents cooking up a momentary time warp, I almost called Nick's name and savored a taste from his stirring spoon. My poor Pavlovian brain could ID only "Nick," since he was the last one to use that stove for anything more than heating frozen pizzas.

In the kitchen, looking shrunken in my shorts and Project Angel Heart T-shirt, her hair tied back in a ponytail, Lottie had resurrected Nick's culinary phantom. Just as she'd shared Nick's affinity for gardens, handsome scientists, and standing in drenching rain, Lottie also loved to cook. She was assembling a real meal out of old rice and seasonings unused since Nick moved out, plus a chicken she'd hunted from the freezer. "I hope you don't mind, Ray."

"Mind?" I poured us each a beer. "To me, other people's cooking is a sacred ritual. Lottie, you've brought the Holy Spirit back to my kitchen."

While the chicken baked, I led Lottie out to the patio for my own specialty, chips and salsa. On the table beside Lottie's cell phone rested *GENETIC WARFARE: A Beginner's Guide.* Scrawled over with marginal comments and highlighted in yellow, it nestled in a stack of real estate papers. "I've done a lot today," she told me. Clients had been called, her supervisor held at bay, and inquiries made to the federal women's prison in Sweetwater, Wyoming. "I think I'm ready to roll first thing tomorrow."

"What about Nick's funeral?"

She set down a chip in mid-dip and looked at me. "I won't be able to attend. Not with Kurt going."

"Won't it kind of get him off your trail, though, if you show up? Prove to him that you're all right, so he stops trying to protect you?" In the morning I had eased her the news of C.A.T.'s invasion of her room and Kurt's surprise visit.

Since Lottie had never given Kurt her address at Chou's, my news had confirmed her theory that Kurt had her under constant surveillance. Now she scooped that chip and said, "Ray, you just don't understand. Kurt isn't trying to protect me. He's trying to control me, contain me, like an infection."

"But couldn't you go in your disguise?"

Lottie smiled sadly, shaking her head. "Ray, a lot of these people have known me since I was a baby. I could go as a geisha or a gypsy, and they'd walk up and say, 'Como estas, Lottie?' I'd be exposed, entangled in Kurt's web no matter what."

Lottie fell silent. She broke eye contact and, blinking rapidly, scanned the maples overhead. Watching her fight against tears, I regretted having pressed the point. She'd probably turned over and over every possibility about attending her best friend's funeral, and concluded it was foolish, no matter how much it hurt to banish herself. She sighed, met my gaze again, and told me, "Besides, with Kurt and Patrick at the funeral, I'll have the perfect chance to head to Wyoming undetected."

Over dinner, the hot afternoon cooled into a breezy evening. We switched to wine while I coaxed from Lottie more about Kurt's real disposition toward her. She discussed their failure to produce a baby during their years at the Utah lab, finally traced to Kurt's sterility.

"Through it all, Kurt was a saint," Lottie explained. "Our childlessness wounded him, but he devoted himself to helping me recover." By the time Dominex recruited Kurt to take over research at the Mamie Doud lab and they'd full-circled back to Denver, their marriage had become a refuge Kurt told her that even if he weren't pledged to secrecy at the Mamie Doud, he might invent it, loving the purity of their time apart from his grueling new research schedule. Even though the mountain house had to serve Kurt's new position, the visiting officials and corporate guests, it was designed to stress private spaces, too. "Our cloistered garden," Lottie said. "Xanadu."

Kurt and Lottie studied high-altitude horticulture, working the soil together as their enormous house grew on the ridgetop. "We both realized we'd been building a monument," Lottie explained, "to the survival of our marriage."

Xanadu, San Simeon, West Egg—that was the scale of what Kurt could offer Lottie now. As she spoke, I sensed that inside that Globeville scholarship kid, that young biology teacher, Kurt left her awestruck even now. "And you still love him," I said, "don't you?"

"So what? I hate him even more."

It occurred to me that instead of high-altitude forget-me-nots, Lottie now cultivated moral outrage. The more she could re-imagine the brilliant Kurt Weiss as evil and corrupted, the less the danger of being yanked back into his gravitational pull. "So when did your feelings change?"

"It was a long process, long before the move to Denver, but I kept lying to myself. Kept making excuses to keep things harmonious. Given the secrecy surrounding Kurt's work, not only in Germany and Saudi, but especially in Utah, I learned how to suppress my own suspicions."

Lottie tapped the cover of *A Beginner's Guide*. "When Larry Lucas still worked at the Proving Ground with Kurt, he and I struck up a friendship. When Larry went across the valley to head the Desert Ecology Project, he and I continued to explore the backcountry, whether on foot or on horseback. Or from the sky, in Larry's Cessna.

"One time, flying low over a dry wash near the Confusion Range, we spotted a disturbed flock of sheep. Several down on their sides, writhing. Some already dead. After landing, we hiked over and discovered that the older sheep were all fine, but the younger ones were wracked by seizures. The lambs were in death throes. And all well fed, wooly coated, bushy tailed, despite their obvious agony."

Lottie and Larry tested water, soil, food, skin, and blood, but found no traces of chemical weapons ever tested in the area. Nor could Larry match the animals with those of any local ranches. It was as if they'd witnessed a ghost flock.

When Larry and Lottie returned to the Confusion Range for more samples, all traces of the sheep had disappeared. No manure, no hoofprints. Even their own footprints had been erased from the salt-sand valley floors. "That's when Larry decided we'd stumbled upon someone else's research project, which had nothing to do with environmental factors or manmade compounds. Something internal had slow acted upon the younger animals. That was the beginning of Larry's big hypothesis, that disease could be imprinted genetically. For military purposes."

"Lottie, that's a lot of evidence to suppress."

"You're telling me. When Larry presented his findings to Kurt and Patrick, they urged him to continue his research. Kurt praised my participation and encouraged Larry to explore more range land all around the Desert Ecology Project. He even arranged funding. Patrick came along for some of our exploratory flights. But we never saw anything like that vanished stock in the Confusion Range."

Lottie accepted another glass of wine. By now, we'd demolished the chicken. In the failing light, our piles of small bones looked especially savage. "So then," Lottie said, "just as I was beginning to doubt the reality Larry and I had witnessed with our eyes and ears and microscopes, I went shopping one Saturday in the nearest town, New Carlsbad. There was a church fair, with wonderful home-canned jams. One of the young mothers had her twin babies in a double stroller beside her booth. They had slight but constant trembling. While I sampled jams, another young mother said a neighbor's baby's tremors were worse. It had developed permanent neural damage.

"When I told Larry, he speculated about rogue scientists within the National Proving Ground who were perverting the research. Technicians, maybe, in the thrall of terror states or corporate opportunists. Then out of the blue, a medical researcher at the National Proving Ground announced the outbreak of a 'natural' neurological disorder in New Carlsbad. Being Mormons, family histories were documented all the way back to the mid-1800s. Genetic nervous disorders up and down the family trees." Lottie stared at me evenly, as if daring me to doubt her. "Just after that, Dominex recruited Kurt. Along with Patrick. Interesting how they came to Denver as a matched set, huh?"

"So how did Nick eventually hook up with Patrick?"

"Blame Nadia and me. Patrick was gay and single and lonely in Denver. So Nadia and I cooked up a dinner party with the express purpose of matchmaking Nicky and Patrick."

"Nick, who was also lonely and single?"

Lottie smiled. "He'd broken up with the normal schoolteacher a few months before."

I supposed that was Lottie's effort to lighten the conversation, but my thoughts swirled within my cranium's own confusion range. I asked her to excuse me while I made coffee and bussed the table.

In the kitchen, I staggered around in the twilight, reluctant to cast light on those bones scattered on each plate. Scattered, too, my mind, trying to focus on genetic manipulation at Utah's military-funded proving grounds and national labs; on those agonized sheep, those damaged children; on Nick mating with Patrick via Lottie and Nadia's matchmaking while I grew used to warmed-up pizza and empty planter boxes.

The coffee maker shuddered and hissed in the deepening dark while I pondered the world through my window screen. Across the street, headlights popped on, but the car just idled there, the driver yakking into a headset phone through the open driver's window. A convertible cruised down my narrow street, pounding a bass stanza of gangsta rap. Behind it, a police car eased by, slowly—slowly—its mini-floodlight cast porch to porch to porch.

Back on the darkened patio, coffee fueled the rest of Lottie's tale. As Kurt led Dominex's research at the Mamie Doud, Larry Lucas stayed in Utah to research the articles that would later be gathered into *A Beginner's Guide*. "Larry argued that an ultimate weapon was under active development at Dominex," Lottie told me. "As a deterrent to terrorism, the weapon threatened an eternal agony for the enemy's future. With implanted genetic mutations, fertile regions could be transformed into deserts of crop failure. Sterility could be genetically programmed into livestock. Even beyond hunger, the human consequences would be unthinkable. To any family, one child could be born without eyes, another without arms, one left whole. Another born without a spine or intestines. Then, twenty years later, that single, whole healthy child would give birth to a pain-wracked sack of blood and organs.

"Larry's insight was that no matter how genetic warfare threatened to give its keepers ultimate power," she went on, "given its imagery—injured lambs, quaking babies—it could also backfire, and do for disarmament what seal bashing had done for Greenpeace.

But the counterattack was already underway. Dr. Kurt Weiss became the face of reasoned science, assuring legislators and journalists that Larry Lucas's speculations were irresponsible, and not only unpatriotic and repugnant, but impossible with present genetic technology. "Kurt likes to call Larry's work a cheesy fifties' science fiction movie, a monsters-in-the-desert fantasy."

Now Lottie's words hit a familiar note, the dim background media Muzak from those months after my relationship with Nick had disintegrated. How local peace groups, inspired by Lucas's outcry, scheduled candlelit protests at the gates of the Mamie Doud labs. How extremists had spawned the Avenging Eco-Angels. Though now defunct, they once scheduled high-profile "actions" throughout the West, gaining increasing credibility until they were implicated in Brandy McConnaughty's botched bombing of Kurt Weiss's main laboratory. With a research monkey killed and a janitor paralyzed, pubic opinion turned against the anti-genetic-weapons movement.

Local attention had turned to Brandy's trial. "She became the scapegoat quite deliberately," Lottie said. "Wouldn't you much rather prosecute a naive seventeen year old than a world-renowned researcher? But with his outrage over Brandy's conviction, it was Nicky who inspired me."

"How, though?" I recalled Nick's suspicions, disclosed in the hour before his own death, that Nadia's fatal tumors were somehow engineered. I still could not quite accept either Nick's or Lottie's certainties about so many speculative, disparate events. "What did Nick inspire you to do?"

"He helped me regain my independence. Helped me get my real estate license. After Nadia fell ill, we worked together to form our League chapter until I finally found the guts to leave Kurt. I was free to work for Brandy's release. And now, even though Nicky's gone, I have the chance to contact Brandy before it's too late for her, too."

"Maybe it's not too late," I sighed, fortifying myself with more coffee. "But consider that it might be too dangerous, Lottie."

"All the more reason to help Brandy, Ray," Lottie said, shrugging. "Can you imagine how frightened she must be? Separated by a harsh sentence from her family, her friends? Even the movement which sent her into the lab abandoned her. She needs me."

When Lottie spoke like this I got tripped on her empathetic overdrive. It just sounded too pat, pasted from some peace-and-justice mass e-mail. Still, she seemed sincere in her determination.

"You shouldn't go alone," I said.

"I don't have any choice."

"Lottie! Think what C.A.T. did to your belongings, your League work. And though we don't know how or why, we do know what happened to Nick."

"Believe me, Ray, I haven't thought about anything else. The real irony is, Nicky is the one and only person I could count on to help me now."

"All right," I said, knowing that I was about to jeopardize better judgment for the sake of sentiment, honoring Nick by helping Lottie. "All right, I'll go with you."

"You're an angel," Lottie said, squeezing my hand.

Not an Avenging Eco-Angel, I thought. A shaky, substandard angel, maybe, who'd lost his training wings and trembled into some godforsaken desert, genetically impaired and probably doomed.

CHAPTER FIVE

By midafternoon Lottie and I reached Sweetwater, Wyoming, a dried-up oil town. Trailers straddled a creekbed of stagnant pools. Fast food fed highway traffic. Traffic in souls invaded abandoned enterprises, with the Blood of the Christian Lamb Church installed in—no lie—a former sheep slaughterhouse.

At some point in Sweetwater's death throes, its lambs' prayers had been answered. The town won the fight for an ever-renewable resource: bad girls from all over America. Other ailing Western towns might fight for plutonium dumps, but Sweetwater as good as put up a plastic marquee at the edge of town, spelling out its welcome: "Send us your teeming female refuse, and we shall deny them liberty." Along the oil-gummed creek banks, ever-expanding in cinder-block and mobile outbuildings, lay the Federal Correctional Facility for Juvenile Women.

Lottie and I had fled Denver in my Subaru just after I'd returned, alone, from Nick's late-morning funeral. After the memorial service, in a painful, bizarre mix of real grief and lame charade at the parish reception, my role had been to present myself, alone, to Kurt and Patrick just in case anyone suspected I was still linked to Lottie. Not that I could explain to anyone why Lottie wasn't there, an absence which mystified and wounded Nick's family and aroused suspicion in Kurt. So, when I'd most wanted to hug Nick's relatives, especially his sister Natalia, and share in the family comfort and grief, I had to slip away and drive Lottie to Wyoming's desolate center.

At the corrections facility we found the reception area, a mobile unit so flimsy it shook in the wind. We were offered metal folding chairs and the promise that Brandy McConnaughty would appear behind the mesh-and-glass cage cut into the paneling. A security guard, her thumbs jammed into her gun belt, hovered behind Lottie and me.

Lottie offered a weak smile to the guard and took her seat. Her glasses lost in the C.A.T. burglary, she had to wear her prescription sunglasses indoors, which made her seem inscrutable yet pretentious, like a celebrity wannabe.

I wasn't smiling. I felt foolish, out of my element, along for the ride even though I was driving. When the door behind the mesh cage opened to hammering construction racket and a blazing shock of blue sky, a skinny girl slipped through, her stringy hair wind whipped. The guard pointed her toward the folding chair against the mesh partition.

Perching on the chair's edge, Brandy leaned forward but hung her head, her feet shuffling. Her tiny gray eyes copped a glance at my crotch, then met Lottie's before they retreated to the floor. It was so quiet that under the muffled whine of a power saw outside, I could detect the starchy rustle of Brandy's pale blue prison smock.

I'd expected to feel sympathy, at least, for this locked-up kid. But to my surprise I disliked Brandy in the flesh with burning, irrational intensity. In return, I could feel her hostility to me just as purely, half-expecting her to stick out her tongue at me.

After introductions, Brandy studied Lottie, a flicker of confusion in her eyes. "You're Dr. Weiss's wife, right? I saw you at the trial. And you've wrote me, then they told me you'd be coming up from Denver. You want to help me?"

"That's right, Brandy." Lottie's smile seemed pained, her voice extra gentle. She removed the sunglasses, squinting. "You see, Dr. Weiss and I are separated. We're on opposite sides of your case. I've been trying to organize for your release. I think the public needs to know the truth about your case, and I—"

"Wait! I don't get it." A flush swept Brandy's pale cheeks. "What do you mean, the truth?"

Lottie smiled tightly, as grimly patient as a teacher stranded in an after-school tutorial. "Just how the bombing was intended to expose what the lab was doing. Not to hurt anyone."

"Yeah. I must'a told them that a thousand times."

"Well, I listened, Brandy. I believed you. Have you had any support from your family?"

"That's a laugh. Sherry and Daiquiri won't even write to me."

"Oh, no," I said, unable to suppress it.

Lottie pressed my hand in reprimand. "Your sisters . . ."

But Brandy had turned her gray rodent eyes to me. "You think it's funny, dude? So my stupid mother thought it was cute. Now we're all stuck with her cute names, and she's gone. Ran off with her fag boyfriend when I was in middle school."

"That's terrible," Lottie said. "But what about your father?"

"My dad says he's got half a mind to join C.A.T. himself."

"Citizens Against Terrorists?" Lottie asked. "Why?"

"He says he's ashamed of fathering a traitor. He says I got what I wanted anyway. That I get to sit around and freeload meals and watch TV all day. That's what he thinks."

"You must be lonely."

Faced with Lottie's sympathy, Brandy fell silent, her eyes searching the linoleum again. Then she looked up, her head cocked. "I don't have time for lonely. They got me taking school tests, even studying this damn speller made for sixth graders. Like I'm gonna need spelling, when I got women's prison to look forward to next year. For the rest of my life. But, yeah, I got a speller. And stupid sessions with this fag shrink. He wants to know why I won't 'open up.' I just want to know how he got to be so ugly and nosy."

Lottie leaned closer, her voice lowered. "I'm afraid there may be people here you can't trust."

"You're telling me?" Brandy's laugh was scornful, a quick extended "HA!" She spoke loudly, as if taunting the guard: "I got threats from C.A.T. My floor warden won't show me the letters, but she tells me all about them and how they're working on tracing them. Like they've got the brains to hunt down the guys who write 'em." On a signal from the guard, Brandy rose. "Those guys at C.A.T., they've got people on the inside who think life in prison's too good for me. They want to kill me."

By the time Lottie and I rose to our feet and Lottie could blurt something about visiting tomorrow, Brandy was already being led out the trailer door into the gritty wind.

An hour later, Lottie and I sat in webbed chairs on the motel deck, indulging that universal ritual of cheap American lodging, cocktails in plastic cups full of round, hollow ice. Actually, the motel was a string of mobile units atop a bluff overlooking Sweetwater's mobile school and mobile post office. The temporary mobile cells of the Federal Corrections Facility for Juvenile Women, sprawled just below us, backed against the sheer sandstone bluff.

"Brandy's in even more danger than I expected," Lottie was saying. "I thought I'd presumed the worst from Kurt's quarter. But I never dreamed C.A.T. would threaten her, too."

"But look at it this way," I said, "where could she be safer?"

"You're assuming the prison system's interested in her safety. But I've never felt such strong intimations of something phony."

"Like her grammar? Sometimes she'd say, 'they got,' then change to 'they've got'."

"Maybe she's actually learning something in these English classes. I meant she was hiding something from us, since the guard was there. Playing dumb."

"You're assuming she isn't just dumb."

"She had brains enough to infiltrate a high-security national lab."

"But it was botched!" I said. "And her boyfriend, the Avenging Eco-Angel, put her up to it, right? And probably left her holding the bag."

"Everyone did. The judge and jury. Kurt and Dominex and the entire weapons establishment. This is a frame-up if I ever saw one."

"Ingenious, though, framing a poor kid with no constituency. Nobody looks out for the legions of dumb-shit, black-eyeliner white girls."

"The League does. That's why we're here."

"Yes, the all-powerful Ray and Lottie. And I'm not even a League member. It is brilliant, though. 'They' framed the most pathetic kid on the planet."

Lottie swigged the last of her vodka tonic and stared toward the horizon. Twilight had dulled into night. Under the black humps of the Rattlesnake Range, Sweetwater's streetlights switched on, feeble in contrast to the sharp stars puncturing the desert sky.

Lottie jangled the hollow ice. "Ray, don't you think Brandy's tormented by the damage she caused? I'll bet she's only acting so callous to cover up her guilt. And of course she was a pawn. She bungled someone else's plan. You can't expect a dumb-shit white girl to have an original idea, right? And damn it, she wasn't wear-ing eyeliner."

"You're right. I don't think Brandy has any eyelashes at all. Just bald lids, like a reptile."

Lottie stood to toss her ice over the railing. Then she squeezed the plastic cup and pointed it at me. "I'm surprised at you. If she's no beauty, no great genius, she still doesn't deserve anyone's scorn. She's probably had nothing but doors slammed in her face. I got out of Globeville in part because I was lucky enough to be considered pretty. But nobody rescues the Brandy McConnaughtys." With that, she retreated behind our sliding glass door and left me alone in the echo of her words.

OK, I did feel ashamed for making fun of a scrawny kid. Abashed, I watched as scores of lights below were extinguished in the long concrete blocks and mobile units of the prison. So sudden, like lights-out in a brutal summer camp. We were perched right over the entry gates, behind which the guards' quarters were still warm with yellow light and the flicker of TV sets. I couldn't help but think of those young girls lying in that enforced darkness, their sentences final, their boyfriends lost, their letters unanswered. I couldn't help but think of that damn Brandy, either, ostracized by a decimated family. She cut a far more vulnerable and pathetic figure than the news media's image of a hardened, precocious terrorist.

I stood, catching a glimpse of Sweetwater's earthbound galaxy below. There was no lights-out for Kmart, Burger King, and Exxon. And Union Carbide's billboard had probably been ablaze for decades, since the company's pesticide plant in India exposed a half-million people to toxic gases: TODAY, SOMETHING WE DO WILL TOUCH YOUR LIFE.

I woke to Lottie's weight on the edge of the bed, her warm hand on my bare arm. "Ray, wake up! Something's happening at the entry gates."

The sliding door was wide open to a hint of sunrise over the Rattlesnake Range. A breeze chilled the room. I'd fallen asleep on the bedspread in a T-shirt and boxers, but temperatures had fallen hard. I yanked a blanket over myself and asked Lottie why she was so alarmed.

"I woke up a while ago and couldn't fall back to sleep. Got some coffee at the cafe, took it out to the deck just in time to see this pickup going through the entry gates. There was just enough light to spot who was in the passenger seat. Though I wish I had my regular glasses. I'm pretty sure it was Brandy."

"What kind of pickup?"

"A big one. Red. The kind with double wheels in the back. The guards waved it through. No checking for papers. Whoever was driving parked right beside the concrete cell block, then led Brandy through a side door." In the shorts and sweater she'd borrowed from me, Lottie shuddered. She gripped my arm. "I'm scared."

"What do you think's going on?" I accepted a sip of her luke-warm coffee.

"I keep thinking the worst. I don't know. Interrogations, God knows what. Ray, what if they're hurting her?"

"Come on, Lottie. It might be a routine health check."

"Before sunrise? If I uncover any mistreatment, I'm going to raise holy hell. If officials can't explain this, I'm sure there are re-porters who'd be interested."

I freed my arm from her grip, then clasped her hand. "Look, we'll visit Brandy today, right? Maybe she'll have a perfectly rational explanation."

"OK. OK. Sorry, I just get to the point where I don't trust anything anymore." Lottie indicated the wide, brightening Wyoming sky, meaning, I guess, the federal corrections system, the U.S. attorney general, the whole human shooting match. "But thank God I've got you, Ray, here with me." Her hand in mine squeezed back, warm.

After breakfast we got the bad news. Because of a "staffing shortfall," there would be no visiting hours that day. Furious, Lottie pressed her case in the front office, complaining that we'd driven hundreds of miles and had to move "heaven and hell to set aside this time."

"Don't you mean," she was corrected, "'heaven and earth'?" Regrets were offered; Wyoming's low taxes blamed. We would have to wait until the next day for our allotted half hour with our teenaged terrorist friend.

So we had a whole day to kill in Sweetwater, which led us inexorably to Kmart for binoculars. Lottie also needed clothes, since mine were so ill fitting on her, given that I was half a foot taller but lacked her extra measures in the bust and hips. With her curvature squeezed into my jeans, Lottie inspired long second looks from many males in the vicinity, while certain women squinched their brows in disapproval. We needed no such attention and decided Lottie needed to be as covered up, as local, and as uninteresting as possible.

Sweetwater's Kmart featured ranch wear: Wranglers and pearl-button blouses, leather vests and jeans jackets. I enjoyed having a legitimate excuse to investigate the women's wear and apply my purblind queer eye to Lottie's makeover. Lottie had fun, too. She held up a blouse to me, complimenting its creamy silks against my "delicate complexion." I cinched a broad cowboy belt through her Wrangler loops, then asked a saleswoman, who was already frightened by our hilarity, if Kmart Corporation could emboss the belt's rear end with enough stamped letters to write "Charlotte Vjiovinovic." When Lottie finally picked jeans and tops, and I helped carry the choices to the fitting rooms, she slipped with them through the door, smiling and calling, "Thanks, Nicky!"

She didn't come out for the longest time. When she finally emerged, looking convincingly ranchette in a checkered blouse and Lady Wranglers, her eyes were red. "I'm sorry," she said, posing for the mirror. "Nicky and I used to shop together like this, laughing like that, and I had a brain crash."

"It's OK. I keep thinking he's still here, too."

Despite her modeling for the three-angled mirror some ill-fitting selections, we couldn't muster the laughter again.

We endured a long restless afternoon. Over early dinner at a steakhouse, Lottie disclosed more of why she felt so drawn to Brandy's case. "The day she was sentenced, facing a mass of news microphones outside the courthouse, she seemed so scared, so naive. So detached from exactly what she'd done and what had just happened to her. She was no older than my students had been, and apparently not as bright as many of them. Just a brave girl completely out of her depth."

Then Lottie revealed a fact she'd kept back: "Brandy's also a Globeville girl, you know. Went to the same elementary school Nicky and I had attended. Then when her mother abandoned the family, her father moved the girls into a trailer park down in Sheridan. So I had more reason to feel that we were connected, Ray. Maybe she'd acted as my agent, my shadow self, in trying to alert the wider world about the real nature of Kurt's work at Dominex. Maybe I need to help her because I'm really campaigning for my own release."

High beams flickered behind me, proclaiming pursuit. But as my Subaru charged over the embankment, my own headlights didn't reveal a creek but a salt desert.

My footprints disappeared the moment they made impressions in the sand. Sinking sand. With one arm, Lottie tried to pull me out of my waking nightmare.

Above where I lay on the motel bed, she clutched the binoculars. "Ray, wake up! It's happening again. That pickup's going through the checkpoint."

The clock radio showed only 9:37 P.M. After dinner, after a shower, I'd dozed off on the bed.

I pulled on a shirt over my boxers and followed Lottie to the deck. Twilight had dissolved into another pitch-black night, though faint moonglow silhouetted the Rattlesnake Range. Lottie offered the binoculars: "See for yourself. They've got Brandy in that pickup. It's just been sitting there, at the guard station, for three or four minutes."

I studied the huge Dodge 4x4 Dualie. I could make out two people in the cab, a large guy in the driver's seat and a smaller figure pressed against the passenger door, but no detail. "What's to see?"

"Brandy's in there, take my word it," Lottie said. "I saw them lead her out. Through the same rear door she entered this morning."

A uniformed guard stepped out of the checkpoint booth to pass a clipboard to the pickup's driver. Then, on the guard's signal, the cross arm went up and the pickup eased through.

"Ray!" Lottie cried, witnessing it from the deck rail. "Let's follow that damn truck! Come on!"

I stepped into my sneakers without realizing I hadn't pulled on my jeans. I grabbed them and ran out. Lottie was already waiting at the Subaru, hand on the door latch. I threw my jeans in the backseat and hopped behind the wheel.

We squealed downhill on three switchbacks carved into the bluff. It was agonizing to be so close to the pickup as it disappeared straight east while we zigzagged downward.

Skirting the prison along mobile home lots, the pickup bridged the creek bed, in clear view but farther ahead. "Step on it, Ray!" Lottie cried while I wondered how this would look to the police, this speeding through Sweetwater's residential back streets in my boxer shorts in the company of a beautiful, desperate neo-brunette. How would it go over when I explained we were pursuing a felon who'd been extracted from the prison?

In open country, I pressed the gas even harder, dipping into stomach-fluttering dry washes. The pickup's taillights would vanish, then flare into view three or four gullies ahead.

I had the Subaru floored now, but my four cylinders were no match for the big V-8, which naturally for Wyoming did ninety on roller coaster back roads. Up ahead, it turned rangeward, atop a plateau. Once we reached the junction, at least we could see the Dodge's progress far into the distance, bound, it seemed, toward where the thin crescent moon rose over the Rattlesnakes.

"Oh God, Ray, what if it's Citizens Against Terror? Where in hell are they taking her? What if this road heads over the range into some crazy maze of jeep trails?"

I had the same thought. My Subaru had all-wheel drive but not the suspension for axle-breaking desert two-track. The map I'd glanced at earlier showed rugged, folded ridges rising to eight thousand feet, then a dry-creek void stretching fifty miles to the next paved road.

Luckily, far ahead, where the crescent fully rose over the range, the pickup finally slowed. It turned abruptly west, lights wobbling toward a cluster of dim lights nested under the dark ridge. The Dodge stopped, headlights killed just as house windows lit up.

We were in the midst of an old ranch community with rough-hewn fence posts, collapsed shacks, and side roads veering over cattle guards. One of them led into the squares of the house lights. The ranch was announced on an aluminum mailbox that glimmered in my headlights as I drove past and rose toward the ridge.

"Where we going?" Lottie asked. "Didn't the pickup turn here?"

"We can't very well go in, headlights blazing, and shout howdy."

"No, I guess not." Lottie released a breath. "Sorry, I'm being stupid."

"Well, neither of us have practiced the procedure. You know, for approaching an abducted felon."

"Hold on! See that road?"

I killed the lights, glad the moon was just bright enough to reveal the roadway's outline. At the base of the ridge, the side road led under a crooked archway. Beyond that a field of upright boulders, leaning every which way, caught the moonglow.

"A cemetery," Lottie said, lowering her voice. Yes, they were gravestones, not boulders, buckled by a century's freezes and thaws. After the last tablet, the faint lane disappeared in a wide expanse of darkness. Were it not for the faint lights of the ranch complex coming into view, the Subaru might have crept through the crisp sage and right over a bluff.

When I cut the engine and set the parking brake, we each suppressed a gasp. I remembered to switch off the interior lights before we eased out simultaneously, then leaned side by side against the hood.

The Dodge truck was parked not fifty feet below us, right at the bluff's base. The ranch house screen door slammed shut before we could see who'd gone through it. Porch lights revealed a row of doors opening to a long breezeway. Lighted outbuildings were scattered between the house and the bluff. Beyond the breezeway, a figure moved into the darkness.

Chickens squabbled in response. Then a girl's voice cried, "Momma! Here, Momma! I've got a treat for you, kitty cat."

"Brandy," Lottie whispered.

I thought the voice sounded too sweet and high to be Brandy's, and besides, the behavior was hardly in character, unless she planned to grab the momma cat by the tail and use it as a bludgeon against her abductors.

The screen door screeched open again. A heavyset man appeared in the doorway, stripped to his undershirt, a holster strapped across his chest. Leaning around the door, he yelled to the darkness, "Come on! You know the rules. Get your ass in here. I told you not to bother with another damn cat."

"It took the milk I set out last night. I'm sure she used to live here."

"Any stray would take milk." The man rested his hand idly on the holster, then raised his ball cap briefly. "Come on, leave it be."

"Just one second, Mortimer, OK? I think she's right here, just up the bluff."

"Did you hear me, Ferret-face? I don't have to mention the rules more than once. You know what happens."

"OK, OK." The shrubs below us rustled, and after a few moments, Brandy appeared at the edge of the porch's light, cradling a scrawny calico cat in her arms and advancing toward the house in a halting, hunched gait. "But, see how calm it is? It's like it knows it's come back home."

"I don't give a damn. And I'm not going through this song and dance again. Drop the damn thing!"

Brandy halted at the porch's edge and immediately released the calico. But before it had a chance to scramble far, Mortimer drew his pistol and shot. The cat jolted, then lay still, its forepaws poised for flight.

Lottie swallowed a scream. She edged forward, then thought better of it, and settled back. Absolutely motionless now, she gripped my wrist.

Brandy, meanwhile, regarded the cat's execution with calm. On the porch, she stared at the carcass for only a moment before she dropped her arms and headed through the screen door. The big guy followed, slamming it shut.

"What the hell was that?" I wrestled my wrist from Lottie's grip and wrapped my fingers into hers. "So C.A.T. actually assassinates cats?"

"When I first saw him pull out his pistol, I thought he might take aim at Brandy."

"Me too."

"Well, we've got to get down there somehow." Lottie leaned forward, then shoved off from the car hood, yanking me forward with her. "It's not that steep. I think there's a trail here, Ray. Yeah, it traverses the slope."

Lottie started down a faint outline of bare soil through the sage, probably a livestock trail. Then she halted so I could pass, and slid behind me. "You lead. I can't see so well with or without these sunglasses."

So I squinted into the dark and crept downward. My legs felt chilled in the breeze, and I realized for the first time since leaving the car that I was still in my boxer shorts.

Down the hill, we found a roadway that connected the corral with two barns stacked high with fragrant hay. "Sure smells like a real ranch," I whispered. "What the hell is Brandy doing here?"

"They've got to be C.A.T., right?"

"You'd think so. Except that the guards waved this guy, Mortimer, through the checkpoint."

"Why couldn't the guards be involved with C.A.T.? I mean, who'd be easier to convince that we need more prisons, longer sentences, harsher conditions?"

Lottie and I crept around the first of the outbuildings, avoiding the light by bashing through brush. Thorns pricked my bare legs as we stole across the side yard. "But why would C.A.T. need

this elaborate ruse, a working ranch? Why would they keep shut-
tling Brandy back and forth to prison?"

"Who says she's being shuttled? Ray, this may be her final destination. You saw how they trashed my room. You saw that poor
calico. Maybe they're trying to force information out of her, from
the trial. Maybe for some kind of publicity stunt . . ." Lottie cut off
her muttered theorizing when we reached a row of cottonwoods.
We now faced two bright windows, curtains open. Peering in,
Lottie and I could watch the supersized TV seemingly over
Brandy's shoulder.

Hunched in an armchair, Brandy flipped through channels so
the TV shifted from scene to scene incoherently. After stopping
for a few moments on a women's mud wresting gala, she settled on
Nickelodeon. *Gilligan's Island.* So we watched Brandy watch inter-
minable scenes, the castaways all the more ludicrous in silence.
The faint titter of the laugh track competed with the dull stirring
of cottonwood leaves overhead. Lottie touched my hand and
whispered, "Maybe they're brainwashing her . . ."

I was about to say, "with *Gilligan's Island*?" when the big guard
appeared in front of the TV. A Rockies cap pulled low over his
brow, he blocked Brandy's view. Popping open a can of beer, he
spoke to her, harsh and continuous.

Brandy put her hands to her ears. Mortimer laughed so hard he
spit up his beer, but Brandy continued to writhe in the chair, curling
more and more into herself, her hands tighter against her ears.
Swigging his beer, Mortimer grabbed the remote and switched the
channel back to the mud wrestling. He gaped, standing, his hand
rubbing his belly. Brandy turned away from the screen, digging her
hands into the chair's arms as if forcing herself to stay calm. When a
commercial came on, Mortimer drifted out of the room.

Brandy turned up the sound so much we could detect a skeletal
actress singing the praises of SuperPuffy Cheez Puffs. Reaching

for a box of tissues, Brandy covered her face and sobbed. The Cheez-ditty camouflage not providing enough privacy, though, she switched off the lamp beside the armchair.

At that instant, a shot crackled from the ridgetop behind us. On the main road, a motorcycle backfired again as it crested the incline. Mortimer charged to the front porch with a rifle aimed at the motorcycle's retreating lights.

He lowered his rifle. But instead of going back in, he cocked an ear to the darkness, stepped off the porch, and prowled around to the side yard. Luckily, the motorcycle backfired again, down at the junction.

Lottie and I had just enough lead time to lope back to our route through the sagebrush. We didn't stop until we'd hustled behind the corral, where we took shelter behind a shed. With Lottie breathless, leaning around me, I sidled forward to see Mortimer scanning the side yard with a flashlight, its beam steady under the cottonwoods before it guided him back to the porch.

When the screen door slammed, Lottie and I scrambled toward that faint trail and back to the graveyard above. Catching our breath at the top, we surveyed the ranch rooftops. "I don't know why I didn't anticipate this," Lottie said, "given that everything so far turns out worse and worse. We've got to take her out of here."

"Enlist the aid of some humanitarian agency?"

"We are a humanitarian agency, Ray. We're the League, aren't we? I've already beaten down the doors of all the agencies, remember?"

We started toward the Subaru, but Lottie stopped in her tracks so suddenly I almost stumbled into her. "Not even the Catholic Church would listen, Ray, wouldn't even post Brandy's picture in their human rights display. As if she weren't even eligible to be a child of God!"

The faint, toppling tombstones gave way to straighter, larger headstones. Suddenly Lottie gasped, grabbing my arm. "Watch out!" she cried, halting just at the edge of an abyss. I could feel the string boundary against my shins. "Damn these sunglasses," she said, removing them to regard the freshly dug grave at our feet.

We sidestepped the excavation. Beyond it, a smooth mound of earth was topped with a metal identification marker.

Nearer where the Subaru perched on the bluff's edge, I could spot where Sweetwater's mobile houses and prison cells glinted in the dry basin below. In these flimsy, flypaper towns, marble monuments in their graveyards always seemed reassuring. The West's transient lives ended up, at least, in a permanent home. I reached for Lottie's hand, but she wasn't beside me.

She stood over the fresh grave, bending to read the marker in the dark. "Ray, go ahead. You should put your pants on."

Yeah. She needed a moment alone. Nick's grave would be something like this, though covered over now, the flowers massed and fragrant tonight in Denver's late-summer heat.

Back in the driver's seat, I grabbed my jeans from the back and lazily covered my bare legs under them, absorbed by the pathetic tableau under the bluff. The dead stray still lay exposed, floodlit in the porchlight. Like a warning? If we followed through, somehow attempting to rescue Brandy, would our carcasses be sprawled there, then bound for some dusty ditch?

Lottie took the passenger seat in silence. I offered her a tissue from the glove box, which she took without comment. While she dried her eyes, I combed my fingers through her hair. She leaned over, resting her head on my shoulder. "Please don't think I'm crazy, Ray. But we've got to help her. People who treat a young girl this way are capable of anything." She touched my arm. "I'm so glad you're here. Imagine how helpless I'd feel if I'd discovered this by myself."

"What exactly are we going to do, though?"

"They've abducted her. So we abduct her right back."

On that note, the cops arrived, announced by crunching gravel and high-intensity headlights. Before one of the policemen reached us with his flashlight, Lottie had the presence of mind to knock my jeans between my legs and down to the floor. She shuffled even closer and began unbuttoning my shirt. By the time we were caught in his beam, Lottie made a show of shuffling back to the passenger seat, then tidying her hair.

I rolled down the window so I could hear the cop say, "Oh. Sorry, folks. But we're always finding kids making trouble here in the cemetery. Underage drinking, you know. Sorry."

"It's OK," Lottie said, smiling at him. "We shouldn't be here, either, no matter our age. But it's our anniversary. It's silly, but since this is where we first . . . you know . . . We always come up here to celebrate."

"God, I'm sorry, lady. But you know, this cemetery is private property. First Christian Church, lock, stock, and barrel."

"Yeah. We'll be going, officer," I said, reaching for my jeans and covering my crotch. "We didn't mean to trespass."

The cop looked young, gawky, trying to suppress a big smile. Finally he shoved off, doused his flashlight, and said, "Ah, hell, who cares. Go ahead and . . . finish. Enjoy your anniversary, folks. Good night."

After he disappeared, I stepped out, and before I forgot again, climbed into my pants.

CHAPTER SIX

"You can't sleep, either, buddy?" a square-jawed man asked me at one in the morning. He'd been glancing my way while he chatted with the barmaid about the genius of Johnny Cash. Every time

I glanced sidelong at him, he caught my eyes. Now he sent a glass of wine my way. "I never can get a wink of sleep in this town."

In the cocktail lounge of the swankier motel across the highway from ours, I hadn't planned on this. Really. Not in the dead center of Wyoming. I only meant to drink myself into grogginess.

Lottie had crashed, hell-bent on getting at least six hours' sleep, but after two hours of insomniac writhing, I'd given up. According to Lottie's plan, we'd be rescuing Brandy McConnaughty from her cat-killing abductors before sunrise.

Through my sleeplessness, an alarm kept sounding, not a wakening blare but an inner alert.

I was the first to admit I'd agreed to drive Lottie to Wyoming out of questionable motives. Lottie's apparent plight had aroused my stray manhood to limp chivalry, more or less in Nick's honor, in concern for his friend's safety. My puzzled but overwhelming suspicion about Nick's death factored in, too. Plus, I had seized the last chance for summer adventure before the school year dropped like a curtain in a multipurpose room.

But, sweet Jesus. When had I signed on to help kidnap a federal prisoner? Especially when I was now bound to abduct her in a sleep-deprived stupor? My best shot now, if the chardonnay did its wonders, would be to stagger back to the room for a few hours' shut-eye.

The barmaid cut the soporific lounge music and popped "I Walk the Line" into the sound system, laughing for the square-jawed man's benefit. He took the stool beside me, eager to know if I liked the wine.

"Thanks," I said. "But I really can't accept it."

"You've got to, buddy. I already paid for it, and I'm concentrating on the hard stuff." He raised his straight whiskey.

I downed the last of my first glass and surrendered, toasting him with the new glass before I sipped. "I'm just trying to get sleepy."

"Is that pretty wife of yours too much of a distraction?" When I stared at him blankly, he explained that he'd seen us earlier. He was staying in the mobile motel, too, a few doors down.

"Oh, she's my sister," I lied. So much for the equally fictitious anniversary Lottie and I had just celebrated in the country graveyard.

"That's nice. Whose kid are you here for?"

This took me a second, too. "Oh. Hers. Her daughter—Amy—from her first marriage. My sister—Nicolette—well, she made some mistakes when she was young, and now her daughter's followed in her footsteps."

"My Gina says she'd go nuts in the facility if she couldn't count on a regular visit from her dad. So I try to show up as often as I can."

Dad. The square-jawed man would make a wonderful daddy, I thought, with his dashing physique, graying temples, and liquid, honey-brown eyes. In both his looks and take-charge manner, he reminded me of Nick, or what Nick would be like in ten more years. Would have been like.

"Is your wife with you?" I asked.

"Oh no. She's been . . . out of the picture . . . for many years. How about yours?"

"Oh no. No, I'm single."

"Nice lookin' young devil like you? Huh." His knee brushed my thigh. "So what do you do with yourself here in exciting Sweetwater?"

I admitted that it wasn't so exciting, especially with the visiting privileges delayed until tomorrow.

"They did a great job, didn't they, putting this prison in the middle of absolute nowhere. All the waiting they make us do for these damn half-hour visits, and nothing to do in the meanwhile." His knee did another slow journey along my outer thigh. "Have you and your sister gotten out and toured the countryside or anything?"

"Is there something we should see?"

The square-jawed man laughed. Then he looked straight into me. "No. But there's definitely some territory you and I could explore, if you're up for it."

I was. Up for it. After downing our drinks, we crossed the highway.

I soon found myself naked beside him in his queen-size bed. Found myself kissing him, consoling myself with the Nick-like swirls of curly hairs on his chest.

Afterward, the square-jawed man wasn't one of those indifferent daddies who dismisses you or sinks immediately into private sleep. When we were done, he sat up on the pillows and pulled me into an embrace, my head on his chest, and asked me why I was crying. "Did I hurt you, baby?"

"No, no. You were great. I just, you know, lost someone. You remind me of him."

"Oh, I'm sorry."

"No, don't be. I'm not really sure why I was crying. I was enjoying it. Then I was overwhelmed."

"Well, you just made my visit to Sweetwater a lot sweeter." He pulled me closer, squeezing me gently. "It's hard to believe that so many of us could have a little girl in this rotten place, huh? Is your niece doing OK?"

My niece?

"Amy?" he prompted. "Your sister's daughter?"

Oh yeah. "Oh, yeah."

"So, you heading back to Denver after your visit tomorrow? U.S. 287 back to Rawlins, then the interstate?"

"My sister keeps talking about the scenic route."

The square-jawed man laughed. "They could drop the big one on this whole damn state and nobody'd know the difference."

I might have risen to Wyoming's defense. Instead, I snuggled closer, soaking up the rare intimacy while I tried to ignore the terrible errand just ahead.

Killing the engine and headlights, I was able to coast down the ranch road. An hour before sunrise, Lottie and I slipped behind the barn, parking the Subaru out of sight.

Inside, four squares of hay provided a platform beside the barn's window. As the sky brightened behind the ranch house, we had a clear view across the driveway. The slaughtered cat still lay midway between us and the assassin, who appeared in the kitchen window as a light flipped on.

Mortimer filled a coffee pot and set it to boil on the stove; Brandy's guard apparently did double duty as the house chef, fixing a gargantuan breakfast. When Mortimer slid open the window, we could hear the bacon sizzle.

"Makes me hungry," I whispered to Lottie.

"Not me. My stomach's doing somersaults."

Her breathing shallow, grim, and intent, Lottie studied Mortimer's every move. Without coffee or breakfast, she and I had worked out our plan to rescue Brandy as we packed up the motel room and hustled across the plateau's cool darkness, rehearsing and revising. Now our contingencies met this hay-and-bacon scented, dead-cat reality.

I was oddly calm. Though I'd had almost no sleep—I'd showered in the square-jawed man's room and slipped back into ours for maybe an hour's dozing—I felt maniacally lucid. No matter how straight-faced and ardent I played for Lottie's sake, I was now certain that nothing would happen according to our plan. We'd have to abandon the whole scheme and return to Sweetwater for eggs and bacon. Then I'd persuade an exhausted Lottie to head home to Denver.

Lottie touched my hand when another light went on. Brandy appeared in her bedroom window, pushing back the drapes and staring, it seemed, right at us. But I supposed she was just confirming the cat's murder by the dawn's light. Sure it wasn't a nightmare after all, she snapped the curtains shut.

Soon Brandy, in a bathrobe, made a brief appearance in the kitchen window, accepting a platter heaped high with pancakes before she vanished from view.

"At least they feed her well," I muttered.

"They're manipulating the poor kid," Lottie hissed. "It's a classic."

Classic what? I wondered. Were pancakes part of the Gilligan's brainwashing scheme, too? We had nothing to do but ponder poor Brandy's manipulation until minutes later. When she showed up fully dressed at the back door, at the end of the long breezeway, I began to wonder if we might not have a chance to follow our plan after all.

Then Mortimer came out the kitchen door, the opposite corner from Brandy. He adjusted his Rockies cap and began to cross the driveway. He headed straight for Lottie and me.

We hopped into the skinny space between the hay bales and the window. "I hope he didn't get a sudden notion to grab some hay," I whispered to Lottie as her knee jabbed into my upper thigh.

We sprawled there, awaiting either jabs, discovery, and/or point-blank gunfire from the Mortimer's trusty holster pistol. Like two uncoordinated fallen pilots, we were stuck in the pose we'd struck upon landing, my elbow pressing the top of her head, her hands clinging to my waist.

Jesus, what if Mortimer went behind the barn and found the Subaru? It was light enough now that we saw his shadow passing the window above. He was probably headed toward the door opening directly onto the driveway. Sure enough, that door creaked open, letting in a shaft of sunrise.

I suppressed my breaths but my heart seemed to pound audibly. I couldn't hear footsteps on the dirt floor, so after a few quiet moments the metallic rattles seemed sudden, disembodied. Great, Mortimer was going for a pitchfork. Not only was our plan screwed, but our lives were about to be scrapped.

Lottie must've come to the same conclusion, her eyes shut tight, her teeth clenched, her clinging hands digging harder into my waist. Our only hope was that Mortimer would fork the topmost bales without noticing the two fools hunched under the lower.

After the rattles, only more silence, not even footfalls. Like an astronaut on the lunar surface, Mortimer must've been bounding around the barn freed from noise and gravity. Silence, silence, then the door creaked shut. The slab of light disappeared. A shadow crossed the window again. Relief felt so total, so palpable in our hunched and awkward bodies, that I almost feared Mortimer might hear our muscles relaxing.

Extracting knees and elbows and climbing out of the skinny space, we rose to the window, glancing out sidelong. Mortimer had taken a shovel, and now he scooped up the dead cat. Using the blade as a stretcher, he conveyed the carcass toward the soft, tilled soil of the kitchen garden. "Here's our chance. Plan A," Lottie said. "Before he puts back that shovel!"

There wasn't time to ask her what the hell Plan B was. While Mortimer dug the cat's grave, Brandy was feeding bites from her breakfast to a kitten hidden under the breezeway. Heading through the barn's back door, Lottie and I separated, she taking the long way around the cottonwoods to disclose our scheme to Brandy, and I back to the Subaru.

I reversed down the driveway, then halted near the kitchen door. Slamming the door and calling out hello, I walked around the house to the kitchen garden.

Mortimer glanced up from his unceremonious burial, shoveling dirt over the shallow hole. When he'd filled it, he stuck the shovel in a furrow and faced me. He lifted his cap enough to reveal his bald head, then tamped it back. "What can I do for ya?"

"Sorry to bother you," I said, leaning against the ramshackle fence. "I'm lost."

"I figured that much. No other reason a stranger would end up way out here." Close up, Mortimer wasn't quite as evil looking as I expected for a teenager-kidnapping, cat-shooting Citizens Against Terror vigilante. Granted, he was bigger than an outhouse and could dismember my person with his bare hands. But he had a smile that spread crinkles around his eyes. He acted as if he were glad I happened along, just for the distraction. "Where you headed, buddy?"

"Somebody told my sister and me this road would take us back into Casper. A shortcut. But we ended up at a dead end in the cemetery."

"Well, they told you wrong. You should've gone east, back to Alcova."

"Where the heck's Alcova?"

"Listen, come on inside. I got a road map fairly handy."

Mortimer led me through the kitchen, where he washed his hands at the sink, then led me down a long hallway past the bedrooms. He stopped at the open door of Brandy's room, calling her name. "The girl's got to get ready for work," he explained, "and she always shilly-shallies."

I had time to glimpse Brandy's room as her guard looked in:

two overstuffed armchairs, an expensive sound system, a computer, a shelf full of pristine paperbacks, CDs, and DVDs; a king-size bed laden with stuffed animals under a framed poster of a hunky country singer, shirtless under cowboy hat and guitar strap. "Yeah," Mortimer said, reading my expression, "she's spoiled, all right."

He directed me through the den, where we'd seen Brandy watching the big-screen TV. Like Brandy's room, it was crowded with new, expensive stuff that ill-matched the creaky old house: plush carpets new in their chemical scent, brass lamps, armchair loungers, pool and foosball tables. It looked like a ranch family's name-brand spoils, fresh from victory on a TV game show. The whole atmosphere, including Mortimer's implication that he was Brandy's indulgent father, struck me as stagy—out of a script for when strangers happened by. Maybe Lottie was right about C.A.T.'s power and subtlety, considering how they must've created and managed this velvet trap for the puny prize of Brandy McConnaughty.

Mortimer took out the road map and spread it across the pool table, expertly redirecting me back to Casper. From the den he led me onto the breezeway through the same door that Brandy had used to sneak out and feed the kitten. I held my breath. Had Lottie had enough time to complete her stage of Plan A?

Plan B, I realized, was simply whatever followed the failure of A, our instant and bloody demise at the whim of Brandy's armed guard.

I sucked oxygen again, though, when Mortimer and I emerged onto the breezeway's empty planks. We strolled around to where Lottie waited in the Subaru's passenger seat. She glanced into the visor mirror and fussed elaborately with her hair, then smiled sweetly for Mortimer as if just aware of him. She rolled down the window, then went on dragging a comb through her dark locks.

"That girl's probably out pampering her horses," Mortimer told me as I took the driver's seat. "Or playing around with this kitten she thinks I don't know about. It's the same song and dance every morning."

"A teenager?" Lottie inquired, sighing in sympathy. "Why do they have to be so contrary?"

"That's the perfect word for my girl," Mortimer said. "She's ornery as a three-legged mule. Well, you folks have a good trip. Though I'll be goddamned why anybody would be in any hurry to get to Casper."

Less than two hours later, I sat on a picnic table, Brandy's no-name kitten in my lap and a map of Wyoming spread out before me. In the opposite direction from Casper, in a state park outside Lander, I waited for Lottie and Brandy to emerge from the ladies' room and wished the sun would rise above the canyon walls. Either emergence could take a while. The canyon was deep and women seemed to indulge in lengthy absences when they visited lavatories in pairs.

Our flight from Sweetwater had been uneventful, Lottie and I giddy with relief. Brandy, however, grew silent and sullen from the moment she emerged from her hiding place under our coats in the backseat. Clinging to her fugitive calico kitten, she defied Lottie's attempts at conversation, stuck in a stubborn "Yes, ma'am, no ma'am" mode. From what little she was willing to say, I gleaned that Lottie had had no trouble convincing Brandy to come along for the ride. The only non-negotiable item had been the kitten, which Brandy refused to abandon to the guard's violence. "That son of a bitch shot her momma in cold blood last night," she'd seethed.

In the interests of keeping the peace, I didn't mention that if the kitten had meowed while Mortimer stood beside the Subaru, we'd all have been at his pistol's mercy.

Ears fastened to local radio for bulletins, we'd hurried west over a two-lane blacktop near Lander expecting roadblocks and

gaggles of highway patrolmen on high alert for an old maroon
Subaru, an escaped adolescent felon, and two adult kidnappers.
We skirted town, though, on a back road that would climb over
the Wind River Range and back to points south.

South of Lander in Canyon Sinks State Park, we powdered our
noses in a chilled chasm. This deserted picnic area beside the Popo
Agie River was completely concealed by high shrubs.

Now that I was alone, with time to consider our predicament,
my stomach took its turn at somersaults. In one quick gulp of
Wyoming landscape, I had gone from expecting an anticlimax to
expecting arrest on federal charges. I could also add one more loss
to this summer, along with Nadia and Nick: my teaching career.
Without giving this abduction a moment's intelligent analysis, I'd
probably exchanged our blind-lucky rescue of a sullen prisoner for
a long sentence of my own. It felt as if all my co-scheming with
Lottie in the wake of Nick's death had been under a crazy enchantment. Now the spell was wearing off fast.

On the drive, I'd tuned in as Lottie inquired about the exact
nature of Brandy's confinement. Why the shuttle back and forth
to the luxurious ranch house detention? Was C.A.T. really behind
it all? Yes ma'am, Brandy sure was glad we'd saved her from those
vigilante wackos. No ma'am, she didn't understand what they
planned to do with her, either. The nearest I could figure, C.A.T.
meant to try Brandy in a kangaroo court of their own, in cahoots
with rogue prison guards, showing off their hostage as a publicity
stunt. Here's how my own short but scintillating conversation
with Brandy had gone:

"So, what did you find out about C.A.T., Brandy? Are they
linked to the militia movement?"

"What's that?"

"You know, nuts with guns who hate the government? Like
Timothy McVeigh."

"Who's he, some fag?"

So I was left to my own theorizing. Was Brandy's capture designed to expose weaknesses in the federal prison security system? Was the stunt designed to promote C.A.T.'s critique of too-lenient justice and too-lax prisons? Was Brandy's detention deliberately luxe to convince the media that their aims were honorable and completely political?

The sun finally grazed the sandstone tip of the canyon's jagged rim. Now orange-red rock blazed over the cottonwoods, but the sight seemed beyond savoring now. We needed to get the hell on that back road. What was taking the ladies so long?

At last, Lottie crossed the footbridge a few yards upstream, Brandy behind her. They stopped for a moment at the railing. Lottie suddenly hopped, causing Brandy to lose her balance, which caused something else, unprecedented: Brandy laughed. Giggling, she recovered her balance, then imitated Lottie's hop, so that Lottie lost hers.

When they came forward to the table, out of breath and still chuckling, Lottie announced, "We came back on that nature trail along the opposite bank. It's got a guide to the whole riparian ecosystem."

"Wonderful," I said, rising. "Now, let's—"

"Oh, look, Brandy," Lottie said. "There's one right here. A sego lily. This place is absolutely teeming with wildflowers. An oasis."

"Wonderful," I repeated. "When the cops get here, you can include them in your riparian lecture."

Lottie sighed. Brandy snatched her kitten from my grasp and paced away, nuzzling her face against its fur.

"Sorry, Ray," Lottie said when Brandy was out of hearing. "I needed a few minutes alone with her. To see if she'd open up to me. We've got to get her to trust us, tell us more about the abduction,

C.A.T., and whatever they were planning next. What kind of press conference can we call if we don't have any facts?"

"We're calling a press conference?"

"Of course. Once we've got Brandy safely sequestered somewhere. Once we expose the way C.A.T. mistreated her, I don't think we'll be the ones who need to worry about the cops anymore."

"So, there's a safe place for us?" I rattled the map, then smoothed it on the picnic table. "Where to? Mexico?"

Brandy had wandered back into earshot. "That far?" She squeezed the kitten.

"Well," Lottie said, "we'd have international immunity."

"Ever heard of extradition?" I asked.

"Hey, I never mentioned Mexico, Ray. You did!"

"What about California?" Brandy asked. "Like, Hollywood?"

"I've been thinking of Utah," Lottie said. "I know just the place, hidden away from practically everything, where we could plan our press conference and our next steps in peace. Plus, I have a friend there to help us."

"Not the Confusion Range." I said. "Not the National Proving Ground."

"I hear Utah sucks," Brandy added.

"Trust me, folks," Lottie said, "it'll be perfect. Larry Lucas is very interested in Brandy's case, and he knows all about handling publicity. Plus, he'll do anything for me." She pointed at the map, her forefinger tracing a looping route on faint, squiggling secondary roads out of Wyoming and into Utah's Uinta Mountains, through the Bad Land Cliffs and Wasatch Plateau, around the Mount Nebo Range and across the Sevier Desert toward Utah's southwestern edge. "Plus," Lottie said, "it's really not that far."

Though they reduced the odds of roadblocks and highway patrol vigilance, those empty back roads also raised an out-of-state car to the status of an event. Yet we had to pass out of Wyoming and across all of Utah undetected.

Brandy leaned against the table. Her gaze, aimed over the kitten's head, followed mine out of the chasm, the gravel road climbing on rugged switchbacks toward South Pass. Then she asked Lottie, "So, what's 'riparian' mean?"

"Oh, it's just a fancy word for a desert zone where plants and animals can survive along waterways. Where, otherwise, life wouldn't belong at all."

Past noon we were already ensconced in Little Antarctica, a massive truck stop/tourist trap dominating the interchange where our back road intersected with the interstate. Just north of the Utah line, its glorious capitalist offerings beckoned in the form of powerful "bottomless cup" coffee-shop coffee, and omelets, and coffee, and pancakes, and coffee. We'd circled the complex three times, expecting to elude the highway patrol lying in wait for us, but with the place busy as hell and devoid of cops, we indulged ourselves.

In the gift shop Brandy and I sampled a selection of obscene wooden door pounders—"great knockers"—while Lottie collapsed into sleep in one of the 333 "air-conditioned (brrrr!) modern rooms." Plan C was for Lottie and me to take turns sleeping while the other amused our teenaged fugitive. Then we'd drive under night cover all the way to New Carlsbad, Utah, the closest town to the National Proving Ground and Larry Lucas's defunct Desert Ecology Project in the Confusion Range.

"He'll do anything for me," Lottie had bragged of the renowned Dr. Lucas. Well, la-de-da; somehow, his powerful genius was sucking me another five hundred miles from my leafy, peaceful neighborhood.

The back roads from Lander had been empty but still provoked

Lottie's penchant for roadside distractions. When we'd crossed the Great Divide near Atlantic City, and Lottie found out Brandy had never crossed to the Western Slope, she ordered Brandy to spit into Pacific Creek. "Now your saliva will float to California, not the Atlantic." (Brandy responded with "No shit?" and a smile.) Lottie also took the chance to hold forth on the telltale alpine habitat of Richardson's ground squirrel and the unmistakable characteristics of the common flicker bird. Brandy actually responded with a flicker of interest in the warbling vireo until I spoiled the nature study by reminding them that we were under avid pursuit by C.A.T. and the federal corrections system and the sheriffs of several counties, and politely urged them back to the car.

Now I babysat Brandy in the gift shop. She cradled the kitten in her arm's crook while she studied a selection of ceramic kitty cats. I inspected redwood slabs with inlaid ashtrays proclaiming PARK YOUR BUTTS HERE, fascinated by the certainty that I'd seen identical artwork twenty years before when my grandparents took me to California's Drive-Thru Tree. As an eight year old, I hadn't thought it was very funny, either. Was this the true American nightmare conspiracy, an enormous underground sewer pipeline connecting the nation's souvenir shops, Cape Canaveral STICK IT UP YOURS plastic rockets shipped to Arizona while the Petrified Forest's MINE'S HARD TOO stony woods were vacuum-tubed to the limp, mucky Everglades?

"I love this store," Brandy said, actually smiling as I approached. "I haven't been able to shop for so long."

I raised my eyebrows in silent tribute to Brandy's capacity to appreciate anything, even if it was this crap. "You wanna buy something?"

Brandy shrugged. "No money."

"You want one of those kitty-cat knickknacks? Hey, I'm loaded."

She opened her squinty eyes as wide as they would go. "You'd do that?" Dropping her eyes to the kitten she muttered, "I didn't think you liked me."

"Why wouldn't I? I don't even know you, kid."

"Kid? I'm not a kid. I've gone out with guys your age."

"No way. I'm practically a senior citizen, child. Come on, pick one out and let's go."

Showing her sharp little teeth again, Brandy turned back to the shelf. Just as she reached for a ceramic kitty cat, the clerk appeared at her side. "I'm afraid you'll have to take your kitten out of the store."

"Why?" Brandy asked. "This kitty's not hurting—"

"Store policy. That's why, missy."

"That's stupid!" Brandy hollered, shoving her face within inches of the cashier's. "I was gonna buy your cheap piece of crap here, but you can have it, OK?" She hurled the ceramic kitten at the clerk's feet. The astonished woman had to do a little Mexican hat dance to avoid ricocheting shards. Brandy bolted outside cradling her kitten in both arms, yelling, "I hate your store!"

I apologized, helped the cashier clean up, and paid the extortionist price. I felt compelled to cover our tracks. "Poor kid's under medication," I told the cashier. "But it's wearing off. Family's on the way to see Amy's specialist in Salt Lake."

"I'll pray for you, young man."

I hurried out to find that Brandy had vanished. Immediately, my guts tensed as I sensed she'd run off. But why? Without money, wheels, wherewithal, or a destination, she needed us.

Still, I fought a panicked flutter as I searched the complex of shops in the warm, steady wind, then checked our room at the motel. Lottie remained alone, sound asleep. I checked the parking lot, where I'd hidden the Subaru between a huge dumpster and a Cowboy Van Lines truck, though I didn't know why Brandy would want to hang around a locked car. Then I heard voices on the other side of the Cowboy rig.

Brandy had set her kitten on the cab's running board while she chatted with the tall, handsome young driver. He spat, laughed, and set more chew under his lip. When she asked him something, all I could hear was "California." The driver shook his head, patted Brandy's shoulder, and stepped toward the running board, which startled the kitten. It leapt down and scampered under the cab.

"See what you did, you bastard?" Brandy yelled in her charming fashion. "You selfish son of a bitch!"

The driver just laughed, hoisting himself into the cab while Brandy hustled around it.

I rounded the cab after her, just as the truck's engine growled to life. I overtook her as she loped toward the "33 gleaming gas and diesel pumps," through which the kitten had already maneuvered. "Look! Ray! My kitty!" she yelled as I passed her.

Taken aback by hearing my name fall like a toad from her traitor's mouth, let alone in such notes of pure distress, I stumbled forward. The kitten hurtled into the open door of the gas pay station as if it caught the scent of its martyred mother inside.

But, at the door, I caught the scent of the square-jawed man. He'd scooped up Brandy's kitten after he'd paid the cashier and faced me at the threshold. "Well, I'll be damned. We meet again, so soon! Your little cat?"

"My niece's." I indicated Brandy, who appeared beside me to accept the kitten with a real smile between hard breaths.

"Dang little critter ran straight up my shoes and clawed my cuffs," he told Brandy, smiling. "Must've smelled something—or someone—familiar on me, huh?"

"She's just a very friendly kitty," Brandy explained, and thanked the square-jawed man.

We all moved off the hot, gas-pungent asphalt toward the shade of a quick mart overhang. Brandy sat on a bench to comfort her kitten while, freaked out, I pulled the square-jawed man out of her hearing range. "This is a hell of a coincidence."

"Not really. Everybody on I-80 stops at Little Antarctica. But I thought you were heading back to Denver."

"Well, remember my sister and the scenic route? We ended up getting sidetracked. Canyons, nature walks. See, Nicolette's a biology teacher. Birds on the brain."

"You're a hell of a long way west," he muttered, smiling.

"And what are you doing way out here?"

"Change of plans. Boss sprung a company meeting in Salt Lake on us. Hey, that was fun, last night. Wish I could pack you to my lonely hotel room for company tonight." He took my hand, as if to shake it, but held it briefly. "Seriously, if you have any chance to get away, we could have a good time. After the meeting tomorrow, I'll take you back to Denver, safe and sound."

Oh my God. As his gaze bore into mine, I turned away, glancing at Brandy. No niece I'd ever claim, she smoothed the kitten's coat, cooing nonsense baby talk. What, what I was doing here?

"Well, my car's still at the pump," the square-jawed man said. "I better get going." He nodded at Brandy, raising his voice. "So, this one came along to see her sister, huh?"

"Yeah, my sister, mister." Brandy joined us, hoisting the cat. "I thought she'd get a kick out of my new pet, but the damn guards wouldn't let the kitten into the visitors' room."

"Sounds like Sweetwater, huh? No common respect for the families. Well, great running into you folks. Have a safe drive back to Denver, OK?"

As Brandy and I watched the square-jawed man pace to his car, a sporty BMW, I suppressed a powerful desire to escape with a handsome traveler, just as Brandy had tried to do. Why not run off with the square-jawed man for nonstop hotel sex in Salt Lake City? I'd done my part, hadn't I, risking my life to rescue Brandy? And for my trouble, I'd sunk into deeper jeopardy, accomplice to an entire volume of federal crimes and pursued by vigilantes. My brain must've been just as addled as Lottie's when I agreed to this fiasco. And now that I felt more clearheaded, I seemed to be losing my false bravado. What else would compel me forward? What good was I now?

Apparently I was no good at all. Not only was I an unmitigated slut, I was a slut of the evil variety who'd abandon a damsel in distress for drive-by sex. Well, two damsels in distress.

The square-jawed man lingered at his platinum BMW coupe, waving at me but standing still to hold the door open.

Oh my sweet baby Jesus. All I had to do was ask Brandy to give Lottie my keys and my best and bolt for the Beamer. I could call Lottie from the road, explaining how she'd be better off without me, traveling lighter to Utah. After her liberating press conference with Larry Lucas, all would be well, and she could drive the Subaru back to Denver.

Brandy sidled closer to me, staring at the square-jawed man as he stared at me. "He's not bad lookin'," she informed me. "Who is he, Ray, some rich fag you guys met in Sweetwater?"

So this was my fate, to squander my last days of freedom in the company of America's Little Sweetheart of Conscience?

Conscience. How I hated that word. I waved, at last, to the square-jawed man while the damned kitten trounced from Brandy's grip onto my shoulders.

Crestfallen, cringing as the kitten clawed through my T-shirt, I studied the Beamer's long good-bye. It looped slowly, lagging along the frontage road to the on-ramp, then gunned to merge with the westbound traffic.

I shrank under the day's nervous excitement. I finally felt the physical cost of our constant anticipation of radio bulletins, drag-nets, lone-wolf sheriffs, and maybe even aerial surveillance, none of which had yet materialized.

I collected the kitten, which had wrapped iself around my neck, and handed it back to Brandy. I forced myself to say something positive as I pointed Brandy across the asphalt, toward our room. "You handled that pretty well. That was cool, jumping in with the story about the visitors' room."

"I'm not as stupid as you think."

"Maybe not. But that was definitely not cool, having a temper tantrum in the gift shop. Missy."

"She was a bitch."

"So were you. And now you owe me 22.95 plus tax."

"You said you were buying it for me!"

"I don't buy broken merchandise. And what was the drama with the truck driver? What the hell were you doing, asking about California?"

"Were you spying on me?"

"Damn right!"

"I was just being nice to that stupid nigger trucker. Give him the thrill of his life. A little attention from a white chick."

"You're one hell of a political idealist."

"What?"

"Aren't you the brave martyr who bombed the Mamie Doud lab in the name of peace and humanity? I'm disappointed. Turns out America's Prisoner of Conscience is just another racist."

"Racist? I don't have nothing against blacks. There was all kinds of black chicks in Sweetwater. Spanish girls, too. Who do you think my friends were? Not those stuck-up white bitches."

I sighed, opening the door to the humming motel room. Lot-tie was awake now, smiling at us from the bedding's orange-chintz splendor, hair tangled in the pillow. I collapsed on the other bed while Brandy told Lottie an abridged version—minus her encounter with the stupid nigger trucker—of her "bad wittle kitty's" near-escape.

Lottie just smiled indulgently at her prize, this abducted human rights case, this illiterate, unpleasant, rickety ignoramus of a girl. Brandy dangled the kitten into Lottie's open arms.

Lottie cradled the critter. "I'll bet she was just overstimulated from having seen all those birds this morning, up on the divide," Lottie said. "All that temptation! I'll bet she was trying to make a run for freedom."

Twisting southward over wet ranges and arid valleys on narrow highways, I dreaded any light clusters flickering ahead under the sliver of moon. Each might mark either the next tiny town or a roadblock. Each pair of headlights, like the ones following us at an even distance along a tight-curved ravine, could be Citizens Against Terror vigilantes happily fingering their triggers.

Since I was the last one to take a sleep shift at Little Antarctica, I was still groggy when Lottie drove the Subaru into Utah at twilight. I truly did expect a full-blown federal dragnet at the state line with both state patrols lending extra vigilance. But at the border, the only party inspecting us was teenaged boys passing in a Mustang convertible. They hooted, rolling down the windows as they overtook our lovely driver, screaming, "Hey, hot momma! Meet us for a beer in Vernal!"

Lottie waved and smiled, but I could tell she was restraining the same anxieties as I. Like underage Wyoming boys who'd blundered into the wrongest state of all for scoring forbidden beers and wild women, we might be delusional fools. Criminal fugitives now, we'd crossed out of wild and empty laissez-faire Wyoming into the very heartland of law and order. Utah had a decided disdain for bomb-wielding terrorists. Ours was lying down in the backseat, cooing over her kitten between bouts of soft snoring.

Whether it was the teenaged boys or restlessness, Lottie grew animated as I fell back into drowsiness, launching a conversation about our teaching careers. "I started young, too, Ray. Even at twenty-two, I always visualized myself as a lifer. I thought I'd be inspiring city kids to love the natural world until I was an old lady."

Hence—despite our status as fleeing fugitives—Lottie's pit stops at wildlife refuges for Brandy's edification. "So you miss teaching?" I asked, ever the dutiful shotgun passenger, even as I craved to slip into a nap.

"I just feel like I'm living a parallel life somehow. As if it were a fantasy, my becoming the wife of a globe-trotting geneticist. As if that young teacher's still out there, organizing mold labs or biodiversity samples, pushing forty while her sophomores are always fifteen."

"When I started, I was never that sure about teaching. Sometimes, I'm still not . . ."

"I am, Ray."

As I finally surrendered to sleep, another voice replaced Lottie's. "I can tell, when you come home all jazzed about the genius girl you've cast as Abigail in *The Crucible*. Or when you torture me at dinner with your students' insights about Tennessee Williams."

"But I never tell you about the panic in my guts. When I'm driving to that school at six in the morning and I've got no idea whether my whole plan is going to dissolve into chaos. If my supervising teacher will dismiss me for incompetence . . ."

"Get over yourself, Ray! Every single job worth doing involves panicky guts."

"But even if I get a real teaching position next year, I'll barely make enough to pay off my student loans and pay the rent. I could make a lot more if I just went full time at your agency, Nick."

"So you wanna be a full-time office boy? For a bunch of snarky real estate agents? When anybody who's spent five minutes enduring your student-teaching braggadocio knows you've got that spark? If you give up now, Ray Fucking O'Brien, how could you ever deserve to be in love with anybody as wonderful as me?"

I started, coming to as we passed the distant lights of a ranch house. Lottie squeezed my wrist. "Are you OK, Ray?"

"Why? What was I . . . ?"

"You were talking in your sleep."

"Dreaming," I said, forcing myself awake. "Nick."

"God, maybe that's how he'll live on. He was always so involved with his friends; I don't see how he'll be able to stay away."

"Yeah. Messing with our brains any way he can."

Lottie laughed, then asked me to scan the radio dial once again. For a while, we'd received an all-news station but listened in vain for any mention of Brandy. So was a notorious terrorist's flight from the Federal Corrections Facility just not news, at least in faraway Salt Lake?

"Maybe the guards," I wondered aloud, "have deliberately failed to report Brandy's absence."

"Yeah," Lottie added, "since they bungled so badly?"

"Meanwhile, C.A.T.'s just lying low, planning to pursue us on their own."

"Yeah. Who knows how deep the connection is between the Federal Corrections and C.A.T., anyway?" Lottie asked. "Could be all kinds of crossover."

I agreed, but kept one more suspicion to myself. Who the hell was the square-jawed man, anyway? Maybe his "boss" was really C.A.T., and his mission was to follow us. If so, I had lusted my way into one more colossal screwup. Thank God, at least, I'd had the wherewithal to mislead him about who we were.

Still—damn!—he'd seen Brandy herself at Little Antarctica.

As those headlights kept steady behind us, I debated telling Lottie about my Sweetwater indiscretion. I still hadn't told her about my tryst with Kurt, either. Suddenly it seemed like I had a lot to hide. Had I inadvertently become a sexual traitor to our cause?

"All this paranoia's exhausting," Lottie declared, pulling into a turnout and asking me to drive. The headlights behind us slowed but kept on the road. As I got out and swung around to take the driver's seat from Lottie, I caught a glimpse of a big Volvo sedan. To my relief, it kept hurtling ahead.

"Anyway, Ray," Lottie said as we proceeded up another piney summit, "whatever role C.A.T. has, before long the regular prison officials have got to be aware of a missing inmate."

I glanced back to see what Brandy thought, but she was sleeping facedown, the kitten curled up on her rear end.

"We'll be in New Carlsbad," Lottie went on, "an hour or two after midnight. Then we'll all feel better . . ." She seemed to be drifting off to sleep.

I didn't know what magic New Carlsbad was supposed to work. I foresaw only more bumbling and risk. With the guidance of Larry Lucas, Lottie planned to focus her press conference on C.A.T.'s mistreatment of Brandy and her subsequent rescue by that force for freedom, the League. Through further magic, this would turn public opinion to favor Brandy, who would somehow remain safely cloistered until the feds granted her release. Then Larry Lucas would hold forth on the genetic weapons dangers that had led to Brandy's attack on the Mamie Doud National Laboratory.

So the whole scheme was predicated on a furor over Brandy's disappearance. The all-news channel remained stubbornly silent on that subject until it faded out. Now, on a praise-Jesus station, a team of Christian psychologists gently counseled that my best bet for overcoming my promiscuous state of sin was to surrender myself to Jesus.

Trouble was, whenever I fantasized about surrendering myself to Him, He always struck me as a major Hunk.

Lottie slept, now, too. Even the Jesus station was damned to pure static.

Once Nick and I, driving around the wilds of Idaho on vacation, suddenly couldn't receive anything but urgent bulletins on the local AM. Static so bad we couldn't grasp anything but the blurted names of surrounding towns. Caught in the middle of what seemed to us an invisible but urgent crisis, we could only speculate: terror attacks, neo-Nazi militia shootouts, nuclear explosions at the Atomic City bombing ranges?

After weaving miles wondering if the world as we knew it had been blasted to hell, we got stopped at a roadblock. We learned of a massive manhunt for escaped prisoners who'd already killed two guards, a cop, and a tourist who got in the way. From there, every time we crossed a junction, we had to endure more questions, identity checks, and trunk searches. By the time we reached Wyoming, the relentless scrutiny had drained and shaken us so much we began to wonder if we somehow really had transported felons. Or, as Nick said, "Maybe we ought to take it up."

Now, five years later, I was transporting a real terrorist on identical highways. But the lack of surveillance and the uncanny silence made me feel just as closely watched.

CHAPTER SEVEN

Lottie woke me at half-past nine, meaning I had had maybe six hours' sleep. My eyes first focused on the smiling-but-weeping painted clown over the dresser.

Even though we'd only spent a few nights on the road, it seemed like I'd already misspent most of my life in cheap motels.

Another stained, crispy carpet; another wall-mounted tissue dispenser, broken and empty; another TV stuck on a channel devoted to right-wing screamers. Lottie pressed a Styrofoam cup of instant coffee into my hand. "Compliments of the Wah Wah Motor Court."

"Ah, this is living." I heard the shower pounding. The kitten prowled the bathroom door, guarding her terrorist mistress. "But where are we, Lottie, exactly? And why?"

"I can't answer existential questions," Lottie said, laughing. "Not before noon." She settled on the bed, her bottom against my hip bone. "Tell me, does this cowgirl outfit make me look thinner?"

Talk about existential questions. "That's just like 'does this dress make my butt look big?' I'm gay, OK? I get a pass on all that."

"Come on. You can be honest. I get the feeling all this anxiety is, at least, chewing up all my flab. Which is good, since I don't need to be fat and ugly for Kurt anymore."

"Which is also good, since there's another scientist you'd rather impress?"

Lottie smiled, eyes cast downward. Embarrassed, I thought. Barely able to contain her giddy, girlish excitement over seeing the great Dr. Larry Lucas in just a few hours. She sipped her coffee, ignoring my question. "Once Kurt finds out I've sprung the Mamie Doud's mad bomber from prison," she said, "he'll never want to see me again. Fat or skinny. Except behind bars." She reached for a plastic store bag. "Anyway, Brandy and I have already been shopping, while you were sleeping. She needed a change of clothes."

"So, what'd you get me?"

From the bag Lottie produced a cap with an inscription over its brim: NEW CARLSBAD: AMERICA'S PROVING GROUND She set it on my head, adjusted it, and leaned back to evaluate the fashion statement. "You look cute with just that cap and your bare chest."

"You flirting with me, now, skinny cowgirl?" I started to push the covers down. "Wanna see the rest of me?"

Lottie halted the sheets' slide. "I already have, remember? The hot tub. You don't have to show off, Ray."

As the shower noise abruptly ceased, Lottie turned toward the thin wall. Pipes rattled and shuddered. The kitten pawed the door, mewling. "God, I meant to tell you something before Brandy gets out of the bathroom," Lottie said, lowering her voice. "I think something horrible happened at that ranch outside Sweetwater."

"For a cat killer, that guard didn't seem like such a bad guy."

"Or such a bad actor? When we were walking back from the shop, Brandy hinted that Mortimer was abusive. But I'm not sure she knows what sexual abuse really is. I'm serious. Considering her boyfriend—who let her take all the risk and all the blame for bombing the lab—I'm sure she thinks exploitation is normal. No wonder she thinks you're the cat's pajamas."

"She can't stand me!"

"That's not what she told me. You're probably the first gentleman she's ever met, Ray. Just, please, go on being nice to her. She's a lot more easily bruised than you might think."

I immediately flashed back to fragile Brandy's tantrum in Little Antarctica, those ceramic shards flying. Not to mention her lascivious plot to escape with the Cowboy Van Lines trucker.

On that thought, the bruised creature herself appeared, drying her hair in the sink alcove, wrapped in a towel too small to conceal her scrawny, freckled shoulders and long, skinny bowlegs. I noticed her big, flat feet. Her toenails were painted pink.

I wondered why Brandy had told Lottie anything positive about me. Though I helped save her bony butt, I hadn't been especially pleasant to her.

When Brandy slipped back into the bathroom to try on her

new outfit, I got dressed. I admired my new image in the mirror, the cap adding just the right local-good-old-boy touch for our afternoon adventure at Larry Lucas's place in the mountains. His ever-present best seller, *GENETIC WARFARE: A Beginner's Guide*, was face down atop the dresser.

I glanced at the book jacket's biography. Even though Lucas's studies of the environmental, military, and moral catastrophes at the Proving Ground had made him a national celebrity, Lottie insisted he was "a self-exiled recluse." Since there was no author photo, and I couldn't recall any of his appearances on cable chat shows or magazine covers, I envisioned an Edward Abbey type, a womanizing, grizzled literary roughneck: long, bleached, thinning hair, sun-damaged skin, and the full beard that grows wild on every environmentalist's chin. But earlier, according to the brief bio, Lucas seemed to have been just another macho-jock-military-science-genius. After conquering collegiate basketball as Most Valuable Player, he served as a Navy test pilot, then saw action in humanitarian operations in the Balkans, "a hero to his comrades in the air and the beleaguered civilians on the ground." With Kosovo safe for democracy, Lucas returned to Stanford to "pioneer doctoral study in the evolving field of genetic ecology . . ."

Brandy tapped my shoulder, then fell into place at Lottie's side. They smiled, striking exaggerated runway poses. Brandy's cowgirl outfit—pearl-button blouse and Lady Wranglers—almost matched Lottie's Kmart ensemble. "What do you think, Ray?" Brandy asked me, beaming beside her voluptuous mentor and savior.

"Just like twins," I heard myself utter. Yeah, like I was quintuplets.

I could play cowperson, too. I narrowed my eyes at Lottie, then lowered my cap's brim like a Hollywood rustler. I winked at the redneck-looking dude in the mirror. But I knew on Brandy's authority he was every inch a gentleman.

"When Kurt and I lived out there, on the other side of the Wah Wah Valley," Lottie announced on our ten-minute comprehensive tour of town, "New Carlsbad was our only contact with civilization." I followed her gesture to the stark, sandy range a few miles west of town.

We were so deep into desert that although the surrounding summits reached nine and ten thousand feet, they had few clouds to catch. Reflected mirage-like in saline wastes, the peaks were just as barren of life. In fact, we were so far west that for all intents and purposes we were in Nevada (except for the purposes of gambling and prostitution and free-flowing liquor).

Sight unseen, arriving in the dark, I'd expected to despise New Carlsbad as just another smug Mormon town where the people were too damned happy and the graveyards too damned big. But the main drag was beautifully seedy, the Rocket Burger and Guided Missile Cafe aiming their rooftop namesakes toward the flawless cerulean sky. Between a vacant savings and loan and a closed, padlocked Environmental Protection Agency office, a metal arch stretched over Atomic Avenue to proclaim NEW CARLSBAD: GATEWAY TO THE NATION'S PROVING GROUNDS. The town's only stoplight eternally blinked yellow, as if warning investors and endangered species to proceed with extreme caution.

Like an atrophied diorama of the West's booms and busts, the town had specialized in broken dreams. We drove past a vintage twenties department store, huge and elegant, but converted into a farm equipment warehouse, tractor-trailers and clodhoppers posing in its plate-glass windows. Lottie explained how the town meant to prosper in the roaring 1920s as "Utah's Pleasure Ground" on the promise of a rail spur that would deliver tourists to its mineral hot springs. When rivals deliberately bankrupted the rail line, the town almost withered.

In the fifties New Carlsbad flirted with the uranium boom, then got jilted in the uranium bust. Pleasure ground to proving ground, it was only the influx of military, corporate, and research personnel to the National Proving Grounds since the eighties that kept the town alive . . . but comatose.

"So the end of the Cold War meant grief," Lottie said, "in this corner of Utah." She pointed out one of the decades-old "new" structures in town, the Ronald Reagan Medical Center, named to attract funding during the reign of that American philosopher-king. As if to embody Reagan's vanished golden age, the shiny metallic box, complete with false porticos and pointless spires, stood empty. Its broken windows stared into the encroaching desert.

"Remember that shut-down savings bank?" Lottie asked us, driving past the chain-link barrier enclosing the hospital. "Its president hustled phony loans for the hospital's construction. Then he ditched town to buy a beach house in Malibu. The funding for health care never arrived."

The more I saw, the more I appreciated the forlorn town. Around the last bend of Atomic Avenue sprawled the great stone ruin of a three-story hotel, all Italianate colonnades and arches, its grand circle drive now fronted by a humble metal sign: NEW CARLSBAD WORLD FAMOUS HOT SPRINGS AND POOL. OPEN TO THE PUBLIC. FEE REQUIRED.

Lottie confirmed that the springs were still open, a rag-tag survivor after "the vice president of the savings and loan hustled a failed redevelopment scheme. He allegedly involved Mel Gibson and Neil Bush on the promise of a world-class resort, a posh soak on the way to Aspen." A flock of gray birds alighted from the grand hotel's paneless windows. "Now the vice prez lives in Palm Beach."

As we swung westward toward the desert mountains, Lottie said, "We'll treat ourselves to a soak in the springs after our press conference. To celebrate!"

It struck me that Lottie was dazzled by more than this vaunted publicity stunt. She'd called Larry Lucas earlier to confirm that we'd be welcome "out at the Project" and really seemed to be in a dither over hooking up with him again. She also seemed mighty pleased with herself for delivering our prize flesh-and-blood, anti-genetic-warfare icon—you know, Brandy—to her hero's doorstep. Instead of the white knight, rescuing these damsels in his trusty Subaru steed, it was becoming clear I was nothing more than a queer sidekick.

So New Carlsbad played host to yet another crew of cheaters, schemers, and charlatans. We were its first, I'll bet, in the human rights terrorist-liberating business. I suspected our little plan would petrify, then flake away like all the others under the Confusion Range. As the town receded and we passed a skeletal quick mart beset by buzzards pecking at a jackrabbit carcass, Brandy poetically observed, "This place sucks."

After dead-straight miles across shimmering salt flats, we climbed into the mountains. The Subaru chugged up bare slopes and past eroded rock spires, sand-choked streambeds, broken cattle guards, and faint two-track roads into defunct uranium claims. Near the top, the road got so steep the windshield aimed straight into a deep blue sky scattered with thin-stretched, rainless clouds.

At the summit, Lottie directed me onto a gravel road twisting along the ridgetop. A fading sign, DESERT ECOLOGY PROJECT had been splashed by a red, spray-painted skull and crossbones. A fresher, smaller sign beneath read CLOSED.

As we crested the ridge, Lottie indicated the broad, white sandy plain to the west. "The National Proving Ground. That's where Kurt and I lived. See where that side road heads toward the mesa? Our place was under that notch." Her cheery tour leader's tone now betrayed a twinge of tension. What would living in such a void do to a person's psyche? Maybe I was right to expect Larry Lucas to be a bit cracked and cantankerous.

"Are we practically, like," Brandy asked, "in California?"

"Not really," Lottie said, almost swallowing her sigh. "We're five or six hundred miles from the coast."

"Is it all as crappy as this? I mean, I thought Wyoming was bad."

"I'll show you some pretty country," Lottie said, "I promise. After Larry helps us organize our press conference."

I appreciated Lottie's soothing tone, knowing she didn't have the vaguest idea what would actually happen to Brandy—and us—even if we managed to bring off the press event.

The gravel road widened as we passed the abandoned buildings of the Desert Ecology Project, windows boarded, doors padlocked. Near a laboratory, a toppled refrigerator had been shoved to the ground and left for dead. High on a rooftop pole, a shredded earth flag slapped in the west wind.

Beyond, a maze of fences marked empty animal pens and corrals. Three spindly, bare-branched apple trees slowly died of thirst. Around them, neat lines of stickers surrounded a scarecrow whose stuffing had exploded. Gutless, it leaned forward, bowing to no one's applause.

"I expected this, but it's still a shock," Lottie said. "The last time I was here, the place was thriving. Labs, schools, families." As we passed weedy, phantom gardens and pens, she added, "Back when the life sciences got a few pennies left over from weapons development."

Now residential buildings ringed gravel cul-de-sacs. Tidy metal dwellings faced outward. Resin chairs waited in dooryards as if the residents might slip outside at any moment, chips and lemonade in hand. A tricycle waited near a doorway. With the material spared and the humans vanished, the Project looked like a city murdered by that other Reagan legacy, the neutron bomb. Swings swayed, childless, in a plastic playground.

The gravel roadway ended. A two-track road dipped into a gully, then rose again to the ridge's crest.

After New Carlsbad, though, this place wasn't really that weird. The entire West was littered with towns that had failed when minerals ran out. Still, here was a town gone ghostly when we'd given up mining for knowledge.

"I used to love visiting Larry and his crew up here," Lottie went on. "And especially spending time with the animals."

"Did they keep horses?" Brandy asked, cuddling her kitten.

"A bunch. Those biologists came out here from the coasts and went cowboy in a big way. We used to go on long rides, overnighters, deep into the Confusion Range."

"Did Kurt go along?" I asked.

"Oh, Kurt wasn't much for the great outdoors. That's why I was so grateful to have Larry's company out here."

Yeah, you betcha, I thought. Those bedrolls must've been smokin' long after the campfires were doused.

The road hugged the ridge's western edge now, offering glaring vistas of the National Proving Ground. The airfield's tarmac crucifix stretched toward the far mesa. A jet took to flight, tiny and silent, and soon streamed a contrail far over Nevada.

"So did you have much of a social life," I asked, "with Kurt and the geneticists over at the Proving Ground?"

"Not really. Most everyone except Kurt and me had deep military affiliations. These guys made Dr. Strangelove seem subdued.

LEE PATTON

They'd hold dead serious dinner conversations about Iraq or Iran secretly invading Texas. If it weren't for Larry and the other biologists up here on the project, I'd have gone completely bonkers."

After a few miles we passed through a roughhewn gate flanked by waist-high junipers and pinyon pine. Ahead a small house trailer nestled, shaded by a corrugated shelter, its roof wide enough to cover a Jeep and a sixties' Triumph coupe.

As we pulled up, a black Labrador rounded the trailer's corner, barking—inquisitive, not unfriendly. Lottie hurried from the car immediately, bending down to pet the dog, who didn't hesitate to lick her face. "Felicia!" Lottie cried, "at least you haven't changed, old girl."

"Just what I was going to say," came a booming baritone around the corner, echoing under the high metal roof. A tall blond man appeared, clean shaven. "But I see it's not true," the man said. He dropped to his haunches beside Lottie and the dog. "Old girl, your hair's almost as dark as Felicia's."

"Incognito," Lottie said before the two of them attempted an awkward hug from their dog-level positions. But then they rose gracefully into a long, sighing, heartfelt embrace, smooching cheeks and nuzzling. Felicia leapt, one paw on Larry's leg, one on Lottie's.

Old lovers, all right.

I stood beside the Subaru. Brandy remained in the backseat, cradling her kitten, regarding Felicia with fear.

When Lottie led Larry to us for introductions, he stared at me in that straight-guy reflex, sizing me up. With his extra inches of towering height and extra pounds of muscle, Larry seemed to calculate that I wasn't much competition. He let go my attempt at a firm shake with a jock's condescension. Then he turned away and forced his arm through the Subaru's back window. Larry smiled broad and toothy at Brandy, extending his hand.

134

Hardly touching his palm, Brandy clung tighter to the kitten.

"It's an honor to meet you, Miss McConnaughty," Larry said without the least sarcasm. "The way I see it, we all owe you a great deal for what you attempted. I'm just so sorry it backfired. Come on, your kitten doesn't have to be afraid of old Felicia."

"You sure?" Brandy said, all trembly and girly. Her timidity surprised the hell out of me. With the habitual hostility erased from her face, she stared at Larry until—shock of shocks—she accepted his hand. He helped her exit the Subaru with her dignity intact. "She sure is a big dog, mister."

"But she's no cat hater," Larry said. "You give Felicia a little time to get used to her guest, and she'll be inviting your kitten to a game of penny-ante poker."

Brandy giggled. Giggled, like a normal teenaged girl. Not only was Lottie smitten in Dr. Lucas's presence, but so was even our timorous, delicate Brandy! I suppose her alleged admiration of me was already forgotten, and who could blame her. Larry Lucas was not exactly the hairy Thoreauvian hippie mad scientist I'd expected. Ruddy-cheeked, his blond hair close-cropped, he looked more like a central-casting astronaut, the All-American white boy at forty. His basketball champion's build was well preserved.

Lottie took Larry's arm as he led us to his "terrace," some beat-up director's chairs huddled around an old metal table under the metal-roofed shelter. The plants around us, including a succulent garden along the ridge crest, looked freshly watered. "You smell good!" Lottie cooed. "Not at all like a desert rat. Or a biologist."

"It's all for company," Larry said, urging us to get comfortable. "Normally I don't bother with a clean T-shirt and my best khaki shorts. I just hang out shirtless, the whole summer, in my boxer shorts. Felicia doesn't seem to mind."

"I'd like to see that." Lottie smiled, sly.

"No problem. I strip at the slightest provocation, as you know,"

Larry said, "for a small fee." Larry winked for Brandy's benefit, then helped scoot her into the chair at the table's head. "You're our guest of honor, young lady. I didn't expect you to be such a wisp of a girl, though. Considering the size of your courage."

Brandy hid her embarrassment with a bout of kitten nuzzling. Larry's forthright, sincere admiration flabbergasted me. He seemed to be Lottie's male counterpart, ingenuous without being a chump, idealistic without being too uncool.

"Well," Lottie said, "there's so much to tell."

Here we go, I thought, swallowing hard as I sat facing the vista over the ridge crest, the Proving Ground's airstrip crucifix. The Confusion Range slumbered on the horizon. Above it, criss-crossed contrails formed a vaporous cursive, like a code writer's private joke squiggled across the western sky.

"You think they hurt, inside?" Brandy was asking me an hour later. "Them lambs?"

After Lottie had brought Larry up to date on our misadventure so far, he'd excused himself to make sandwiches. Lottie offered to help, following Larry into the trailer. So Brandy interrogated me about the animal experiments that Larry and Lottie had witnessed in the Confusion Range. "Did they have, like, seizures?"

"According to what Lottie told me, yes. They seemed to have advanced nervous disorders." As I paraphrased what little I knew, I felt ridiculous. Lottie's stories of mysterious animal ailments called to mind the old tales that swept Colorado when I was a kid, crop circles and cattle mutilations. "In humans," I went on, regardless, "that kind of pain can send victims into shock or even a coma. I'm sure it's the same for most mammals."

Brandy rose from her director's chair, her face scrunched with annoyance. "Nobody told me about that." She stared out over the desert, rocking her kitten, her back to me.

"Who do you mean?"

"I just mean . . . why wasn't it in the news or anything?"

"Larry's been all over the country talking about it. And it's all in his book."

"Have you read it?"

OK. OK, I had to admit I was a hypocrite: "No." But I wasn't the one bombing science labs. Our abducted terrorist remained so enameled in ignorance, even of her own supposed motives for the tragedy she'd unleashed for the janitor and the lab monkey. Not to mention the sharp, lasting fear she'd instilled in the workers at the Mamie Doud. I struggled to censor any number of scornful, sarcastic comments. "It's probably one of the reasons that the ecology project we drove through is a ghost town, Brandy. The weapons testers took their revenge on Larry for revealing the scary stuff they're unleashing over there."

"Weapons testers? What does hurting animals have to with testing?"

I pointed toward the Proving Ground. "Well, imagine if they could demonstrate the horrors in livestock, then threaten the same disorders in humans. During wartime."

Brandy raised her kitten to her shoulder, swaying her skinny butt. "I just don't see how they can hurt helpless animals."

"I just don't understand why you're surprised," I cried, unable to contain my anguish. "According to Larry, Dominex is about to perfect systems a lot scarier than destroying lambs' nervous systems. I thought you knew all this. I thought that's why you bombed the goddamn Mamie Doud National Laboratory in the first place."

Brandy stared, her eyes slit, two mean little lines. "Why are you swearing at me?"

"Maybe I'm tired of misanthropes who are such big fans of all the other mammals."

"Don't use such big goddamn words!" Fighting mad, Brandy turned away, hunched over her kitten. But when she turned back, visibly restraining her temper, she lowered her voice and spoke slowly. "You know I never meant to hurt anybody, Ray. They told me that lab was doing experiments that would hurt children all over the world. Someday. But nobody ever told me they were already starting to use them on real live creatures."

"And they have, Brandy, on real live people, too," Larry said, his deep voice echoing under the high metal roof. The trailer's screen door slammed shut. On the trailer steps, Lottie conveyed a tray of sandwiches and the disappointed face she must've used on students who'd quarreled in her absence.

Larry took the tray from her and urged Brandy to sit down, then made sure we all had a sandwich before he continued. "That's one of the main reasons I agreed to do TV interviews tomorrow in Salt Lake City, for the Sunday morning shows. Now that the *Beginner's Guide* is coming out in paperback, I wished I'd had time to revise it in light of what I've discovered. I have definite evidence of genetic mutations in humans. Here in Utah."

"What about the local family's genetic disorders," Lottie asked, "that supposedly went back generations?"

"Well, that family's been in touch with me again. The mother had her fourth child in July. Died a few minutes after birth. Perfectly normal nervous system, except that every nerve ending and capillary was horribly exposed. See, the baby was born without skin."

We all set our half-bitten sandwiches on our napkins, staring at Larry.

He sighed. "Now researchers are studying this family tree for this 'genetic disorder' that's never been seen before. I've also been following a study overseas, where a whole Kurdish community in northern Iraq has gradually developed beta thlassemia. That means all red blood cells are unable to produce protein. A gradual but certain death for the entire village. Apparently they were selected as beneficiaries of a free 'inoculation' during wartime. I'm certain they were actually genetic implants. I'm almost as sure Dominex supplied the biotechnology, developed at the Mamie Doud National Lab."

Lottie set her sandwich aside and pressed Larry for other new, technical details. What I gleaned from Larry's summary was how genetic manipulation was far more advanced than many experts in the field suspected. Much of the original research had focused on therapeutic treatments, implanting healthy genetic structures into diseased ones. But Dominex's new studies all involved exploring how this process could be reversed. "It seems to be much easier to create disease and grotesque deformities," Larry remarked, "than to produce health. Especially if you're willing to wait for new generations to bear the worst damage you've unleashed."

As absorbing and terrifying as Larry's revelations were, Brandy had recovered her appetite. In fact, she gulped down a second sandwich. Suppressing a belch, she could not disguise her boredom at the very issue that had led her to unleash destruction of her own.

"Why don't you give Felicia the rest of my sandwich, dear?" Lottie said.

Brandy smiled at the diversion and, passing her kitten to Lottie, went around the trailer in search of Larry's dog. We soon heard Felicia barking happily. Larry laughed.

I snarled. "I don't see how Brandy even got convicted. I can't believe any jury thought she had the will or brains to bomb the Mamie Doud. I've never met a more unlikely terrorist."

"She may not be a rocket scientist," Larry said gently, his voice lowered, "but she's no terrorist, either. She certainly had the best intentions."

"I don't think they were her intentions, though."

"At her trial," Lottie said, "it was pretty clear that her boyfriend set her up. It was obvious she didn't understand the issues very well."

"Very well!" I cried. "She doesn't even know what state she's in. The Avenging Eco-Angels must have used some powerful persuasion. But why? Why would they want such a dumb cluck?"

"Ray, have a heart," Lottie said. "Maybe it was precisely because she was so easily led. People with low self-esteem will do just about anything to gain approval. Especially when there's a love relationship involved."

"Thanks, Oprah."

"Ray! Come on. Consider how much courage Brandy showed in the service of ideals she didn't fully understand." Lottie turned to Larry. "And there's more. I'm almost certain she was being abused, psychologically if not sexually, while she was being detained by the Citizens Against Terror. At that ranch. It was amazing to see what expense and trouble they went to."

"I'm sure her escape will be in the news," Larry said, "by the time I reach Salt Lake tomorrow."

"There hasn't been a word about Brandy," I put in, "over two days and six hundred miles."

"C.A.T. may be afraid their complicity with the prison officials is too obvious," Lottie said. "Maybe they've completely hushed this up."

"Then I guess," Larry said, "we need to make a federal case out of the cover-up."

"I expected to state our case in opposition to all the media hype, but this way it's almost better."

"Exactly, Lottie. This way we control the story from the beginning."

"We focus on Brandy's mistreatment in C.A.T.'s hands . . ."

". . . and imply the corruption of the federal corrections system."

"Meanwhile," Lottie said, smiling, "we turn the media's focus to genetics weaponry."

It struck me how the two activists fed each others' passion. They might be more compassionate, but weren't so different from C.A.T. or the Avenging Eco-Angels in their eagerness to use Brandy as their mute and hapless wind-up doll, crucial to the cause but negligible as a human being. I could see Brandy now, up the ridge where the road met the gate, teasing Felicia into ever greater leaps with chants of "Good girl! Good girl!"

"So we stage a big press conference here in New Carlsbad," Larry went on. "I'm sure I can arrange coverage with Salt Lake affiliates. Maybe I can talk that Mormon family into an interview."

"This is exciting!" Lottie said, covering Larry's hand with hers. "I haven't felt this encouraged since Ray and I left Denver."

"But we still need to be cautious," Larry said. As if on cue, a helicopter suddenly thwacked into sight. From where, though? None of us had seen it rise from the mesa or airstrip.

Larry reached for his binoculars. "It's just the usual government-issue chopper, folks, checking out the local lunatic on his ridgetop. I get a visit several times a week."

As the chopper buzzed away, Larry trained his sights on the far mesa. "Ah, there it is, Lottie. I can make out your and Kurt's old love nest. There, under the notch. Third red roof from the far left."

"No need to remind me," Lottie said, petting the kitten.

Larry's gaze roved directly north along the ridgetop. "You're right. We ought to focus on happier times. You know, I don't have to fly to Salt Lake until late afternoon tomorrow. Why don't we take my jeep and head into the Confusion Range in the morning? Scout around, maybe stumble on some fresh evidence. Maybe genetic mischief in the Blindfold Valley?"

Lottie thought it was a great idea, and I was sure it had less to with the prospect of spastic livestock than nostalgia for the backdrop of her trysts with Larry.

I asked Larry to point out the range. Standing, he placed the binoculars in my grasp, taking my shoulders in his firm grip to aim me in the right direction. "See those dreamy hunks of geology? Just northeast of here."

Dreamy? They appeared like any other humps of desert rock, summits piled two thousand feet higher than Larry's ridge, bare except for scattered pinyon and juniper. Their only claim to uniqueness was spooky-looking formations, hollows like empty eye sockets peering blind from barren slopes.

So I scanned west across the horizon to the mesa, searching for those roofs he'd mentioned, under the notch. Yes. Four or five houses, a water tower, a shock of emerald lawn, cottonwoods. The salt desert between the ridge and that oasis glimmered, flat, a seaway mirage.

I wondered, before I returned the binoculars, if Larry had stood here on lonesome twilights years ago. Did he scan that point of green like Jay Gatsby yearning for Daisy, his dream a false promise, fatal to pursue?

CHAPTER EIGHT

"I love this country," Lottie announced to the ravine enclosing us. "I miss it more than I realized."

The next morning, Larry Lucas aimed us toward a pass between two rounded peaks of the Confusion Range. With his jeep tottering in the steep, uneven, two-track trail, Larry fought to steady the steering wheel. Lottie, in front beside him, grabbed the roll bar to steady herself. In the back, Brandy and I kept knocking into each other. I almost lost my cap as Felicia plunged from lap to lap.

Eating dust, I wondered what Lottie saw that I didn't. Maybe her extra-dark sunglasses tinted the scene in pleasant hues, but the barren landscape I was choking on didn't exactly inspire love.

At the two-track pass, the few clouds seemed within grasping distance. As if guarding the summit, deep-browed caves stared down, those skull-like eye sockets in the green-gray shale.

Shallower ruts dropped us into the Blindfold Valley. Our range of sight shot from sky to earth in seconds, though my stomach was still in the air. Glancing aside to check on Brandy, I was surprised that she laughed, quick rat-a-tats, and pulled Felicia toward her fluttering belly as if to share the fun.

But when I tried to make eye contact, she turned away. Still resentful over my outburst yesterday afternoon, Brandy had barely graced me with a civil word all morning. When I'd offered to take the kitten to our motel hostess for catsitting, she'd snatched the kitty from my hands and made the arrangements herself.

Lottie turned, beaming her smile at us backseat kids. "Isn't this fun, guys?" she cried over the brake squeals on the switchbacks. Indicating the valley with a sweeping gesture that promised eyefuls of bleached grasses, dry, salt-caked ponds, and half-dead pinyon pines, she dared to repeat, "God, I do love this country."

"Yeah, it's that sense of sanctuary," Larry said, braking hard to crawl down a jagged patch of rock. "Once you get over the summit, you leave all that restricted territory behind, the Proving Grounds . . ."

"The Wendover Testing Range," Lottie put in, "the Desert Test Center . . ."

"And suddenly, up the slope and around this bend, we're sheltered from it all," Larry said, reaching to squeeze Lottie's hand. "On good, old, wide-open public land."

A regular Shangri-la, I thought, studying the point where the last dying shrubs surrendered to a vast lifeless plain. Though Larry and Lottie seemed to recite this geographic tutorial for our backseaters' benefit, it also seemed to be an incantation, a private, erotic ritual. Like teenagers going gooey over the dumpy drive-in where they'd lost their virginity, Larry and Lottie infused sexual sentiment into these humping barrens. A rattlesnake void enlivened by starry, snuggling nights in bedrolls. A lover's lane for adulterous grown-ups, with Brandy and me along for the farewell tour as the pretend kids, or maybe just two more affable pets.

But I really wasn't so affable, was I? I didn't quite understand these surges of jealousy. I usually wasn't so big in the jealousy department. When I first heard about Nick's acquisition of Patrick, it refreshed my heartbreak, but I didn't battle much with the green-eyed monster. So who knew why I resented Larry's open affection for Lottie. Maybe because she and I had held fast until now, snoozing together, inventing our own mission and route as we went. And, after all, Lottie and I had been the original surrogate parents, managing Brandy as a team. Now, Larry had stepped in as The Man, The New Dad, and I'd been reduced to the Queer Foster Child.

It didn't help that Larry was so good-looking, confident, and accomplished in the manly arts. College athlete, Navy pilot, humanitarian, outdoorsman, science star. Being around older straight guys like Larry put that instant kid-brother chip on my shoulder, and though I might crave a pissing contest or rock toss to prove my mettle, I knew I was sure to humiliate myself.

Lottie had taken to scanning the valley floor with the binoculars. Her falsified dark hair fluttered wildly under her cowboy hat. "Don't seem to be any animals grazing today."

"Yeah, I half-expected this," Larry said. "I'm sure the publicity has led the research team to cull the afflicted herds."

144

"Or maybe," Brandy called out, "all them lambs are just dead by now."

"I hope so," Larry said. "Death is usually better than living with the chronic nervous afflictions I've seen."

As we bounced down the last switchback, I surveyed the valley's tufts of white grass and wondered if it weren't this hellish grazing that had killed the poor beasts—the scant sage, locoweed, and leached forage.

Crossing the valley floor, we reached a dry creekbed where Larry stopped to investigate deep tire tracks. "They're recent," he said, before proceeding up the bank.

"Let's hope it's some rancher checking on his stock," Lottie said.

"I'd sure like to see his herds somewhere," Larry said.

"It's so dry here," Brandy remarked. "What I don't get is how you guys watered your horses on those campouts, Lottie."

"Let's show her Paradise Gap," Larry said, turning around to grin for Brandy's benefit. "We've still got time, before I have to head to the airport."

"Yeah!" Lottie cried. "Since we're not going to see any stock today, let's give Ray and Brandy the grand tour."

Larry steered the jeep toward the sheer face of rock abutting the valley floor. We'd slow every now and then to find fresh tracks in sandy stretches, only to lose them on hardpack a few yards further. The faint road rose now, up a rocky knoll, then seemed to dead-end ahead, where two pale, upright boulders met a sandstone cliff.

"See how it gives the illusion of a solid rock face?" Lottie said, turning back to Brandy and me. "But look again, where that dark shadow falls between the boulders? That's the way to Paradise Gap."

"Hey Lottie, wasn't it just about here?" Larry slowed the jeep in on a grassy ledge, "where we first spotted those damaged lambs?"

"Looks about right," Lottie said. She caressed Larry's hand where it rested on the gearshift knob.

Heading between the massive boulders, the jeep growled up a surface more rock face than road, then settled onto a steep, faint two-track. "We're on the remnant of an old pioneer trail," Lottie announced. "Blindfold Canyon."

The canyon walls seemed to become ever narrower. The track's snaking progress along the sand-and-slickrock surface prevented any vistas ahead or behind.

In a longer sandy stretch, Larry stopped to inspect the fresh tracks. "Well, our visitor must've turned back. The treads are going both ways here."

My mind was back with those much earlier visitors, the pioneer migrants. I wondered how desperate they must have felt in these narrow passageways, creeping forward in rigid wagons. Only a half-mile in, we could see nothing but sheer sandstone ahead, behind, and to each side. We eluded even the noon sun, shafting in directly overhead, and kept slithering into shadows.

"Damn!" Lottie cried out as we rounded a steep, sloping bend. "When did this happen?"

A rockslide spilled over the entire width of the ravine, too high and chaotic even for Larry's intrepid jeep. "Now we know why those tracks doubled back," Larry said, then reviewed our choices: a ten-mile drive over the next pass, then several more miles back along the ridgetop, or a short hike uphill into Paradise Gap.

Felicia decided for us by bounding out of the backseat and scrambling up the rock pile. Larry shut the engine, grabbed a day-pack, and followed Felicia's lead, signaling us to follow.

On the other side of the pile, the canyon felt even more claustrophobic. Our hikers' pace made its twisting labyrinth seem boundless. Larry and Lottie were undaunted, however, animated by the hormonal adventures of yesteryear. Taking the lead with Felicia at their heels, the toothsome twosome turned back to Brandy and me, enlightening us further on the local history.

"Blindfold Canyon was a pioneer trail only for a short while," Lottie said, "the only known passage between Cove Fort and Carson City."

"Then they discovered the passage you took on the highway yesterday, across the Wah Wah Valley and over my ridge," Larry put in. "After that, this ravine was abandoned."

"Just wait till you see what's around the bend," Lottie cried out, hurrying ahead.

I expected a pile of pioneer bones and ancient wagons with broken axles. Horses' skeletons, arrow-pierced skulls, bullets blasted into bone. The fossilized lower extremities of my poor fellow souls—stout-hearted males in their prime who'd headed west. They'd left grief behind only to lose their way in a region where delusional, beautiful heterosexuals forced them up infernal gulches toward the rumor of paradise.

Instead, Lottie halted before something far less histrionic, but more haunting. Into an especially flat sandstone slab, at just the height of a man reaching from a wagon's seat, names were etched and jabbed, dated from the mid-1800s. Big earnest signatures: Joseph MacIntire, Late of Green, Green Vermont; Joshua P. Field; Thomas Brandon Adams With All His Family, among scores of others. High over them all, a longer message stretched. Schoolmarmishly, Lottie asked Brandy if she would read it to us.

"God help . . ." Brandy began, then hesitated. Was she having trouble with the pioneer cursive or just basic phonics? "God help these bewildered and deluded travelers," Brandy finally finished, halting, "wending lost through this damnation."

"Amen," I said.

Brandy did not waste a minute contemplating the bitterness in our pioneer past. She coaxed Felicia away from Lottie's side and teased her into running ahead. When they were out of sight behind the next bend, we could hear Brandy's laughter echoing, then Felicia's happy yaps. Their excitement reverberated with that weird Utah-slickrock amplification. Silence itself seemed a bedrock that purified and isolated every noise, every syllable or giggle or sigh.

"I love to see Brandy enjoying herself so much," Lottie said. "I think it's finally dawned on her that she's free."

I glanced back to the pioneers' forlorn graffiti before joining Lottie and Larry's ambling pace up the ravine. "I think it's finally dawned on her," I muttered to Lottie, "that you've risked your own freedom to rescue her."

"Somebody had to," Larry said, turning back to me with a curious wink.

"Brandy doesn't deserve a thing that's befallen her," Lottie said. Her voice faltered, losing its determined cheerfulness for the first time all morning. She seemed like a besieged mother dropping her brave front as soon as her child was out of earshot. Brandy's echoing laughs grew a little more distant. "And it helps me, you know, to encourage her and keep up my spirits up for her."

"Yep, I do know, Lottie." I dared to take her hand. "On account of another lost soul from Globeville."

Lottie squeezed my fingers, then pecked me on the cheek. "Did you know Larry and I once took Nicky this way, to Paradise? He loved it so much."

I scanned my brain for Nick's mention of Paradise Gap during a Utah sojourn with the mysterious Charlotte Vjiovinovic Weiss, but came up dry.

"Yeah, Nicky did pretty well," Larry said with a laugh, "for a city boy who smoked a pack a day and expected a martini bar at the top of the canyon."

So that was it. Larry knew all about Nick, and Lottie had doubtless told him that I was Nick's ex. So Larry was amused, having another "city boy" along for a guided hike into the wilds.

But Lottie wasn't amused, or even tuned in to where the conversation had meandered. She let go of my hand and ambled forward alone. Even under hat and sunglasses, her devastation was obvious. I was sorry I'd mentioned Nick, even obliquely, in the first place.

It was windless, and, with our silence punctuated only by Felicia's faraway barks, seemed a lot like wandering amid an unfinished surrealist painting. Around the next bend, I wouldn't have flinched to find melting watches or the detached, flaming shadow of a runaway wagon wheel. Lottie trudged forward without eagerness now, shrunken within her cowgirl jeans and blouse.

I was some friend, wasn't I? Since we'd met up with Larry, I'd been resentful of Lottie's resolute escape from grief. Maybe I'd envied Larry's power to help her recall better times. By wedging my way back into her graces with that "lost soul from Globeville" line, I'd done nothing but aggravate her sorrow. So I tried to cheer her back to better memories. "On those campouts here," I asked, feigning curiosity, "did the whole crew from the project come along?"

"Sometimes," Lottie said, staring ahead. "We were like kids, most of us, the way we looked forward to riding the range. We all regressed to horseplay and ghost stories. And we all became amateur astronomers, didn't we, Larry?" She pointed toward the slot of blue sky with a smile. "There's nothing like staring at the desert sky on summer nights."

Sure, with Larry and his Big Dipper stretched over you, I thought, still glad that I'd roused her out of her silence. "Did Kurt ever come along?"

"God no. He wouldn't leave his research at the Proving

Ground to camp in the desert. But at least then Kurt's obsessions still had a strain of idealism. He'd actually say he was on the verge of 'unlocking the secret of life itself.' So how could he possibly waste time horseback riding?"

"Plus," Larry said, "Kurt was snobbish about the Desert Ecology Project. He thought our work was pseudoscience. Touchy-feely flora-and-fauna trivia."

"Did you always go along with the gang to this Paradise place?" I asked Lottie. "Or did you and Larry ever go just by yourselves?"

Lottie glanced at me, peering sidelong over her sunglasses. Then she smiled. "We went by ourselves a couple times." She took Larry's arm. "Just the two of us."

"Wasn't Kurt jealous?"

"God no. He was grateful I had the diversion. Kept me out of his hair. Besides, Larry and I had the bond of our passion for flora and fauna, right?"

"For Kurt, Utah was a void," Larry said. "For Lottie and me, it was a plenum. Lottie's company helped keep me sane, too, and Kurt appreciated that. He was once my best friend, you know. We used to dream the same dreams. At Stanford, we expected our research to save the planet and end human suffering." Larry laughed. "How could it be otherwise?"

So my prurient probing had only launched me back, smack-dab into the toothsome twosome's dignity and idealism. Damn it! They seemed to harbor such deep respect for creation. Even more astonishing for smart, modern people, they didn't bother to filter it through irony or angst. It was as if Barbie and Ken had repudiated consumerism and joined the Sierra Club.

Larry paced ahead. "I'm going to check on Brandy and Felicia. I don't want them to get too far ahead. They might overshoot the side canyon."

When he rounded the next bend ahead of us, I finally had my chance. Maybe I could never achieve Larry and Lottie's moral altitude, but, sometimes, I did have this stray fondness for the truth. "So, Lottie, tell me. Were you and Larry lovers, then?"

"Ray!" Lottie slapped my shoulder lightly. "Where did you get that idea?" Lottie pranced ahead to the first green sprig of life in miles. "Of course, we loved each other, if that's what you mean."

"You didn't answer my question, Lottie!"

Stopping ahead, Lottie pointed toward seepage from a natural spring. It shot from the canyon wall to water a small cluster of lush grass, rabbit brush, and dense junipers. Lottie nodded further up-canyon. "Can you hear it, yet, Ray?"

Before I could answer, she bounded ahead. I did detect the faintest resound of birdsong. Around the next twist of sandstone, Lottie indicated an opening in the canyon wall. "We're almost there. Paradise."

I followed her, several paces behind, as we climbed up the even narrower side ravine. More springs produced green gashes in the limestone, algae caking little mud bogs. Felicia's paws and three sets of boot prints marked the soggy route until the walls widened, the sky seemed broader, the distant birds in fuller cry. Felicia's yaps echoed less. Unseen around the next bend, Lottie cried, "We're almost there, Ray!"

The side ravine widened into a broad oval crammed with green living things. Halted, hand over her chest, Lottie seemed to inhale nostalgia in deep, satisfied draughts. She pointed to a fissure in the smooth stone rim opposite. "That's where we would've come in, Ray, if we'd taken the long way around in the jeep."

"I'm glad we walked," I told her. "This is more dramatic, after seeing all that desolation." I scanned the oval gap, tuning in to birds' peeps and leaf rustling as if I'd been lost in this desert for months. Above, a white lip of Navajo sandstone outlined the dry ridgetop. Under it, sagebrush took hold on a pink ledge, then a redder ledge spread like loge seats in a giant's amphitheater. Junipers scattered across the layer like early arrivals for a performance.

The stage below was the entire compact oasis. Closer to the gap's floor, pinyon pine grew ever more dense, encircling a lusher stand of alder and a cluster of gnarled, ancient cottonwoods. In the center, a freshwater pond fed by multiple seeps reflected the shades of green shimmering all around. Felicia chased a flock of bluebirds while Brandy fished a stick from the muddy bank. Larry inspected an old campfire site.

I expected Lottie to hurry toward that spot, where Larry no doubt pondered an old flame's ashes for any sign of spark and sizzle. But she took my hand and led me there slowly, meandering through the thickening greenery. "Oh, Ray," she said, her tone softer than usual, "I feel like we've really made it. Like there's more than a good chance we'll actually succeed in exposing the truth. Thanks to you."

I squeezed her hand, but after all my jealous peevishness, I cringed at her generous words. Was Lottie blind to what a detached, tentative, sluttish tagalong I really had been?

We followed a little stream now, its banks lined with coyote willow and wildflowers. "There's a pool further up," Lottie said, nodding toward a seep-splashed opening in the rock face, "where Larry and I and all the guys used to bathe. But look at this, Ray, this gorgeous little pond. God sakes. It's even more crystalline, more sparkling than I remember."

"I guess the pond's had a recent visitor," Larry called from the campsite. He'd plucked something from a branch and wagged it. "Somebody who doesn't appreciate the scenery."

When we approached, Larry uncrumpled the evidence: a fresh-looking Little Debbie pecan pie wrapper. Lottie inspected it closely, as if it were the uncanny artifact of some vanished tribe, then folded it up and slipped it in her back pocket. "I hate to think of some litterbug invading our Paradise."

"Litter might be the least of the invader's crimes, I'm afraid—" Larry said, cutting himself short. He pivoted toward the commotion across the pond.

We all watched as Felicia yowled then tore through the brush. She emerged on higher ground, giving sleek chase to some unseen rabbit or chipmunk. Raising the mucky stick, Brandy whooped and sprinted after the dog.

"I'd better keep an eye on those two," Larry said, about to head off when Lottie touched his arm, a gentle restraint.

"I'll go," she said. "Larry, why don't you and Ray check out the upper pool?"

"Good idea," Larry said. "We'd better make sure no goon with pecan pie breath is still lurking somewhere. You wanna come, Ray?"

I nodded, a little disconcerted. It dawned on me that we were penned in on all sides by Utah's guided-missile cowboys and survivalist desperadoes and bigamist renegades. Meanwhile, our posse consisted of a sweet-tempered retriever, a skinny, clueless teenager, a former biology teacher turned human rights activist, her city-boy sidekick, and our fearless leader—an avowed pacifist who seemed to be completely unarmed.

My stomach clenched as I followed Larry back along that little stream. Where it cascaded down the lion-colored cliff, we clambered up a boulder slide, rock-hopping and zigzagging until we reached an algae-caked notch. Heaving himself over the rim with a grunt, Larry offered a hand to yank me up the rock face's lip.

I muttered thanks to him and tried to gain my macho balance. But with my heart racing and breaths quickened, I tottered on the rim like a quivering fairy.

"Hey, Ray, isn't this something?" Larry indicated the upper

pool with a proprietary sweep of the hand. "And we seem to have it all to ourselves."

It was something. I surrendered to pure astonishment. We faced a solid rock terrace, swirls of smooth orange-red sandstone encircling a deep, clear pool. Spring-fed, it gurgled over its stone rim to feed the little cascade. The blazing sun overhead, the ochre rocks and flawless water combined to radiate gold shimmers over the stone terrace.

At the pool's edge, I stared past my mouth-agape reflection into the gorgeous azure depths. Larry, beside me, crouched to untie his boot laces. "I don't know about you, pal, but I'm dying to dive in. I've got road dust in just about every nook and cranny of this tired old carcass."

"Um . . ." I said. "Ah . . ."

Meanwhile Larry kicked off his boots, yanked off his T-shirt, and unceremoniously unzipped his khaki shorts. Leaning to undo my own laces, I stole a glance to inspect that tired old carcass. Almost naked.

Whoa. I wouldn't say old and tired. His pale torso was taut, his muscles defined but not in the overdone gym bunny way. Instead, Larry exuded robust health.

He slipped out of his boxers and dove in, giving me only a sliding glimpse of his smooth, white butt. He had the straight-guy tan—burnished on neck and forearms, but not upper arms; on calves and knees but not thighs. Coming up to gulp air, he yelped, then slapped water in my direction. "Get naked and get in!" he cried, swimming away. "It's great, Ray!"

Yes it was. I would've loved, though, to have just stayed put, dangling my legs in the water and studying Larry's backside as he glided around the pool. Slipping out of my vile, dust-crusted T-shirt and shorts, I felt self-conscious, not really wanting Larry to see my regulation-issue Speedo tan lines, not wanting to confirm my status as an orthodox gay stereotype. I kept my AMERICA'S PROVING GROUND cap on as if it might lend some macho credibility.

Now, down to my boxers, I hesitated on the verge of the water's temptation. Though it seemed an epoch ago, it'd been hardly a week since my similar crisis of modesty on the verge of Kurt Weiss's hot tub. How quickly, that night, I'd bubbled from bashful to butt-fuck. Now, toes in the cool, seductive pool while my fingers trembled to shove off my shorts in front of this attractive man, all my sins flooded back to me. I slipped into the cool water, praying that all the dirt smearing me would sink to the forgiving, sandy bottom.

"You and Kurt Weiss," I asked Larry, surfacing after my first dousing, "you really were best friends at Stanford?"

"I'm afraid so. And lab partners, inseparable." Larry swam closer, then relaxed against a smooth indentation in the pool's rock rim. "Of course, back then, Kurt hadn't sold his soul to Dominex. We had a lot in common."

"Such as?"

"One thing, we were so deadly serious about our studies. Total science geeks, convinced genetics was the key to all mysteries."

I found a smooth edge of my own opposite from Larry and leaned into it. "Sounds like you never gave up on that quest. You know, to save the world."

"Maybe so. But I never thought for a second, back at Stanford, that the number one obstacle to the world's salvation would turn out to be my lab partner."

"But you've got to admit," I said, "Kurt probably thinks he's saving the world, too."

"Yeah. With an arsenal of eternal nightmares. Just what the world needs."

I closed my eyes, imagining the road dust sifting out of my skin, enjoying our conversation. Around men like Larry, I often managed to channel my inner butch guy. Times like this, stereotypes be damned, Ray O'Brien could pull off being a man among men.

So Larry's kiss should have surprised me, but when he took advantage of my resting, manly moment of bliss to slip across the little pool and plant his lips on mine, I felt the paralyzing shock of the inevitable.

Not a bad shock.

His lips were full, and warm, and once it became obvious I was enjoying them, he pressed harder, hungry and urgent. One hand pushed back my cap while the other slid along my side and clutched above my hip, buoying me up and pulling me closer. Our kiss persisted; our mouths opened and tongues wrestled while my hands explored his shoulders, back, and butt underwater. I loved the unearthly floating lightness of seizing his strong legs. I loved entangling them in mine.

My consciousness still whacked within the endless kiss, I opened my eyes to find his dark blue eyes boring into mine, the lashes still wet, his eyes' edges crinkling into a smile. But his lips couldn't form that smile because they were sucking and lapping and sliding against mine, though almost broken by a laugh that we both suppressed at the exact same moment, determined to press on smooching. The yellow light caught in my wide-open eyes flooded the moment in renewed intensity. The kiss took on a golden taste, almond liqueur or cognac and—more delicious, more delirious—demanded closer pressing, closer tasting, tongues probing for even sweeter, drunker sensations.

Agitating our liquid groping underneath and permeating the golden air above, a Western cold front blasted snowfall into the moment, one of those sideways March howlers that creams the western side of everything with mastic, heavy gobs of pure white. No—I knew where I was, simultaneously soul-kissing Larry

Lucas in the Confusion Range deep in August, but also holding on to Nicholas Sanchez for dear life in March, seven years before, while snow slammed against our skulls.

The first time I'd really talked with Nick, at an Art Against AIDS benefit in the foothills above Denver, he was exactly as advertised, a playboy with a great laugh and rapid-fire, dazzling but trivial conversation. I told him I had to head back to town before the storm outside froze I-70 through Mount Vernon Canyon. You scared of a little ice? he'd teased. I admitted I was and hurried to collect my coat and search for my car among the other white lumps parked along the rural road, but, under the canopy that covered the house's entry—a slate bridge—I felt someone wagging my sleeve. When I turned around, Nick pulled me into a kiss right there in the blowing snow, the tiny white lights shaking in a spiny hedge, a kiss like this kiss with Larry that we could not undo or cease despite the wind slamming snow into our hair and ears and down our collars, only now it was the sun slamming pure honey light, pressing into me that same startled, dizzy sense that my singlehood was about to end, even if the kiss never did.

It took Felicia to do that, barking from afar, down in the lower reaches of Paradise Gap. "Well," Larry said, finally separating his lips from mine, "I guess it's just a matter of minutes before all three females join us up here."

I was incapable of comment, overcome under a crushing yet tranquil inertia. A thousand times, critiquing student scenes that involved fairy tales or parodies of them, I'd advised students to "really believe you're under the spell of an enchantment." Now for the first time in my twenty-eight years, with no need for belief or waving wands, I'd fallen under a true spell. Nick had compelled me, fascinated me, obsessed me, but he'd never really enchanted me the way Larry just had. I felt a ridiculous urge to hurry home and listen to jazzy, oblique, classic love songs, "The Good Life" and "Midnight Sun," while staring glassy-eyed at the moon in my window and dreaming of kissing Larry again.

He glided out of my arms, but trailed his fingers as he went so that he clasped my hand. "Thank you, Ray. I needed that. I plotted to do just that, kiss you here, like crazy, all night last night."

"I would've, too," I said, struggling out of my incoherence. "But Lottie didn't tell me you were gay."

"No, she wouldn't."

"So you both robbed me of the chance to torture myself all night, in that motel room, plotting to kiss you. No fair, man."

"Well, Lottie couldn't help revealing that you'd been Nicky's partner, before Patrick. I'm sorry you've lost him."

"Thanks for saying so." I took a breath, avoiding Larry's kind but steady gaze. "But I really lost him two years ago. I'd hardly seen Nick again until the night he died. And I may have been the last person to have seen him alive."

"Do you think he was killed?"

Recalling brakeless, treadless tire marks in the grass at Cherry Creek and a cat shot with merciless efficiency, I heard myself say it: "I don't have any doubt."

"Yeah. We've got to focus now, on exposing this. I can't wait to get to Salt Lake and provoke the media. And when I get back tomorrow night, Ray, I was wondering if you'd like to stay overnight at my place. At the project."

"Sure." I smiled. "Our motel room is awfully cramped."

"Yeah, we'll tell Lottie and Brandy it's for their sake. More privacy for the ladies, right? But understand that I only have one bed in my trailer."

"Understood."

Larry smiled and pulled me into one last, quick kiss. Small, puffy white clouds massed together, blocking the sun and dulling the glare. Felicia sounded closer now, and by the time we'd hustled out of the pool and into our clothes, she appeared, tongue dangling between hard breaths, at the top of the rock slide. She ambled straight to Larry's waiting hands to be petted and good-doggied before she lapped up gulpfuls of the pool.

Larry and I pulled on our boots and hurried to the terrace's ridge to lend a hand to Lottie and Brandy as they clambered up the final rise.

"No further sign of Little Debbie," Lottie reported, "and we went as far as the north opening." She removed her sunglasses to stare at us, each in turn, eyeing our wet hair with a suspicious smile. "And what did you two explore?"

"I'm afraid we took a dip in the pool," Larry said.

"Wow!" Brandy regarded the terrace's liquid wonders, her squinty little bloodshot eyes widening as far they could. I expected her to join Felicia at the pool's edge, but she stooped to a bouquet of wildflowers poking from a seeping crack in the sandstone. "This whole area is totally riparian, isn't it, Lottie?"

"Yes, it sure is," Lottie said, bending beside her to inspect the flowers. "I'm proud that you remembered that word."

"It's so pretty here," Brandy said. "These red flowers right here, with, like, feathers. We saw them in Wyoming, remember?"

"Yes, narrowleaf paintbrush. Very good, Brandy!"

Oh God. So Lottie and Brandy had been reprising their Annie Sullivan–Helen Keller routine. The world, after all, was a biology teacher's classroom, and even the most severely handicapped of students was too tempting, here in Paradise, to leave unenlightened.

"Not only is this a riparian garden, seeming to grow out of solid stone, but there are some rare specimens up here. Over there," she continued, pointing toward greenery at the edge of the rock terrace, "we once found death camas. Beautiful but poisonous. And in that little bog, moonlily. It folds its blossoms in daylight, then opens trumpet flowers at night."

Just like our own flower of Sweetwater, opening only to live at night, stupefied by satellite TV in her plush armchair. That vacant look had already returned to Brandy's face. Twirling her mucky stick, she drooped now, Lottie's words having tested her feeble attention span. But then, leading with the stick, Brandy wandered toward the green patch under an upheaval of rock to inspect, dutifully, the flowers in Lottie's lesson.

"Maybe there is some faint hope for your protégé, Lottie," I muttered.

"My star pupil is blossoming, isn't she?" Lottie said, nudging me hard in the ribs. "I think we've won her over. I think we're going to stage one hell of a press conference, Ray. Brandy wants to read a testimonial about how she's been manipulated every step of the way."

Including the steps along her way with us? I wondered, while Larry coaxed Felicia from the water's edge, readying her, I suppose, for wherever we were headed next.

Just as Felicia barked sharply, Brandy screamed to us, "Hey, you guys!"

I turned in time to notice Brandy, at the base of the rock upheaval, along with a glimpse of mobile white that flew from sight. Brandy called again, "It's one of them wild goats!"

Felicia shook and squeezed her way out of Larry's grip and bounded for the base of the upheaval. She barked in fury but refused to climb toward Brandy. The poor dog hurled herself into each yelp, throwing her legs forward but falling back as if an invisible barrier immobilized her.

Brandy, who'd climbed halfway up the jumble of rocks, now called out a less shrill "Oh, my God!"

Felicia was hysterical now, in a frenzy over whatever terror crouched in wait beyond the rock crest. Larry tried to calm his pooch as Lottie and I took off after Brandy, scrambling upward behind her.

I overtook Lottie midway up. "Go ahead," she called after me, "I'm taking it easy in this bouncing light. These damn glasses . . ."

At the top, I found myself on a second smooth sandstone terrace. It formed an open bowl under jagged granite teeth. I quickly got my lesson in why so many places in Utah were called "Sliprock." Seeping springs and slick sandstone combined to make my hustle after Brandy and the goat a slapstick caper of pratfalls and tailbone scrapes.

Upright again, I picked my way among dry patches, turning back in hopes that Lottie would copy my route. All the while, Felicia's yelps echoed against this arching rock bowl. Near the far granite edge, I eased myself toward Brandy's side.

She leaned over a fallen mountain goat, a kid really, her hands suspended inches above its shaggy hide as if offering an incantation. "Ray, it's like, shaking . . . ." she said, her first direct words to me all day. Her tone seemed strange; flatter and more vulnerable, less urban hillbilly: "I saw the poor critter stop running. It kind of staggered, and just fell on its side right here. Then it starting having all these . . . like, little shakes."

I leaned on all fours opposite Brandy, my heart pulsing like a cautionary strobe. I'd always admired the wild mountain goats, having encountered many climbing Colorado's Fourteeners with Nadia. They embodied calm, even wisdom with their zenlike composure, intelligent, peaceful black eyes, and monkish beards. But this young, tortured kid's eyes were coated with a yellow gel. As if gaping with terror, its mouth opened wide, then shut spasmodically, punctuating the horror it struggled to communicate. Tremors shook all its limbs. Spasms pulsed along its trunk.

I spotted Larry on the rim, Felicia at his heels. He'd been

surveying the scene, aiming his camera toward us. Approaching, he photographed the adolescent goat from several angles, and even narrated a quick film and audio clip for his digital camera, speculating about the yellow gel.

Shaking its head ever more to one side, the wild goat attempted to rise, hoisting itself a few inches off the ground. It soon collapsed again, but immediately roused itself, almost recovering its full power, struggling to its shaking feet so rapidly that Brandy fell back.

Lottie called from the rock bowl's verge. "It's so slippery here."

I called, "Try to circle around that drier—"

"Oh damn!" Lottie cried. "I've turned my ankle!"

Brandy gasped, shoving off from the ground to head toward Lottie, but fell backward on the wet slickrock surrounding the wild kid, who'd collapsed again. So I crouched beside Brandy, meaning to help her up, then go back for Lottie. "You OK?"

Brandy groaned, now splay-legged, rubbing her boot. "It's my damn foot. I twisted it into that sharp . . . goddamn . . ." She pointed toward a knifelike granite slab poking from the smeary slickrock.

I helped her out of her boot, checking for blood. The skin was intact, though her heel was raw and red. "You're gonna be OK," I said. "Let me go check on Lottie."

Larry rose just as I did, hurrying ahead to Lottie. As I grasped for Brandy's tossed-away walking stick, gunshot tore through the momentary silence.

And my shoulder. I threw myself forward, covering Brandy under me just as the gun blasted again.

The first bullet had only grazed my shoulder and nipped a bit of flesh. The second bullet had been aimed not at me or Brandy, but the wild goat.

The gunman, who disappeared over the jagged granite ridgetop, didn't appear again. After inspecting our injuries and re-assuring us, Larry had produced a bandage from his pack for my bleeding shoulder.

Hustling, Larry and I managed to ease Brandy and Lottie down to the upper pool, each one hobbling on a different foot. Wide-eyed, gasping, Brandy and Lottie really were twinned in their sudden injuries and fearful of managing the rocky descents. Confronted with the rock slide, Larry and I chaired Lottie down on our arms while Brandy slid from rock to rock on her butt. From there, it was a fairly easy hobble across flatter land, through the seeping side ravine, and back to another hesitating scoot over the slide blocking the jeep trail.

At the jeep, Larry wrapped Lottie's ankle from a first-aid kit. Despite the torturous, dust-choking jeep route back, before too long we'd cleaned up and nursed our injuries at Larry's trailer.

When Larry expressed reluctance about leaving for Salt Lake City, Lottie insisted he proceed as planned. She even talked him into videotaping my and Brandy's eyewitness account of the mountain goat's convulsions.

With Lottie's blessing, then, Larry opened up more, revealing the true importance of what he'd captured on camera. "It's too bad we didn't have a chance to haul that carcass back with us. This mountain goat represents a whole new escalation in their powers. That they'd dare to manipulate wild herds, to test out genetic in-jections in animals they can't contain—it's just blind hubris."

"There's no shortage of that at the Proving Ground," Lottie said. "Or Dominex."

"Yes," Larry said, shaking his head. "Genetically impaired

wild animals loose in the Utah backcountry? Culled by hired guns? I'm going to have to put this at the top of my press release."

By the time we dropped Larry off at the airfield, he seemed assured that we were all going to survive without his guidance and first aid for the twenty-four hours he'd be gone.

When we'd reached cellular range nearer the New Carlsbad airfield, Larry had managed to phone advance appointments and confirm interviews, with photos and tape for the 10 o'clock news. Then he further tantalized his news contacts, inviting them to a follow-up, on-the-scene press conference here in New Carlsbad.

Amid fellow pilots and airport crew who'd gathered to cheer on Dr. Lucas before he climbed into his little Cessna, the airfield manager's wife—the principal of New Carlsbad Middle and Senior High School—pulled Larry aside to gush over a volunteer teaching gig he'd scheduled for September.

This irritated me for two reasons. First, it reminded me that somehow, if I eluded capture, arrest, and torture for my part in abducting Brandy McConnaughty, I had to return to my own teaching position soon. Second, the principal's gushing deprived me of any chance to gush over Larry myself.

Before disentangling himself from the principal and hurrying to his plane, Larry shook my hand, then pulled me close for a whispered confidence: "I'm entrusting our fair maidens to you, Ray. Keep as low a profile as you can till I get back, OK?"

"I'll give you a full report, Dr. Lucas," I promised as he hustled to the cockpit. "Here, take this as a memento." I passed him my AMERICA'S PROVING GROUND cap. "From Lottie to me to you."

Larry slipped it on. "OK, Ray. See you tomorrow night. For a long, full report." He winked at me, then waved everyone good-bye.

I tried to wink in reply, as usual without success, and kept waving like a lunatic long after everyone else had ceased. Elated, I squinted to follow Larry's glide north into the windless blue.

CHAPTER NINE

I stared down our motel room's only artwork, a cardboard portrait of a crying, smiling clown, as Lottie applied more hydrogen peroxide to my wound.

Late in the afternoon, the three of us sprawled in convalescence at the Wah Wah Motor Court. As a precaution against Citizens Against Terror vigilantes, goat-killing gunmen, and/or geneticists gone bad, I'd parked my Subaru in the alley and asked the innkeeper—a heavy, gruff, but helpful grandmother—to please keep our presence unknown if anyone inquired.

"Motels exist only to keep secrets, darlin'," she'd assured me when I'd picked up Brandy's kitten. "I've kept a million in my day. Anybody asks, I never see nothin'."

I fell back against the pillow as Lottie dabbed at my wound on the Vibrato-Queen mattress. I flinched from the sting as Lottie tossed the cotton swab and applied a fresh bandage.

"No sign of infection," Lottie said, "thank God."

"Thanks, nurse. How's your ankle feeling?"

"It's nothing," Lottie insisted, but the way she grimaced when she eased her lower leg back on a pillow betrayed the pain. She sipped the whiskey we'd bought in Sweetwater and smiled for me, a gorgeous fraud. With the Ronald Reagan Medical Center nothing but an empty promise, we were on our own, determined to heal ourselves and gorge on takeout until we picked up Larry at the airfield the following evening.

Brandy lay on the other bed, the kitten on her stomach and

her sore foot resting on Felicia's back. Peering around the animals, she ignored us to concentrate on some late-afternoon soap about a blind girl who'd had corrective surgery. Now the girl waited with heroic patience for the bandages over her eyes to be removed. Little did she know that the doctor and nurse were deep-kissing behind a partition. I was just getting engrossed when cheesy over-the-kiss music signaled a station break. A perky redhead inserted a teaser for LiveNews's next broadcast: "Now this. Catch the award-winning Utah author and scientist tonight, only on LiveNews at 10 . . ."

"It's Larry!" Brandy cried. "How can he already be on TV?"

"It's not possible . . ." Lottie said, glancing at the clock. "He's got to be flying over the desert somewhere west of Delta."

But LiveNews only featured a brief bite from an earlier taped video interview. Larry declared, "Pandora has already opened the box, and we have to find the courage to realize the world is dramatically more dangerous." Broad brow crinkled in concern, dark eyes big and sincere, Larry intoned: "Blinded by genetic engineering's promise, we haven't confronted its potential to destroy and keep on destroying for generations." The redhead killed her smile in the wake of Larry's video warning and delivered the teaser: "Dr. Lucas claims to have new evidence on actual genetic manipulations in southwestern Utah's Confusion Range. Stay tuned for our exclusive interview on LiveNews at 10."

"Larry's soooo telegenic," Lottie cooed. "God sakes, he could sell a Bible to a Saudi mullah."

"Wait till he tells them what we saw today," Brandy said. "I hope they'll run pictures of that poor goat."

Suddenly Lottie's delirious scheme seemed almost viable, that they—we—could stage the press conference here in New Carlsbad starring Brandy's surprise testimony and Larry's best-selling, Stanford gravitas. If Larry could lure enough of the regional press down to this fucked-up, fucked-over proving ground, we all might emerge from hiding, freed under the cover of media scrutiny. Mission accomplished.

Tires crackled in the gravel outside our door, which was propped to let the breeze through the screen. I jumped from the bed, startling Felicia, who growled and scurried toward the commotion at the doorway. The retriever slid between my legs, determined to protect us with her best ferocious stare while I leaned out. An old white delivery van did a U-turn in the lot, then turned onto the main drag long enough for me to read the painted logo on its side:

LITTLE DEBBIE SNACKS
FOR UTAH'S SWEETEST TOOTH

When I dropped back to the bed to share the news, Lottie soothed my agitation, her fingers smoothing my hair. "It could just be a pure coincidence, Ray. Little Debbie is big in these parts."

I sighed, stealing a sip of her whiskey. We'd been having an amiable quarrel about the gunman's identity ever since we'd hobbled back to Larry's jeep. While we both assumed he was in Dominex's hire, under contract to the National Proving Grounds, culling stray research animals, Lottie didn't think we were the prime targets at all. She figured our appearance in Paradise Gap had been a total surprise for the gunman. "That wild goat was completely out of its range, Ray," she added now, as if this were somehow apropos of the Little Debbie wrapper and the van. "It must have wandered west from the Fishlake Mountains."

"Then why would a Proving Ground employee be searching for a mountain goat in the Confusion Range? I think he was hunting for the three of us. On behalf of our old friends at C.A.T."

LEE PATTON

"Then why didn't he shoot us, detective?" Lottie asked. "There we were, fish in the proverbial barrel."

I didn't have an answer. But with a sharp stab of apprehension, I wondered how I would ever sleep tonight with visions of that gunman coming through our window after midnight, a mouthful of Little Debbie pecan pies in his grinning maw.

"Anyway," Lottie went on, taking my hand, "at some point in this genetic weapons program, Kurt's team must have become fascinated with wild animals' genes. Obsessed, maybe, by gaining access to a more 'pure' research category. In his book, Larry predicts we'd eventually see damage in the second generation of animals. Though unharmed themselves, parents were implanted with neural diseases to pass to offspring. Set at conception and triggered in the lambs and calves and now, this wild goat kid. So that gunman may have to search these hills on a steady basis, killing strays, a reverse shepherd."

"Why'd he shoot it in front of us, then?" I asked. "Why not just wait until we were gone?"

"Maybe he was sharpshooter enough to take the chance that he could kill it before we suspected anything about its convulsions."

"OK. I admit that's credible. Slightly." I squeezed Lottie's hand and sipped more of her whiskey. "But I'm still not convinced it wasn't C.A.T. That bullet could've had my name on it," I declared, with the great satisfaction of uttering a cliché that felt apt. "Those maniacs could've meant to recapture Brandy and get rid of any witnesses to her abduction at the ranch. How could we have surprised him, anyway? He must have heard Brandy yelling to us when we were standing by the pool. Not to mention Felicia barking."

"I think he'd just rounded the bend," Lottie said, "in pursuit

168

of the mountain goat, when you dropped down to help Brandy. Do you realize, by the way, that you saved her life?"

"That's right, Ray." Brandy turned away from the soap opera to face me with a shy, slight smile. Apparently, my instinctive—not courageous—gesture had actually led her to forgive me. "That bullet would've gone right through me."

In fact, if Lottie's reverse-shepherd theory were correct, I'd simply gotten in the way of a bullet meant for the goat. Or maybe, to introduce a theory we hadn't considered, he meant to kill Brandy, too, and destroy her testimony before she voiced it.

That meant that our unknown pursuers had access to our private conversations. Possibly even our make-out sessions in shimmering desert pools.

I glanced out the window, afraid of the coming nightfall, then looked at the TV, afraid a Little Debbie commercial would pop on. Instead, the blind girl was asking, "What's that sound?" while the doctor, in a passionate frenzy, knocked the nurse's rear against a metal tray.

"Well, whoever the gunman was," Lottie said, "it's lucky you got a glimpse of him."

"Yeah, but it's too bad he got a glimpse of us." I'd seen him for a split second—a wiry, bearded man in a leather vest and one of those Australian hats, brim snapped to the side—before he disappeared behind the rock rim.

When a commercial for a local firearms auction came on, the innkeeper knocked at our screen door. "I don't want to bother you," she said, "but I just picked up a treat for Felicia at the butcher's."

Brandy rose, her smile—how to describe it?—almost sweet and humane. She hobbled to the door, passing the kitten to Lottie and me. Felicia entangled herself between Brandy's ankles to inspect the innkeeper's package of bones. Brandy asked, "Do you know Larry's dog?"

"You kidding, little girl?" The innkeeper smiled. "Everybody loves Felicia. Larry got her from my son-in-law's niece, so I consider this pooch part of the family. We couldn't have asked for a better home than Larry's, either. That man spoils her near to death. Here, babycakes," she said, luring Felicia out with the tantalizing, lovely bones wrapped in butcher paper, "come and get 'em!"

Brandy glanced at us with that same, newly enchanting smile and said she'd be outside with Felicia for a minute.

"Keep out of sight, though," Lottie called. "Stay on that lawn behind the high fence. Please, Brandy?"

Brandy nodded and let the screen door slam behind her.

The kitten climbed up my leg, clawed at my belt, then settled on my stomach. Now was my chance. I'd been dying to ask Lottie more about the triangular "arrangements" at the Proving Ground since I'd learned Larry was gay. I'd also been squirming inside, knowing that I'd screwed around with her still legal husband, and now had fooled around with Larry, and felt I was somehow betraying Lottie in keeping it all clandestine.

I didn't exactly start with courtly grace. "So how come you never told me Larry was gay?"

"For starters, Ray, it's none of your business."

"Come on. Is he in the closet or something?"

"He spent his twenties in the military. Do I have to inform you about 'don't ask, don't tell'?"

"OK. But I mean, is he open with his friends? Himself?"

"Sure. Of course, but he's always had to be careful. He had to pass national security clearances when he was a younger scientist at the Proving Ground. Now, to stay effective as a peace advocate on genetic weapons, he can't let gossip steal his thunder."

"Wait a minute, though." I flashed back to my hot-tub tryst with Kurt. "Weren't Larry and Kurt 'best friends' at Stanford? Who ended up living in the same obscure corner of Utah?"

"But Larry didn't act on his sexuality until after grad school at Stanford. He had a macho self-image as a pilot. He had women throwing themselves at him all during college and military service."

I refreshed our whiskey. Though Lottie sounded so intimate with the facts, I was sure she'd blurred them through heterosexual lenses. She just couldn't imagine a studly buck like young Larry as having been anything but a lady's man or a noble warrior-celibate. But I couldn't imagine a Stanford doctoral candidate staying in the closet so long, not with the temptations of San Francisco a short drive north. "So . . ." I ventured, testing the waters of Lottie's awareness, "how did Kurt react when Larry did come out?"

"It became just another useful fact for Kurt to ingest. Kurt would seduce anyone, man, woman, or mountain goat, if it advanced his research. Or consolidated his power and influence."

"So Kurt's truly bisexual?" I smiled. "And possibly bestial?"

Lottie laughed. "He may never have messed with goats, OK— but he sure is sexually responsive to females and sure has had his fun with other men. But I honestly think Kurt really wants to screw the entire known universe. That's what his hunger for genetic manipulation is. A sexual charge, an urge to penetrate the ultimate womb."

"Mother Nature's?"

"Yes. And once inside, ravage it. But Larry idolized Kurt too much to realize the scope of his ambition until it was too late. Even now, after all Larry's own discoveries about Dominex's genetic weapons projects at the Proving Ground and the Mamie Doud labs, it's been hard for me to convince Larry that Kurt has completely defected from the human moral order."

I could understand Larry's reluctance without too much trouble. Despite all I'd seen and heard myself, despite my suspicions about Nadia and Nick's deaths, I couldn't quite wrap my mind around the full extent of Kurt's culpability. Sure, I was a lustful moral weakling who'd wrapped my naked legs around Kurt's and, faint of heart, kissed him again a few nights later, still in the shadow of Nick's murder. If Lottie was right about Kurt as the ultimate universe fucker, a reverse God, he'd seduced me only to leave me prostrate at his feet.

Because there was also Kurt's natural evenhandedness, his charm, his sincerity about genetics' potential to heal and cure, his concern and care in the face of C.A.T.'s attack on Lottie's room. It was not so hard to imagine that Larry had once felt his best friend's personal attractions, then wrestled with the same contradictions about Kurt's professional crimes.

And what had Lottie's role been? She had seemed to play the matchmaker yesterday, distracting Brandy in Paradise Gap so that Larry and I had time alone at the pool. I was gradually coming to believe that Lottie really was an agent of goodwill, an intermediary for love and compassion. Yet I couldn't quite abandon my hunch that she kept engineering my part in this adventure with such finesse that I was forever doing her bidding, even—or maybe especially—when I thought I was stealing a private kiss.

But I didn't finish exploring these revelations with any finesse of my own. "So . . . you think Larry kind of had a thing for Kurt?" I asked. "That must have been tough on you."

"I'm not sure I thought that, Ray. But if I had, I would've just questioned Larry's taste and judgment. Besides, what can you do with love but respect it? If only Kurt ever felt that way. After Kurt and Patrick realized Larry's work would expose the real nature of their research, I'm certain they moved to destroy the Desert Ecology Project."

Brandy entered with the ecstatic Felicia in tow, both of them smiling wider than usual. After we agreed to order pizza for dinner, Brandy flopped onto her bed for the soap opera's denouement. The doctor had contained his lust long enough to remove his patient's blindfold. In a shot from the girl's viewpoint, fuzzy shapes and lights accompanied her dreamy voice-over, "I can't wait to see all the ordinary things I've missed . . ." As blinding flashes scattered the shapes, portentous music came up and the credits rolled.

The perky redhead returned to announce the teasers for Live-News at 6. Aerial shots of wildfires in the River of No Return Wilderness led the broadcast, then got cut short. With a jerky transition, we were back in the studio with the redhead, who apologized for interrupting the story. "This just in. We have breaking news." She allowed a long pause as she puzzled over a note. "Yes, we have some unexpected news. Only a short while ago, Dr. Larry Lucas, Utah author and ecologist, reported a fire in the fuel line of his small private plane while flying from New Carlsbad to Live-News headquarters for an exclusive interview. He lost radio contact shortly after passing Cedar Valley. Emergency workers who arrived at the crash site in the Desert Chemical Depot report that Lucas managed to land the burning plane."

The redhead hesitated again, the next detail cross-hatched in her brow: "But Lucas could not survive the conflagration that followed. More on this tragedy when your LiveNews exclusive Live-Unit reports from the crash site. Now this."

Early in the morning after Larry's crash, I stirred my chilling coffee and stared at the Guided Missile Cafe's cable news. Over and over, they looped the story of a Texas biotech corporation whose financial officers had raided its assets and destroyed the company. Over and over, they showed the video clip of bewildered office workers wandering Dallas streets clutching family photos and artificial flowers from their ex-cubicles. Brandy, across from me, slid her untouched plateful of pancakes back and forth in a hard silence.

I'd done nothing but watch the news through the night, keeping the sound muffled as Brandy and Lottie writhed in and out of shallow sleep. Lottie would sometimes cling to me. Other times she'd shove herself facedown against the pillow, crying convulsively. Then she'd stare silently at the ceiling.

Brandy had spent the night curled on the other bed with Felicia and the kitten, her face to the wall, immobile but without sleep's steady breath.

After all these days and uncounted miles of relative composure and odd luck, our almost familial concord-spiked-with-discord, would the three of us lose our wits completely now? Brandy shoved the pancakes away and reached for a paper napkin. She dangled it over her brow as if trying to hide her eyes from me.

"Come on, Brandy," I pleaded, wishing Lottie were beside me for moral support and emergency Brandy management. Reluctantly, we'd left Lottie alone in the room. She'd claimed she would sleep and get breakfast later. I knew she wanted to be alone with this new loss, a dagger into the fresh wound of Nick's death. So I tried, hapless, to cheer Brandy myself. "We've made it this far. We'll figure something out. Hey, come on. Please don't cry."

She shook her head as she soaked her face in another fistful of napkins. "I ain't crying," she said, trying to stanch another drizzle of tears. "I hate it when chicks cry in public."

My eyes usually started tearing if anyone else cried, and sure enough, my ducts got busy welling up. But Brandy and I were both saved from more public blubbering by the TV announcement of a "Utah Update." Though the national news kept running a canned clip about Larry's crash, local updates would rivet us, commanding our full attention as if, any minute, the Salt Lake media would disclose their mistake and reveal that Larry had survived the explosion and fire.

But that hope crashed as each report added detail. Alight like an airborne torch, diving into fuel tanks at the Desert Chemical Depot, the small plane's metal melted like twisted flesh. "There could be no human remains," the Tooele County coroner admitted simply. "Nothing for us to identify."

In the local coverage, Larry's intended message, the whole reason he'd flown to Salt Lake in the first place, had been subordinated to the shock of his sudden, explosive immolation. Announcers, many of whom knew Larry personally, resorted to hyperbolic tropes: "Only minutes from his destination, at the height of his fame, in the prime of his life . . ." Along with instant editorials about the need for more regulation of small private aircraft, Live-News kept re-running a "special report on small plane fuel line hazards." Though they looped the clip of Larry's "Pandora's box" analogy over and over, none of the video journalists talked about genetic weapons and the revelations of his book. And none of the reporters mentioned that they'd already been summoned to a press conference in New Carlsbad.

Already, too, from the nation's sewers of psycho bloggers and talk radio, seeped speculation that Larry might have acted as an "American suicide bomber extremist" who took deliberate aim at a federal chemical depot.

In the back of my mind, I marveled that in all those hours of coverage not one millisecond was devoted to Brandy's disappearance. Of course, Salt Lake had a dramatic tragedy involving a controversial Utah celebrity. But why wasn't a controversial federal prisoner's escape worth a sentence on the national news? The more the news media ignored us, the longer we went without any evidence of pursuit by the feds or C.A.T., the more exposed we seemed, like kids who believe they've hidden themselves when they've only covered their eyes.

It was so desolate between Brandy and me, without Lottie's presence, that I had to try to force our attention away from the news cycle. "I wish they'd shut up, too," I said, "but I do wonder why they never mention you."

"Them jerks in C.A.T.—" Brandy began, and stopped. She leaned closer, lowering her voice. "See, they know how bad they screwed up. So they worked something out with those prison guards who were in on it. Like, not to say anything."

"But somebody else has got to be missing you. What about the other guards, the other girls, the officials?"

"Jeez," Brandy said, shaking her head. She poured more syrup on her cold, untouched pancakes. "Sometimes you're kind of dense, Ray. How come you think the officials are so damn pure? Don't you think they might be in on it, too?"

"So, you think C.A.T. paid off everybody involved? Maybe I am dense, but that's kind of expensive, isn't it? And setting you up on that ranch, in luxury—"

"Luxury! That was all their crap, not mine."

"OK, but let's think this through. They were putting out a lot of money to . . . what? Interrogate you? Take you hostage, then present you in some vigilante publicity stunt?"

"Yeah." She pushed her plate aside. "I guess. Kind of like Lottie and Larry are . . . were planning to do." Brandy raised her full glass of orange juice, swirled it, and set it down. "But nobody at the ranch would tell me exactly what was going on, no matter how many times I asked them."

"All right. But if there's this big hush-up, why isn't C.A.T. still pursuing you on their own?"

"Maybe they are." She cast her eyes to the window, glaring across the street to Rocket Burger. "Maybe that rifle guy meant to aim a bullet straight into me. He probably . . ." She didn't finish. She closed her furious little eyes, unable to control another quick cry. "And they probably got somebody else on my tail who's a better shot . . ." She trailed off again, choked by another bout of tears.

"Hey, please, Brandy, they're not trying to kill you. You're, like, the prize."

Brandy stared at me with red eyes and clutched another fistful of napkins. "It's sad about Larry, huh? I don't see why a nice guy like that had to die."

"Me neither," I said.

"Me neither," said the waitress neither of us had noticed, standing by our booth. Wiping her hands on her apron, she was a big-boned gal with a name tag that read VERONA. "I almost didn't open the place this morning. Larry had breakfast here, you know, 7 o'clock sharp, whenever he was in town. Always sat right there," Verona said, pointing to an empty booth. "I was thinking we ought to rename the cafe after him. Guided missiles have sure never done this town any good." She glanced out the window. "Isn't that Felicia you tied up outside? You kids were friends of Larry's?"

"Yeah," I said, amazed at the ready ease of my lie: "Larry was my T.A. at Stanford. We were passing through and stopped for a few days' visit. He even left Felicia with us, at the airport yesterday." I extended my hand. "Name's O'Leary. Ed. This is my wife's little sister, Amy. My wife, Nicolette, she's back at the motel."

"Pleasure. I never knew anybody who had so many out-of-town friends. Now, you'll stay for the memorial, won't you? I was just talking it over with the reverend. We're calling media all over hell—Vegas, Salt Lake, Denver—to invite anybody who wants to come. We're gonna fill up the goddamn First Methodist and show Larry how much we're gonna miss him."

I glanced out the plate window at Felicia, peacefully resting under the wrought-iron bench where we'd leashed her. She smiled, panting, at a pair of kids who strolled by. Laughing, they doubled back to pet her.

"I didn't know," I told the waitress, "that Larry was a Methodist."

"Oh, he never gave a hoot about religion. But after Larry helped the reverend put up the new roof, they became poker buddies. It's not easy running a Methodist church in Mormon Country." Verona glanced out toward the dog. "Listen, you kids want us to take old Felicia off your hands, the reverend and me? Jack," she called to the plump fellow sitting at the counter, who raised his coffee cup to us, "these kids got stuck with Larry's dog."

"We're not stuck with her," Brandy said. "Larry asked me to look after her while he was gone. And that's what I'm doing."

"OK, Amy, honey," the waitress soothed. "But if you change your mind, you drop her off here, OK? Larry sometimes left Felicia with us when he left town."

We all turned to the next Utah Update teaser, this time featuring a chopper shot of Larry's Cessna: a telephoto pan, the plane tiny and molten beside the jagged propane-tank blowhole.

Verona spoke again, facing the screen. "I wonder when the Salt Lake news is gonna start talking about how Larry just had that plane safety checked, prop to tail? That somebody might not have wanted him to reach Salt Lake and talk to reporters?" She turned back to us, then stared at our plates. "Aren't you gonna eat any breakfast at all?"

I had Verona wrap my waffles for Lottie. But when we carried them back to the room, we found Lottie finally asleep. Brandy said she didn't feel so hot, and dropped immediately onto her bed, facedown, the kitten doing laps over her head. She agreed, though, to bolt and latch the door behind me when I announced I was taking Felicia for a short walk.

It would be the first of many solitary strolls with Felicia over the next two days. Together we learned every cranny of New Carlsbad. Lottie never roused herself to accompany us, never left the room, and I got the feeling—strange to say—that Brandy felt too protective of Lottie to let her out of sight for long.

After Nick's death, Lottie's grief must have been transformed into the energy that propelled us all the way to the Confusion Range. Suspicious as I may have been, I still admired how undaunted she'd seemed, her capacities churning us into the heart of the territory. Now, of course, Larry's immolation seemed to paralyze her. Now, I'd be glad to fall back into my sidekick role; instead, I could only coax and comfort her when she'd seize me during her night terrors. I kept wondering if her constant agitation were really an affliction, something we could seek treatment for in a town that offered clinical care. Was this, in fact, a nervous breakdown?

That first walk took Felicia and me through the town's newest subdivision, its wide asphalt street lined by twenty prefabricated ranch houses. Only a handful had signs of life or surviving lawns. Most had federal repossession program stickers in the windows, and most of the windows were broken, most screen doors stolen. It was just a newer version of the Denver neighborhood where I had first met Lottie; cheap, downsized housing for some mortgage of last resort.

At the dead end of empty Moroni Avenue, I realized I was just across a gulch from those abandoned local follies, the Ronald Reagan Medical Clinic and the Hot Springs Grand Hotel. Staring over the tamarisk-choked gulch into their vacant windows, I wondered how soon our civilization would vanish like an enormous Anasazi village.

I sat on the gulch's edge while Felicia huddled against my shins. A west wind off the mountains cooled the late morning air. I wondered, closing my eyes, if I could snooze for a minute, but my mind continued to pace its merciless thought rut.

Maybe my sleeplessness had its source in my standing date to spend the night at Larry's. Maybe as long as I stayed awake, then our date stood against all physics and logic, and I could still look forward to that moment when Larry would take me in his arms.

Felicia stirred and began yapping happily. I opened my eyes. Her sweet dog smile panting and wide, her big eyes followed a plane's descent to the airfield. As it flew much closer, almost overhead, I could detect a company logo emblazoned on the small commercial liner's entire side, wing to nose: DOMINEX. I couldn't see the smaller print underneath, but knew what it said: HEALING A WORLD OF HURT. Felicia didn't care, though, and, circling in self-delight, she wagged her tail and cheered it on with rhythmic yaps.

So, there, feet in a gulch, I lost it for the first time since that moment in the Globeville churchyard. I wept for Nadia, Nick, and Larry. For the mountain goat; for our orphans, Felicia and the kitten. For Brandy and her fears of renewed pursuit and violence. For Lottie.

My love for Nick lost in perpetuity, my kiss with Larry aborted for all time, I howled for myself too. For that clueless wonder who'd vowed to Nadia that he'd climb every mountain in Colorado before the end of his youth.

It took more than forty-eight hours after Larry's crash until Brandy and I could coax Lottie from the motel room. We convinced her that a soak in the hot springs would soothe her ankle. It was either that, I told her, or a long drive to Provo and the university hospital, because despite constant icing, the swelling wasn't going down. As it was, she had to lean on me all the way to the Subaru. Brandy's foot wound was better, though. She hardly limped now as she delivered Felicia and the kitten to our innkeeper's care.

The Grand Hotel's hot springs made an apt setting to bubble away the last of our delusions, cast to perdition in steam and sulfur. From three stories of decaying suites, all windows broken, jagged glass reflected the evening sky. Skeletal hotel wings surrounded the open-air pool. An Italian arcade's classical pillars lined the pool's sundeck and overlooked a vanished garden. Cadaverous, upright remnants of topiary junipers now bordered patches of dirt and weeds. Plaster fountains clogged with beer cans served as bases for statuary, headless angels, a wingless Pegasus. Cupid's bow had been ripped off.

Beyond the lifeless garden, the Wah Wah Mountains undulated under a band of sunset clouds. Their violet light bounced into the pool, softening the cracks in the ancient concrete and dazzling the brackish water's surface. Hunched under this haunted, ruinous beauty, the three of us sat on an underwater bench, submerged up to our necks, each soothing various wounds and aches.

We seemed to have the whole place to ourselves. Even the girl who sold the tickets had left for the day, saying we could stay until an attendant locked the showers at 10. Utter peacefulness, with no possible intrusion by LiveNews or Utah Updates. After a few minutes, even the rotten-egg odor seemed less noticeable. I asked Lottie if her ankle felt any better.

She nodded, dragging her bad leg up to the surface and cutting a circle with her toes. "Just think, originally we were going to come here to celebrate. After our press conference, remember?" She reached to massage her ankle. "Now the best we can do is soak our injuries. So we can hobble to Larry's memorial tomorrow."

"I still wonder, though," I said. "Maybe we shouldn't go."

"Oh, who cares anymore? It's over, Ray. There's no point in hiding. It's Brandy I'm most concerned about. It's not going to do her a bit of good to stay in our company."

I nodded, trying to disguise my relief at hearing Lottie, at last, talk like this again, stubborn as the tenth-grade biology teacher she once was. I closed my eyes and tried to suppress my first smile in days.

Lottie turned to Brandy, glancing around me. "Why don't we arrange for you to stay with contacts in California? Isn't that where you've wanted to go, Brandy? You'll love Palo Alto. I can spare the rest of my cash. Just think, Brandy. A new life." Lottie waited for a response while Brandy kicked the water's surface with quick stabs of her good foot. But she said nothing, so Lottie added, "We could swing by the Salt Lake airport on our way back to Denver."

Staring ahead, Brandy kept kicking. "OK. That's probably the best thing to do. But I sure wish I could go to Larry's memorial."

"Oh, I wish you could, too." Lottie's voice lost its stubborn edge now. She reached across my stomach to take Brandy's hand. "But it would just be too risky, Brandy. There'll be all kinds of potential trouble. With the police, rangers, reporters, Proving Ground staffers, somebody's bound to recognize you."

"Maybe, but my picture hasn't been in the news at all. Maybe everyone's forgotten what I look like."

"It's too great a risk, Brandy. I can't see the point of your risking exposure now."

"I don't know what the point is anymore." Brandy went still. I could feel her hand tighten around Lottie's across my stomach. "It's weird. I never thought it would end up like this."

I knew what she meant. None of us had thought beyond the press conference, which had promised to be the magic event that set Brandy free (somehow) and exposed genetic weapons research (like, wow). Deprived of that magic and Larry's credibility and genius for publicity, what were we supposed to do? Keep Brandy in hiding forever? Still, I couldn't imagine the poor bag of bones making much of a new life for herself in California.

"Well, setting you free was the only thing we've done right," Lottie said. "If you stay with us any longer, we might be putting you in greater and greater danger. We've lost Nick and Larry. I'm not about to lose you, Brandy." She squeezed Brandy's hand and let it go. "Think about that gunman in Paradise Gap. If he wasn't working for Kurt, then Ray's probably right. He was hired by C.A.T. to scare us. At the least. They must know right where we are."

"Then won't 'they' follow us to the airport?" I asked. "I don't see how we can guarantee Brandy's safety by sending her out to 'contacts' in Palo Alto."

"We can't guarantee anything," Lottie said in her new damn-the-devil tone. "Not even that you and I will get back to Denver in one piece. But Brandy, you'll be much safer there than with us. Larry's friends there know what they're doing. And I can send you more money once I do get home. I'm just sorry I bungled this so badly. I meant to get you out of jeopardy, not into it."

"You don't have anything to be sorry about!" Brandy said with unexpected heat.

"I appreciate that, Brandy, but I've had days to mull this over now. My blame goes deeper than you know. Now that you both know the magnitude of Dominex's program, you have to wonder about me. Don't you? Any marriage is symbiotic. How can I not be tainted by all those years when I tolerated my husband's research?"

"That's bullshit, Lottie," Brandy said. "You've been fighting hard. You went through hell to help support the Avenging Eco-Angels. And me."

"That was kind of late in the game, though," Lottie said. "I already had this big scarlet 'A' scored into my bosom. For 'Accomplice.'"

"You're not the only one," Brandy said. "I let myself get

rooked into this. The bombing, I mean. All you tried to do was help me. Nobody's ever done that for me before." She set her neck against the concrete rim and stared overhead. "I keep trying to figure out what it is you get from all this, what you want, Lottie."

"I want you free."

"And I am. If you guys hadn't gotten me off that stupid ranch, well, who knows whether I'd be lying in the dirt like that cat? I'm just . . . going to miss being with . . . Felicia and the kitten. And you guys. I never knew people could be so nice. Or care about anybody else so much." Brandy shoved off from the underwater bench, side-stroking out into the steamy deeps.

For a crazy second I figured we ought to just adopt our O'Leary personas and go on living in New Carlsbad happily ever after. "We could do it, Lottie. The O'Learys. I'll go on being Ed, you're Nicolette, and our little Amy could sign up for community college at the Deseret Extension. We could fix up one of those repo houses on Moroni Avenue."

Lottie actually smiled, taking my hand. Brandy reversed course and swam back to us to stand, hands on her hips, facing Lottie. "But the main thing is, you were gonna do something. Remember, Lottie? Like stage that press conference. It was, like, a way of fixing some of the mess I made with that stupid bomb."

"Yes, we did try," Lottie said. "We almost—"

Brandy slapped the water. "We still can. Is there any reason we can't still hold that conference? Especially with all them big shots in town for the memorial?"

"Yeah," I heard myself say. "Well, Lottie, why not? There'll be all kinds of reporters at the service. All we have to do is arrange . . ." I cut myself short when I heard the metal door of the men's locker room creak open. I actually flashed on the hope that it might be a journalist, appearing as if bidden, some eager young reporter arrived in town early and taking a dip in the World Famous Hot Springs. Could we still bring off Larry's media coup?

The guy appeared along the pool's far end, his phantom silhouette darting between the arcade's columns. A phantom naked to the waist, wrapped in a towel, who strolled slowly toward us along the concrete rim.

Lottie held back a breath and tightened her grip on my hand. My throat went parched.

He sat perched on the rim, catercornered from us, and bid us good evening. "It's just sad we have to meet under these circumstances, isn't it?"

"You son of a bitch," Lottie said flatly. "You dare to show up for this? Larry's funeral service?"

"Dare?" Kurt asked, adopting an incredulous tone. He stood again to slip out of the towel and display his well-toned nakedness, then stepped slowly, familiarly, down underwater steps before shoving off into deeper water. He surged beyond us, his sleek back tinted by dusk a gold incarnadine, inhuman. With a perfect flip, he floated onto his back toward the rim and hoisted himself up. Sitting on his towel, he dangled his feet in the water. "I'm glad we got the chance to visit before the service."

"I thought we'd be spared that," Lottie said, coolly, but still clutching my hand as if for dear life. "I thought the pool was closed."

Kurt laughed—surprised, yet gentle and amused. He spoke, gaily, to me: "Lottie and I snuck in here so many times after closing. Even got a citation once, for public mischief, from an officious deputy sheriff. That's still the only criminal violation on my record."

"I do love American justice," Lottie said. "Remember the time we snuck in after midnight with Larry, when Nicky was visiting us? You do remember them, Kurt? Nicky, Nadia Sanchez's son? And Larry? Dr. Larry Lucas?"

"How can you ask me that? Hasn't this summer begun and ended with their funerals?"

Lottie ignored his wounded tone. "So how did you find out we were here?"

"I happened to check into the Wah Wah Motor Court."

"You—" Now Lottie really seethed. She almost shot from the water, then seemed to think better of it and sank back, facing forward in a cold burn. "You goddamn war criminal. You smug bastard."

"That nice lady at the office didn't think I was such a war criminal bastard. We had quite a chat about Felicia and what a wonderful dog she is, and how much we'll all miss Larry. When I confided that I was your husband, she confided that you'd gone to the hot springs. With the nice young people who shared your room. That's one nice thing about Utah, Ray. These Mormons have prodigious respect for marriage as a union between a man and a woman."

"That is nice," I told him. "Fuck you."

"You wouldn't have come all this way alone," Lottie said. "Where's your entourage?"

"Patrick's on his way. He wanted to jog out here from the motel. Run off that jet lag."

"Well, who can blame him?" Lottie asked, then launched an imitation of Kurt's elaborate, archaic, yet colloquial speaking style: "Whenever I'm grieving for a dead lover or a dead colleague, or both, I often take a hearty jog. Must stay in shape, no matter how my heart might be breaking. And now, Kurt, that you've had your nice swim, why don't you go for a nice marathon across the Wah Wah Valley? All the way to the base of the Confusion Range?

Maybe you'll encounter a mountain goat suffering from lab-induced seizures. Or dead from a bullet wound."

"Listen, Lottie, I'm willing to cut you a lot of slack. I know what burdens, what losses have led you to this. But you've got to cut the sarcastic crap about my supposed crimes. OK? None of this has exactly been easy for me, either. And Larry was a hell of lot more than a colleague. You know that. He was a sweet soul. Our friendship transcended our differences. We were like brothers."

"Oh, way beyond mere brothers. Your tenderness toward Larry always took my breath away, Kurt. Why, I may just get up at the memorial and say a few words myself. The good Utahns may respect the sacred link between a man and woman, but they've got to cherish the deep male bond between you and Larry even more."

Kurt's sincere tone seemed unfazed, despite Lottie's refusal to cut the sarcastic crap: "I loved him."

"Then why did you kill him?"

On Lottie's question, Kurt turned calmly toward the metallic bang of the locker room door. A silhouette with a linebacker's build strolled between the columns against the star-strewn twilight. Naked, dripping from the shower, Patrick set his running clothes beside Kurt on the pool's edge. After greeting us with "Hi everybody," Patrick dove in. He emerged with a satisfied yelp, shook the water from his hair, and rested below Kurt on the submerged bench. "Beautiful evening, huh?" He sighed. "You OK, Lottie?"

"Sure, Patrick. You know how I get. But it's nothing a one-car accident won't fix."

Kurt cleared his throat. "This is truly wondrous, our reconvergence here. In our old playground."

"Despite," Patrick added, "the tragic circumstances."

"If we can get help for Lottie," Kurt said, as if to Patrick while staring at the water, "there's no reason we can't return to happier times."

Lottie, though, had never seemed in less need of "help." She seemed so advanced from the costumed and paranoid Lottie my ego had presumed to be a damsel in distress that day last week, during the Ballet Folklorico and the Saudi women's march. Though the little we'd accomplished was far less than we even realized—having much to learn in those last minutes together—we'd still come a great distance.

Brandy had greeted Kurt and Patrick's appearances with an entrenched, paralyzed silence. Now she slapped her hands flat on the water and cried, "Lottie doesn't need your damn help!"

"Brandy, Brandy," Kurt murmured. "It's good to see you're as spirited as ever. I had no idea how your abductors were treating you, though I assumed they were keeping you reasonably fit."

"Damn you, Kurt! They've treated me a hell of a lot better than . . ."

"Than who, Brandy? Shall we tell them, then?"

"No way, Kurt!" Brandy sank lower into the water. Her tone had shifted into that other range I'd sometimes heard—like a slip in a dialect performance—more assured, less deliberately rustic. Older. "Give them a break, OK?"

"I will," Kurt said, "if you'll please just tell your abductors the truth. I'd like to hear in your own words. A personal narrative. Something in the confessional mode."

"Shut up." Brandy folded her arms and stared at her feet.

"OK. I should've realized you'd come to admire your captors. It's called the Stockholm syndrome, isn't it?"

"Whatever," Brandy said. "I never did admire you."

"Not even after all the comforts Dominex can buy?" Kurt said. "I'm wounded."

Patrick rallied to help his wounded partner with the details.

188

"Won't you admit, Brandy, we provided a slight improvement over the rusty trailer? Didn't you and your punk boyfriend want to get the heck out of Commerce City?"

"Where your well water was contaminated with nerve gas from the Rocky Mountain Arsenal?" Kurt put in. "It's touching. You were willing to give all that up to help us save the free world—well, what we used to call the free world—then have free run of your own Wyoming ranch. Your own horses. Your very own satellite dish and high-speed Internet. But I guess that wasn't good enough."

"Free run? That's a joke. You've all had free run of me."

"I'm sorry, Brandy," Kurt said. "But you can see how heartbreaking it was for me. I couldn't sit by, watching Lottie become increasingly obsessed with her campaign. To free a prisoner who was always free."

"So . . ." Lottie let it sink in. "So, Brandy, they released you every night? Not C.A.T., but through some agreement Kurt made with the guards?"

"Oh, Lottie," Brandy said, rubbing her temples. "People don't have agreements with Kurt," she announced in her new, adult intonations. "They just do what he says."

"If I may help?" Kurt asked. "Under intricate arrangements with cooperative officials, Brandy was only sequestered at the prison itself, and for daytimes only, when she had visitors. We assumed your visit would be for a day or two. Our contacts in Sweetwater were only there to guarantee your safety. Ray, if you remember, we even treated you to a chardonnay and a few hours of pleasant company. Of course, we had no idea you and Lottie would kidnap our employee. That you'd steal her away from her carefree life on her trophy ranch in Sweetwater."

"A place, I might add," Patrick added, "as the name implies, with some of the purest drinking water on the planet."

"That you'd force our Brandy," Kurt continued, "along for her supporting role in your B-grade road movie."

"Lottie and Ray didn't exactly have to force me, Kurt," Brandy said. "Funny how old the carefree life can get with Mortimer forcing his fat ass—"

"We really should speak to Mort," Patrick said. "Where the heck is he, anyway?"

"On his fourth Mexican beer," Kurt said. "They ought to be here by now. Oh well. Lottie, Ray, do you kind of get the picture at this point?"

"So, C.A.T.," Lottie asked, "was just as duped as I was?"

"Not to turn the truth into some phony Zen koan," Kurt said, "but can you imagine how C.A.T. might be just as real, and just as unreal, as the Avenging Eco-Terrorists?"

"So you bombed your own lab?" I asked. "You hired Brandy to take the blame all along."

"And you tore up my room at Mr. Chou's? Sabotaged my human rights organization?"

"Lottie, now, that's just my point. How real, really, was the League?"

"The night janitor, the research chimp," Lottie said, "were perfectly real. And that was no accident?"

"It was an accident, that they got hurt," Brandy said. "That's the only true thing in Kurt's whole sewer of bullshit. I didn't have any idea that injuring them was part of the plan all along. The way they told me, the bomb was going to damage a room full of worthless file cabinets and old software. And I didn't know a thing about the nature of the . . . " She spat it: "Research."

"Ignorance is never an attractive defense, Miss McConnaughty," Kurt said. "And before we all become too confessional, I want to remind this assembly that I haven't implicated myself in any of the collateral damage Miss McConnaughty set loose. But I will point out that since the unfortunate bombing, our work at the Mamie Doud labs has been able to proceed without protesters lining the road to our workplace. There has been a marked decline in membership and Web postings for the lunatic, antitechnology fringe. One chimp's death diminishes us all, but the universe sometimes throws hard choices. Like one man's injury versus an entire civilization in the thrall of terror."

"We're working against the clock, Lottie," Patrick said. "You know that. We have this one brief window of time to develop the counterforce before the terrorist states do. Do you think their leaders are quibbling over moral nuances about lab monkeys?"

"Larry was ready to disclose exactly who gave those terror states their genetic technology in the first place," Lottie said. "Patrick, you know that." Lottie was quieter now, as if trying to hear herself over her mind's racing. "You create monsters, supply them with monstrous weapons, then argue that they're the threat driving us to new levels of monstrosity."

"Yes, Larry did have some wild theories," Kurt said, "may he rest in peace. But Larry's flights of fancy aren't the point. We've been assigned to go beyond counterforce now. We have to end this terrifying cycle of weapons escalation for once and for all. We're developing the perfect deterrent to further terrorism."

"All we need to do is demonstrate the power of genetic implants as weaponry," Patrick added, "with all its drama of generational deformity and disease, and we'll have earned a world of perfect peace."

"At last," Kurt said. "No more fits and starts of strife and civil uprisings. A world of perfect expansion for free markets."

"Expansion!" Lottie cried out. "Expansion for what? Bigger Slurpees, more Hummers, more deformed children into infinity? You have attained perfection, Kurt. You've become the perfect terrorist."

"I have to live with a lot of cruel labels, Lottie, but nobody ever seems to label me the victim. Why is that? Did I invent genetic engineering? Did I invent crazed mullahs and fanatic terror cells? And what I did invent, this genetic deterrent, isn't even mine anymore."

Quietly, three dimly familiar shapes entered from the locker room. Mortimer, the heavy-set guard from Brandy's Sweetwater ranch, carried a half-full Corona. He tipped the brim of his Rockies ball cap to Lottie and me, then sat on sagging wooden bleachers behind Kurt and Patrick.

The square-jawed man slipped beside Mortimer. He raised his ice-rattled plastic cup to me, as if to commemorate our brief mobile-motel romance. As if to remind me that, far more than Lottie, I deserved to wear the scarlet A. For grade-A whore, who'd not only been screwed by Satan himself, but compounded the crime with one of his lesser devils.

Last was the bearded guy, mountain goat sharpshooter, in the same leather vest. Under the strap of his Aussie brimmed hat, I could now detect his hearing aid. At the same time, I saw his pistol, tucked into a holster.

They all had pistols.

The bearded guy apologized for his lateness, explaining that their barroom pool game had run into a tie match. He sat on the highest bleacher, as if seeking that same elevated, unobstructed view for the precise aim he'd had in Paradise Gap.

Who would take the wild goat's place here at the World Famous Hot Springs?

Kurt continued his claim to victimhood, hardly glancing at his three armed men. "Larry Lucas wasn't exaggerating about Pandora's box. If there's one thing I've learned in my dealings with governments and military contractors, they'll stop at nothing to protect expensive secrets. Their secrets have long slipped beyond the horizon of reason, as you know, Lottie. Containing them in a chaotic world is the sole employment of thousands. If you'll pardon me, for far from being anyone's perfect terrorist, I'm just counterterrorism's poster child. Its humble servant. Does Dominex dance to the military's siren song, or vice versa? Do you think I act freely? Do you think I'll ever be as free as Brandy was in Sweetwater? I haven't scribbled a single unsupervised equation since I reported for work under Dominex at the Mamie Doud."

Lottie took my hand under the water again, but stared straight ahead now, her eyes wide, her mouth slightly agape, her breaths deliberate. "I admit—" she blurted, revising: "Kurt, I know there's an element of truth to that."

"Thank you, Lottie." Kurt stood, wrapping his towel around his waist in sudden modesty. Then he crossed to the three of us and sat again on the rim, his knee only inches from Lottie's head. "I'm flattered that you all attribute omnipotence to me. But the real power lies in the terrors I've seen. Terrors more tangible than the genetic fantasies of weapons manufacturers. Do you think citizens with inconvenient secrets only disappear in dictatorships? Then don't investigate drainage ditches outside any research triangle in the U.S.A. East of Dominex, in the Land of Nod." Kurt gently touched the back of Lottie's head, combing her dark hair with his fingers. "So, Lottie, don't you see how your idealism, and all the courage and innocence of your adventure, really did break my heart?"

Lottie stared at Kurt, wiping any defiance from her expression. "But you have to understand, too, Kurt. I was motivated by the only information I had."

"I have no trouble understanding that. In this system, access to the truth is as unthinkable as idealism. My sponsors are ruthless. None of the deaths are accidental. Why do you think I've had you followed so closely? But we'll do our best to keep you safe, to make sure no one else we love is sacrificed to this . . ."

For once Kurt's eloquence failed him. I tried to imagine what euphemism he could dream up—besides "system" or "sponsors"—to distance himself from direct responsibility. None of the deaths were accidental.

I strained toward what Lottie whispered to me. She tugged my hand, her lips brushing against my ear, her words so soft I could only distinguish, "remember, wait. Wait," and, "thanks," and finally, "good-bye."

She held a hand to Kurt, who helped her to her feet, embracing her as he covered her in a towel. "I'm mortified," she said, "when I think I've exposed Brandy and Ray to so much danger. Over a gigantic misunderstanding." She pulled away from Kurt. "I'm humiliated, too."

Kurt continued holding her shoulders, arms extended, as a teacher might to steady a child. "There's no need for that, Lottie. I grasped what you thought you were doing, all along."

"But I've caused so much distress. I've been so blinded, Kurt."

Patrick approached with a hand for Brandy. She ignored him for a moment, to cover herself. Then, on her feet, she leaned to kiss the back of my head and murmur, "I'm the one who's sorry, Ray," in that new tone. I recalled how sweetly she'd called the momma cat in Sweetwater when she'd thought no one was listening. "But think," she whispered as Patrick tugged her away, "we almost made it happen!"

While Brandy had distracted me, some new layer of—what, understanding? Mutual deception?—had passed between Kurt and Lottie. Sleek and pretty as Greek deities, towel-clad, they began toward the locker room, Kurt taking the lead. Finally, Kurt reached for her hand as if to stabilize her still-hobbling gait. Lottie clasped it.

Mortimer and the square-jawed man got up, too, the show over, and followed the hobbling, dripping women and their handsome escorts down the colonnade. But the square-jawed man detoured to the rim after Kurt and Patrick disappeared into the locker room. With a glance to the bearded gunman, he crouched, a hand on my shoulder, and confided in a low voice, "There's no reason you and I need to be enemies, Ray. No harm done."

"Does that mean," I said, my voice clogged by the toad in my throat, "that I'm gonna get out of here alive?"

The square-jawed man slapped my upper arm, laughing, a full-bore, scorn-free howl that echoed in the liquid, cavernous space as he hurried off to join the entourage.

No harm done.

Staying deliberately behind, the gunman stood on the topmost bleacher, his hand resting on his holster. He stared at me, even and unhurried, as if scoping his best shot.

So this was it for me, terminating in a henchman's seductive joke. A fitting fate for the sidekick sidetracked by lust. It was a miracle I hadn't disclosed more than I did, placing Lottie and Brandy in even greater danger with Kurt's "systems" and "sponsors."

I closed my eyes, wondering if I ought to at least slip from the pool and make a naked run for it. But there was nowhere to run. I clung to the bench's edge, scared witless.

I swore I could hear, behind and above, the slide of metal from its leather resting place. In the dark, shimmering silence, I heard Nadia's echoing phrase, among her last coherent words to me in May; that "God must be a Democrat after all, because He'd shown enough mercy to kill me off this fast."

Among her last delirious words were "stop them."

The metallic door slammed. I opened my eyes and turned.

The gunman was gone. My relief was purely physical, the gratitude of a still-beating heart. A piece of meat, beating for what, though, and why? My life seemed so insubstantial, a smear of molecules on the planet's petri dish.

That's probably why they didn't bother squashing it.

I hoisted myself onto the rim. Steam rose from my naked thighs as if my whole being were about to evaporate into sulfur.

CHAPTER TEN

I'd been gone such a short time that the porch bulb I'd left ablaze still lighted my arrival home.

A hygienic zombie, I cleaned and disinfected my bullet wound as it shrank to an ugly scar above my collar bone. I shopped for cat and dog supplies. I christened Brandy's kitten Margarita, in honor of the liquor-laden McConnaughty tradition. I attended the new school year's teacher orientation right on time. During chitchat about summer doings, I mentioned only my job updating the possessions of the dead.

Behind my good-citizen facade, I resumed normal routines. Nobody had to know how deeply our mission in the Confusion Range had failed or how willingly I'd sexed the devil on the way there. Now that I planned to be celibate for the rest of my days, I would encourage my reputation as a single gentleman who'd lost his life's love too soon. Inside my own skin, though, I felt stranded, an impostor, forced to inhabit a younger, discarded incarnation of myself.

With my drama writing minicourses expanding into additional high schools, with new facilities and school cultures to learn, my work stresses surged at August's end. Teaching engrossed me, but couldn't erase my fixation on our delusional errand in the Utah wilderness.

In the evenings on my patio, with Margarita snoozing on my lap and Felicia smiling and panting at my feet, I meant to review stacks of my new students' self-descriptions. But I couldn't concentrate. With Brandy "free" but back in Sweetwater, with Lottie presumably captive in Kurt's concrete palace, the reversal of our original goals stung beyond humiliation, beyond even mere defeat. We hadn't freed anyone. We hadn't helped enlighten anyone about this new peril in the world.

Now, severed from Lottie's moral imperatives, I had to endure a failure's straitened life. When my mind replayed our last hope's reversal in the hot springs, my face stung with self-contempt. If the whole affair began as a fairy's fairy-tale rescue, what a limp white knight I must've looked to that male jury on the bleachers. The gay pretender to manhood, completely unarmored. Naked. I'd blubbered in the poisoned pool while the villain and his blackguards led my damsel away under arms.

Yet I'd never liked fantasy as a genre. OK, I might have failed against Kurt's masquerading gunmen, his seductions, proxy enticements, and phony vigilante committees, but despite my powerlessness, it wasn't my life that was the disgrace.

Wasn't Kurt Weiss the figure of fantasy if anyone was? The wizard humiliated, overwhelmed, and finally enslaved by his own black magic. The genuine potency that had accrued from his brilliance and knowledge now beggared new sources, big-money blackmail, and gunpoint coercion.

So I went on steaming in low-boil frustration. I missed Lottie. I grieved Larry, both for his touch and his humane influence in the world. Out of their reach, my reduced life seemed permanently severed from heady ideals and quixotic quests. In manic moods, I imagined mustering a few imperatives of my own. I would be their proxy agent, a League of one. Then, as the mania receded, I fell into self-disgust, guilt ridden that I'd held close for so long my suspicions about Lottie. It'd been dramatic, and dismissive, to cast myself as Lottie's convenient sidekick, riding shotgun through a willful adventure calculated to rile Kurt and revenge a failed marriage. At least I'd come to understand that Lottie really had been pure hearted in her dual goals of freeing Brandy and exposing Kurt's research, which made all the greater the sacrifice she had made for me that evening in the hot springs. Aborting our quest, hobbling back into captivity, she had probably saved my life.

I plunged into funks of dread, imagining ongoing surveillance: a faint click in the phone line; the friendly, inquisitive bald guy who moved into the rental across from my duplex; the silver Volvo a few cars behind mine on Downing Street on three different mornings, the driver a tall goon in a ball cap. When a student reporter left a voice mail wanting to interview me about my "summer travels, adventures, whatever," I deleted it, my heart hammering my ribs, sure that Dominex's talons now clawed into the refuge of my school life.

My delusional duplex neighbor Myna cornered me one evening; she feared for my safety because a Volvo had pulled up and parked across from my house in the middle of the night. "He had one of those pen lights, Ray. I saw him flashing it into your Subaru at three in the morning. I called the cops, but you know they won't answer my calls. The illegals have black-balled my good name."

Myna said she'd stayed up until sunrise on my behalf, keeping watch until the Volvo goon saw me drive off in my Subaru. She claimed he let a few moments pass, then followed me.

Even though I'd already observed the Volvo in traffic, I certainly hadn't noticed it right across the street on any given morning. As I staggered around in the September dawn, rehearsing my plan for my first-hour class and fixated on the coffee steaming in my mobile cup, it's possible that I'd just been oblivious.

Worse than Myna's "confirmation" of the Volvo's surveillance was the echo of my narrative I heard in hers. If I dared to reveal my own story, from its beginnings in Kurt's hot tub to its nullification in those Utah hot springs, what would any sane person think?

Though the trail of captives, corpses, and carcasses proved my fears were hardly a fantasy, bearing those secrets and horrors alone inside myself warped my mental equilibrium. I came to believe that the clients whose estates I'd catalogued all summer had been most fortunate not in their prosperity or possessions, but for their well-timed passage into death. At least death had freed them from the coming genetic nightmares. Friendly old demons like nuclear holocaust and car-bomb terrorism would seem like mercies to populations trapped in lifelong torment: defective organs, tumors, nervous convulsions, blindness. Survivors would face the promise that future generations would suffer ever more, without remedy, in exponential eruptions of individual tortures.

One warm evening, Felicia and I jogged to Cherry Creek. New sod covered Nick's mud-gouged tire tracks. Especially in the failing light, the patches of bluegrass blended seamlessly into the original lawn. Down on the bikeway, two girls on skates batted a tennis ball with field-hockey sticks, laughing as they wove down the path. In their wake I was alone, for a moment, with the faint gush of the artificial rapids below.

Cherry Creek bled the sunset's tint, trickling between the lighted logos of News9, Channel 7, and Fox News just downstream. Downtown's high-rises glimmered in the crimson light, gorgeous against hazed-out ridgelines. Who would guess that our fair city, so infatuated with its own vitality, was actually on life support, its drip feeding no accurate information, no useful diagnosis? Denver lay isolated, deaf and blind to the global atrocities being hatched in its Rocky Mountain outback.

After work one day in late September, I found myself holding hands with Natalia Sanchez in the basement of the Denver Police headquarters. The cramped room seemed makeshift, a former storage room appointed with metal folding chairs and a box of tissues on a nicked wooden table. Natalia and I sat facing a steel door with a keypad entry and big, black block letters:

DIVISION OF INVESTIGATIONS
EVIDENCE DEPOSITORY

We'd been left alone since the detective who escorted us, a big blonde holding a thickly piled clipboard, confessed her own confusion about our approval for recovering Nick's possessions, the clothes and jewelry taken from what she called the "accident scene." Flipping through the mass of papers, she'd told us the release documentation was "irregular" given that it seemed to "pertain to an active contested investigation." She'd apologized for the delay, assured us it would only be a minute while she double-checked, and gained entry to the evidence room.

Natalia glanced at her watch. "That woman's been gone for ten minutes now." She squeezed my hand even tighter. "What could possibly take so long, after we've already survived all those clearances and signatures and IDs?"

"Maybe scam artists collect victims' personal items from police evidence rooms." I pointed to the surveillance video cam, its red light beaming above the steel door. "Maybe they're studying us right now for signs of imposture. Maybe the big blonde's hiding behind that door right now, waiting for me to slip and call you 'Natasha.'"

"Ray!" Natalia let go of my hand and slapped my upper arm. "I'm nervous enough. Don't make it worse."

"Sorry . . ." I really was. I meant to lighten the tension, but lately my humor only dive-bombed, spiraling darker. Natalia, who'd been so fragile after the body blow of Nick's death, had emerged from her brief hospitalization full of edgy energy. Thinner, she looked even more like her brother. But now, so engaged, so alert to her surroundings, she reminded me even more of her mother, a young Nadia with Russian-blue eyes.

After Nick's burial, Natalia had refused further medication and threw herself into resolving her mother's and her brother's estates. Both involved unexpected tasks and complications (such as contacting her estranged father's keepers in a California institution for indigent psychotics) and arranging her own executorship in the company of lawyers, accountants, and the board of Nadia's BREATHE FREE! organization. Natalia's ventures into Nick's estate involved wary phone contacts with Patrick over the usual extra-legal chaos that arose whenever a gay partnership dissolved in death.

It made my brain throb, wondering if Natalia had even penetrated the first layer of those complications. How many more basement rooms would beckon, how many keypad security doors would release after Natalia discovered that—just for one example— Patrick himself was complicit in her brother's murder?

As Natalia and I reconnected over the weeks since I'd returned, I'd kept such questions to myself, careful to let her follow her own hunches. Familiar with the menace that had already savaged her family, I understood why Nick had only hinted at what he knew and warned me from involvement. I hadn't even asked Natalia if Nick had mentioned any of his increasing suspicions about the real nature of Nadia's position with Dominex's "environmental" extension, his cleanup-as-false-front theory. In the past few weeks, I'd sat through long conversations at Natalia's kitchen table while she and her husband wrestled with their own doubts and suppositions; I'd held close my story like cards I could never play, hoping that they would reach their own, similar conclusions. That might assure me that I wasn't just as crazy as Myna.

All the years Nick and I were a couple, Natalia and I had played up our roles as mutual victims of Nick's big-brother condescension.

Closer in age to each other than to Nick, we bonded by ganging up on him every chance we got, mocking his power trips and engineering his comeuppance. How strange it was now, redefining that childish bond as we wandered this grave, adult wilderness of paper and steel, the legal and material remnants of a life cut dead at thirty-eight.

The door clicked, bionic, opening to reveal a man with dark skin and thick black hair. Abrupt, hovering above us in street clothes and a clip-on ID badge, his appearance seemed more like a metamorphosis, as if the Evidence Depository's soul-stealing, shape-shifting magic had transformed the big blonde. In fact, atop the large plastic bin he grasped with both hands, he bore the blonde's clipboard, which he double-checked at first sight of Natalia and me.

He nodded in my direction, confident. "You're Nicholas Sanchez."

"No." I pointed to the plastic bin. "I think what's left of Mr. Sanchez is in there."

Natalia gasped, seizing my wrist. "This is Ray O'Brien, sir." Polite, she identified herself as the deceased's next of kin.

The black-haired detective hoisted the bin onto the table, retrieving the clipboard but also snatching the long silver scarf. He freed it from his fingers, dropping it back in the bin. "That scarf. That was Mister Sanchez's?"

"No, officer," I told him. "Nick was just wearing it when he died."

"And, Mr. O'Brien, who—" the detective asked, flipping through the clipped papers, "who exactly are you in relation to the case?"

Following my considered pause, Natalia answered, "Ray's a close friend of the family. Very close to my brother."

"*Sabemos el tipo de amigo, si, hermana?*"

"I'm sorry, I don't speak Spanish. And *no soy su hermana, senor.* Please, we already went through all the identity checks with the other detective."

"Well, miss, I'm afraid an urgent matter has detained her. I'm afraid you will have to accept me in her place, is that all right? Now, Mr. O'Brien," he said, again scanning the documents, "could you please identify yourself in relation to Mr. Sanchez."

"Nick and I were a certain type of amigos for five years."

"I see." He scrutinized me. "I see."

He turned to Natalia, as if I'd just lost my credibility, manhood, and any stake in the "case." "I understand that this case is closed, miss, and you're apparently cleared to take possession of the deceased's personal items."

"Yes, sir. Just so you're aware, I didn't initiate this. Your office called me to collect my brother's belongings. I was actually surprised that you were ready to release them so soon."

"Miss, I'm sorry you feel critical of our investigation."

"I'm not critical of anything. There was just an open question, for a while, about whether my brother's accident was the result of tampered brakes, or at least a faulty repair job. But I never received word that any of that had been confirmed or denied."

"I'm afraid that's outside of my purview. This case, I can assure you, is officially closed. My only involvement has been to deliver these personal items to the approved recipients. And while I do see that your certification is in order, it's highly irregular to release them in the presence of an unrelated third party."

After he passed Natalia a release form to sign, the dark-haired detective instructed Natalia to please leave the emptied bin behind on the table. Clicking the keypad code rapidly, he disappeared behind the steel door.

"I don't get it, Ray," Natalia said as we positioned ourselves over the bin on the table. "There seems to be so much outside pressure to avoid a single second thought about how Nicky really died."

"It sure seems that way," I said. "But what do I know? I'm just an unrelated third party."

Instead of smiling, like I'd hoped, she pulled me close and sighed against my chest. "Oh, Ray . . ."

I squeezed her, kissed her forehead, and led her closer to the table. "Let's get this over with." I eased the bin her way.

She pushed it back. "Would you start, please? I'm kind of anxious."

Under the silver scarf, there wasn't that much. The black silk button-down Nick had worn to the party, wrapped in plastic along with his slacks, belt, socks, and his scuffed black Italian loafers. A smaller bag contained even smaller ziplock baggies, holding the gold stud that had been in Nick's left earlobe. Plus, the big plastic GI Joe watch he'd always worn to events he felt were "too foofie." Another bag stored a gold ring embedded with small sapphires, his birthstone, that I hadn't seen before.

Natalia slid right next to me, holding onto my upper arm. "Patrick gave him that. His last birthday."

Nick's wallet, next, presented its own unique folds of apprehension. It was, after all, made of skin. An expensive, silken leather three-flap type, slender, broken-seamed and well-worn, it had spent years pressed next to Nick's own living flesh. Pulling it from the baggie, hardly expecting its supple, warm texture, I passed it to Natalia.

"OK." She held it open, pulling it over her palm with a gentle glide that was enough to shake free two clear plastic inner folders. Landing on the table, one held credit cards. The other was jammed with photographs. Only two pictures showed through the plastic window, though, exactly as they had when Nick and I were still boyfriends: one of Nadia beside Natalia and her two kids, and one of me, in faculty-picture drag, a tie and dress shirt. A grinning sap.

"Let's get out of here, Natalia," I said, gathering the items into the bag they provided. Whatever a person wore at the moment of death fit snugly into a discount store shopping bag.

Passing guarded checkpoints, we emerged from the basement maze into the public spaces on the ground floor. Among the fingerprinted suspects and handcuffed teenagers being shipped to court dates at the City and County Building, Natalia and I must've looked like lost shoppers, eternal consumers in some absurdist police purgatory.

Out in the Cherokee Street plaza, I took in huge gulps of air. "I hadn't realized how stale and suffocating it was in there. Even this smog tastes great."

"Ray, you knew, didn't you?"

"Mine just happened to be facing out, Natalia, just one picture in a stack. He was too lazy to update his pictures. Including your kids'. He carried wallet-sized snaps of you, too, from Globeville Elementary. And from when you were prom queen. Nick was so sentimental about everybody."

"I was never prom queen. And Nick never stopped loving you."

"Why didn't he carry a picture of Patrick?"

"He never stopped loving you, Ray."

"You know, I was so selfish. So wrapped up in my own grief over Nadia that I didn't extend any comfort to Nick, not during her hospitalization, not after her death. I still resented him. Maybe I even wanted to punish him. That's the kind of person I am."

"You were scared and heartbroken. We all were. Just wandering around in the dark, absorbed by our own wounds. Nobody can judge how we grieve."

As I tried to bring the stark, ugly police plaza back into focus, striving for oxygen, I felt hungry for judgment, to serve some just sentence for my smallness, my failures of compassion. Natalia led the way toward her car, where I set the sack on her passenger seat. She asked me if there were anything of Nick's I especially wanted to have.

"For now, I'll just take this scarf," I said, on the whiff of a notion, "and see if I can't give it back to Charlotte Vjiovinovic someday."

"Oh, have you been in touch with Lottie, Ray? I haven't had any luck all month. She doesn't return my calls, and just answers my e-mails with these evasive responses. Like 'I'll write more if I ever get a chance.'"

That evening while Felicia and I jogged the slope above Lake Grasmere in Washington Park, a breeze fluttered the neighborhood's thinning canopy to reveal the southwestern foothills' winking lights. I imagined a solid web of circuits, tantalizing under a wired sky, stretching clear to Lottie's window in the palace.

Her capture under Kurt's force could not be the tale's final act, I was sure. I dreamed up a Lottie-like scheme, that I'd wave the silver scarf and tell the checkpoint guard I needed to return it to Mrs. Weiss personally, considering its extreme and tragic sentimental value. If that didn't work, I'd steal into Kurt's compound posing as a caterer or a Jehovah's Witness and spirit Lottie away to my idling Subaru. We'd dodge Kurt's thugs down the switchbacks. But the fading echo of Lottie's adamant, whispered "wait," stalled any plan in its tracks.

A few days into October, a heavy frost attacked. The park's flowerbeds were glazed, colors brilliant in stasis but fingered for certain death. When I drove to school the following morning, park crews were hauling the floral carnage away, fresh earth heaped in the gardens like burial mounds for the summer.

The sight spurred me to ignore Lottie's admonition to wait. As my opening act, from work I called E. Chou, who insisted he'd never heard of Charlotte Vjiovinovic or Lottie Weiss or anyone of her description. Confidentially, though, he mentioned he did have a room for rent—unexpectedly available—if I were interested.

I kept a close watch on local news, since my deepest, closest, and most justified fears were about Lottie's survival. What would it be, a throwaway item in the obituaries, a renowned geneticist's wife fallen victim to ptomaine poisoning? Choking on a chicken bone? Suicide after weeks of treatment for severe depression? Or would they, in their elegant arrogance, dare to try another one-vehicle death, Lottie's dilapidated jeep slipping off a switchback?

But my close scrutiny of the *Denver Post* revealed an item I might've otherwise ignored. I hadn't realized the Mamie Doud Eisenhower National Laboratory was locked in a genetic race with Denver's Eleanor Roosevelt Institute, which had been mapping chromosomes, the entire human genome, in a long quest to cure cancer. Both laboratories would be honored together at a University of Colorado gala in a few nights. October happened to be International Genetic Research Month.

The local media's science coverage awakened from back-page torpor to offer cute comments and cartoons about the labs' rivalry, "The Age of Terror versus the New Deal," between "Denver's first ladies of research": Mamie's flashy Pentagon contracts versus Eleanor's dowdy decades of tracking chromosomes, funded by private benefactors and charities, in a quest for health. Naturally, the Mamie Doud was up for the most prestigious award. Dr. Kurt Weiss would accept it in a speech he planned to dedicate to his "fallen comrade and fellow dreamer," the late Dr. Lawrence Lucas.

The day that article appeared, in my backstage office at Coyote Creek High School I tried to coach a student while devouring my sack lunch. She wanted to do a cutting from Jane Wagner's *The Search for Intelligent Life in the Universe*, but was struggling with how to interpret the narrator. "Is she really hearing voices from these wise alien sources, or is she just nuts?"

"Does it matter?" I asked. "She believes she's alone with this special knowledge, right? She's certain she's this conduit, this agent for earthly transformation . . ."

"In other words, Mr. O'Brien, she's nuts. Right?"

I chomped into my apple, buying time to form my response, when a student messenger delivered a sealed, handwritten note. On stationery from a familiar realty specializing in government-repossessed properties, it was addressed to "Ed O'Leary c/o Mr. Ray O'Brien, Theatre Instructor, Denver Southwest Unified Schools" and read:

> Mr. O'Leary: In regard to your interest in properties which might make attractive rentals, I have located an appropriate listing in Globeville. It is extremely close to an educational facility and walking distance from a defunct factory. For your inspection, I will hold it open Friday during the lunch hour.
> Truly yours,
>
> Nicolette

Lottie's real estate paraphernalia was set up out front. A carelessly painted GOV'T. REPO—OPEN HOUSE—DEEP DISCOUNT sign leaned against her parked jeep's front bumper. Under a thirsty elm, her cardboard table basked in a spot of shade on what remained of the lawn. A paperback, *Daniel Deronda*, lay overturned on the table beside an open can of fruit juice. A folding chair was pushed back. The front door of the little bungalow stood wide open.

Even from the front steps the racket from the school yard behind the house bounced around, raucous and high-pitched. Though the Globeville block was agreeable enough, identical brick houses under diehard maples and dwindling elms, the street dead-ended at the barbed-wire gate to a shut-down smelter. It was famous to me; Nadia and BREATHE FREE! had fought the factory owners for years to remove acres of cadmium contaminants.

As I passed through the freshly painted front room, I wondered what had caused the owners to fall into foreclosure. This place was actually habitable, a brave and successful renovation. On top of breathing cadmium dust, maybe enduring the school yard din had driven the family crazy?

On the way into the backyard, past gleaming kitchen tiles and appliances, I spotted a dollhouse shoved into a corner of the back porch, its fresh plywood still unpainted.

I stood behind the screen door, bracing myself after I caught first sight of her. Lottie's short-cropped hair was golden again. She looked thinner as well as severe in her business costume, gray jacket, white blouse, long gray skirt, black flats. On the patio, she bent on her haunches to get face-to-face with a tiny boy in a bunny suit. Lottie used a handkerchief to dab the scrape on the boy's wrist, then to wipe away his tears. She brushed back his hair with her fingers, straightened the bunny ears, chucked his chin, and rising, extended her hand to lead him across the alley and back to the school yard. Releasing the high catch on a metal gate, Lottie let the boy lead her back to a circle of pint-sized pirates, Gypsies, and Aztec warriors playing kickball.

I stepped onto the patio, waiting as Lottie chatted with the teacher on lunch duty. Despite the laughing, screaming, yelling, squeal-pitched wall of noise across the alley, the evacuated family had built no barrier. Instead, they'd planted a wavering hedge of cosmos flowers, now freeze blackened, their elongated stalks leaning earthward.

Spotting me, Lottie waved and hurried back through a thicket of Robin Hoods, princesses, and executioners hanging out between the jungle gym and the gate.

She passed through the cosmos hedge and stood still for a moment. She hitched her handbag higher on her shoulder. Her hair shimmered, gorgeous in the noon sun. She stared at me.

I stared back. "Did you make friends with a little rabbit?"

She smiled. "It's an old Globeville Elementary tradition."

"Having Halloween three weeks early?"

"No, it's the Fall Pageant, a whole day of skits and music and costume antics. I myself was an angel more than once."

Lottie pointed vaguely across the alley and went on. "Ray, it turns out that little boy, Carlos, used to live here. He went under that gap in the school fence and hurt his wrist. He actually thought I'd come to take away his sister's dollhouse. He wanted to know if I was another 'mortgage lady.'" Lottie clutched the clothesline pole. "That teacher was telling me Carlos's sister died last year. Rare lung disorder."

"Nothing to do with living next to a smelter, right?"

"They ran out of money, Ray, trying to pay the girl's medication out of pocket. They lost the house."

It was only a few quick paces and Lottie was in my arms. We held on for the longest time, weaving, rocking a little. She felt so insubstantial in my embrace. It was not so much the weight she'd lost as the distracted, almost spectral presence she exuded. Finally she kissed my cheek, patted my windbreaker, and pulled away.

"You're thin," I said. "You could use some brownies."

"I'm eating better lately. I'll be robust again, soon. You'll see. I swear, I plan to be teaching again, myself. Soon."

We sat on a wooden bench built to frame a planter box. Lottie stared straight into the screen door, eyeing the big, unfinished doll-house. "Hard to absorb, isn't it?" she asked. "We have billions for secret weapons of mass destruction, engendered into the neural pathways of wild goats, but we won't help a little girl fighting just to breathe."

"Dominex family values," I said. "Healing a World of Hurt."

She produced a pharmacy vial from her purse. "And here I've got plenty of medication I don't even want. Some tranquilizer I've never heard of. I flush two of them down the drain every day, but I've got Kurt convinced that, on my meds, I'm absolutely tranquil."

"What's it like for you, Lottie, now?"

Lottie told me about the therapist Kurt had arranged for her. "Good company man, a Dominex lifer. He's got this wonderful theory, how my 'delusions' were triggered by the trauma of my miscarriages. See, I was only trying to capture Brandy as a child substitute. Our whole journey was nothing more than a neurotic fantasy, did you know? I demonized poor Kurt, who in truth is trying valiantly to heal the world for family values. But I reversed Kurt's identity into the evil genius villain because, despite his potency in the laboratory, he couldn't knock me up."

"Brilliant. So you're the model patient."

"No talk therapy has ever worked faster. That's because I let the blowhard do all the talking. I'm Repentant Wife of the Month on Dominex's October calendar. So tranquil that Kurt's encouraged me to take on a few listings again."

"He trusts you that much already?"

"Not really. He was having me 'escorted' everywhere. As far as I can tell, this is my first outing without someone trailing me at a few blocks' distance."

"A silver Volvo?"

"No, a plain old white Toyota. This is my first open house since you walked up to my table at the end of July. Kurt knows it's good for me to be seen, intact and well, doing my little inconse-quential job. Helps head off nasty rumors. He's even been brave enough to trot me out for a corporate dinner party. The story is, we're reconciling. Most everyone at the Mamie Doud lab thinks it's lovely."

"And what do you think?"

"This charade is my only successful project. Ever, Ray. Mean-while, Kurt really seems to believe what he told us in New Carls-bad, at the hot springs. Poor Kurt Weiss is the true victim of Dominex's corporate ruthlessness. See, it was Dominex that sold its soul to military fantasias, not Kurt, and it's probably true that with his deep involvement in the research, he'll never get out alive. So he's stuck. We actually talk about it openly now, as if that moment in the hot springs was some kind of turning point. He continues to presume—I think—that I'm sympathetic, that de-spite my psychotic episode, I'm still his only true soulmate." Lot-tie paused. She must have read the skepticism spelled across my face. "OK, Ray. Maybe Kurt and I are locked in mutual decep-tion. But look, you're still alive. And so, by God, am I. But I don't see any way out of this sick symbiosis now. And I haven't even mentioned the position I've put you in."

"I'll take responsibility for that, thanks. I was a willing accomplice."

She touched my shoulder. "You've been a wonderful friend and partner. I hated abandoning you there, in the hot springs. But I had to think on my feet, Ray, and knew I had to make that move into Kurt's arms when he started saying he was a 'victim.' Which always means he's sidestepping his own culpability. That he's trapped himself inside convenient abstractions. Like 'Dominex.' Like 'terror.' I knew then that we were finished."

"Finished!"

"Finished with that effort, in New Carlsbad. We'd crossed heaven and hell and half of Utah, after all, and look where it got us."

"Nowhere. Minus nowhere. But I still don't feel finished."

"Me neither. I'm doing my best, Ray."

"Meaning you continue your phony therapy and sell a few foreclosed houses?"

Lottie sighed. "For starters, I wanted to see you, to tell you in person how sorry I am."

"Sorry for what?" I stood and paced the brick patio. "Our friends didn't quit. Nadia and Nick and Larry never gave up, not willingly. Neither did you, Lottie. You were the one-woman League. Look at you now. I'm not sure I can accept an apology from someone so tranquilized."

"Nadia, Nicky, and Larry were my inspirations, too."

"You were my inspiration, Lottie. In fact, I thought you'd summoned me here for our next mission."

"Ray, Ray! You're still not hearing what I'm trying to tell you. I am planning my next move, but I need to do it right this time. It takes more than will and commitment." She stood, approaching me with her hand outstretched. "I endangered your life because I was so naive."

"I don't think you were so naive. I have a plan, myself," I said, realizing to my everlasting astonishment that I did. I grabbed her hand and pulled it to my chest. "And I'm not going to worry about whether it's naive. But I need to count on you."

"Of course you can."

"I figure that you—we—had the right idea all along, we just abducted the wrong material. Brandy, I mean." I lowered my voice. A bell had rung, signaling the end of lunch break, and the school yard lost its giddy racket. "This time, we liberate the research itself."

"Yes . . . wonderful!" Lottie agreed, but her brow knotted when she looked across the alley. Though the school yard had emptied, Carlos still hung at the chain-link fence, staring toward the house, his rabbit ears drooping again.

We crossed the alley and slipped inside the gate, beside Carlos. "Shouldn't you be hopping back to class?" Lottie asked, crouching down, eye-to-eye.

He nodded, enthralled with the pretty lady. So we each took a hand and led Carlos into a side door to deliver him to his relieved young teacher.

In the hallway, with its polished-wood perfume and waxy, well-worn checkered linoleum, we strolled along display cases. Under the banner FALL PAGEANT: FIFTY YEARS OF MAKE-BELIEVE group photographs lined the walls, interspersed with individual pictures of contest winners and candid snaps of student skits. Lottie scanned them, smiling and sighing. "Here, Ray, look," she called to me. "It's Nicky and me. He's pinning my angel wings back on. What the picture doesn't show, of course, is that Nicky was the one who'd yanked them off."

"Check out his smile!" I said, leaning in beside Lottie. "That beautiful, sneaky, snarky sideways smile."

"I started kindergarten in that same classroom. Carlos's." She lowered her voice, taking my hand. "And Nicky started one year later, right there, Room 4. We walked to school like this, hand in hand, every day until the upper grades, when we both discovered . . . boys."

Lottie stopped in the middle of the hall, smiling, facing me, taking both my hands in hers. "Anyway, Ray, I love your plan. So I go on building Kurt's confidence in me. I wait until I actually have a chance at access. I cultivate somebody on the inside who grows to trust me."

"Now you're talking," I said, barely above a whisper in the

hallway's hush. "Lure some Mamie Doud geek who actually has a thing for beautiful women. There's got to be a true straight guy out there, in this story, somewhere."

"And if straight men prove too elusive, if infiltration proves too difficult, there's always sabotage."

"That's the spirit," I said. "Now, I brought you something." I pulled the scarf from my windbreaker pocket. Unfurling it, smoothing the wrinkles, I draped it behind her neck, each long end falling back from her shoulders like silver wings.

That evening, as a thunderstorm shook branches and streamed surges through the drainpipes, I thrashed in and out of uneasy, unwilling, unplanned sleep. It was already dark. Last I recalled, I had daylight enough through the bedroom windows to read student scripts.

The papers scattered across the bed's empty half. I must've tossed aside my felt-tip marking pen, uncapped, now leaking a green blot into the sheet. Felicia snoozed, sprawled in the V made by knees as I'd slept on my side, cuddled into my pillow. Margarita rested on my hip, her claws occasionally entangled in my boxers when they weren't scratching the bare skin below the hem.

The jazz station, playing "Blue in Green" on my desktop boom box, broke in to recite a weather warning: "unusually severe storms across the Front Range and High Plains."

My elation with Lottie in Globeville had withered, and I woke to my default mood, anxiety. Mixed with self-doubt, now. Even embarrassment. What had that school-hall bravado been but two grown-ups hatching a Hardy Boys–Nancy Drew scheme? Or maybe that was an insult to adolescent sleuths. In the face of our adversary's implacable, steely guise, its planet-wide resources, boundless funding, and drive for self-preservation, the very idea of "infiltration" or "sabotage" only seemed to invite another blind stumble like our abduction of Brandy. Only this time, to assuage my wounded manhood, I'd been the one goading Lottie into folly.

No wonder we'd committed to undermine these weapons of infinite destruction during Make-Believe Day. It figured. My very career involved inspiring schoolkids' fictions, cultivating fantasy, urging improvisations. I taught students to undertake fake scenarios with conviction. My only expertise was in staging facsimiles of human conflict that never resolved grievous realities.

The thunder rumbled as lightning strikes shrieked closer, rattling the roof's joists. Felicia jumped to the floor. She prowled in a tight circle and hounded the lightning with explosive howls. Margarita, roused by the commotion, crept up my side and clawed across my head before she pounced onto the floor to join Felicia.

Renewed wind set my neighbors' chimes into hysterical chattering, each porch agape in a parody of fear, block-long mouthfuls of trembling teeth. Dry branches clattered against each other or whipped the rain in solitude.

Just like that night in May when I saw Nadia for the last time.

I knew despite the drama queen weather racket that I was being dragged back into sleep. I'm opening my eyes, but I'm also behind the wheel of my Subaru shushing forward, nearly afloat through swamped intersections near the hospital. Electric jabs fork into the parking lot and sizzle in rooftop rods. Drenched from the short sprint across the lot, I drip into the darkened room. The nurse I've come to know melts against the doorframe, her face drawn, eyes wet. I liked it better when she was yelling at us, she whispers, I liked it better when she was screaming. Nadia zonked against pillows, hooked to pulsing monitors. Natalia whispers that Nick's just left and, guilt ridden, I feel relief, having planned the late visit to avoid him. Nicky asked when you were coming, Natalia tells me, he waited as long as he could.

Natalia pulls me close, her lips brushing my ear. They say it's like nothing ever seen, this tumor, how it's seized her brain stem to strike the neural pathways. All we can do is pray, Ray, that Mom somehow rallies enough strength to undergo surgery, but it's like her system is in shutdown. Tonight, her circulation's so poor she can't accept a feeding tube.

No one expected this; she's sinking so fast, so I sink into the chair beside Nadia, strong, wiry woman shrunken to bones, her hand a tiny claw in my enclosing fingers. I drop my head on the sheet beside her pillow, feeling a slight tug on my forefinger. I press closer to what she mutters.

Stop them, Ray. Stop them.

In her delirium, the tumor's become plural, so I promise I'll stop them, and her bed's my bed again.

Damn! Something slapped down, hard, right outside. Felicia barked in short bursts as she gyrated. With a yelp, she shot from my room.

I opened the miniblinds wider, enough to glimpse a car slogging down the dark street, wipers thwacking, headlights off. A Volvo. Silver?

Felicia quieted now, sitting up on the rug under the front door, grinning and panting. The door itself was blown open—I'd lay dozing all that time, surfing different nightmares, with nothing between me and Them but an unlocked screen door. I peered through it now, but could not trace the Volvo's progress. It was gone.

Why was I such a wimpy, typical Denver antigun, kumbaya Democrat? Why couldn't I be tough and Republican, with an automatic rifle in every room? What was I going to do, fight off Kurt's henchmen with a toilet plunger? And even my trusty guard dog was some kind of delusional liberal, pawing the entry rug happily and catching the wet breeze through the screen.

Felicia's ecstasy surged as I tried to open the screen door. I had to force her back inside as I eased onto the porch. Sure enough, a huge dead limb had slammed to the ground, just inches from shattering my Subaru's windshield. Gnarled, sharp branches poked in all directions and completely blocked the sidewalk. Behind me, Felicia resumed those brief, happy yelps, as if cheering me on as I hustled into the downpour to haul the woody mammoth onto the lawn. She probably thought I planned to play monster stick toss.

As I turned back to the front steps, a tall figure materialized down the rain-blurry block. Ball cap under a dark, hooded rain slicker. Approaching me with deliberate steps.

I tried to snap off a sharp, twisted branch from the mass of limbs, so I could then hustle inside with my maple spear and actually keep a locked door between me and my assassin.

But I was still fighting to snap free the branch when the figure cried out, "So why are you doing yard work in the rain?" He stepped closer. "In your underwear?"

Felicia rose up on her front paws against the screen door, her hind legs fairly dancing, her tail a metronome.

So I was stuck in another shallow-sleep fiction, aware I was dreaming but unable to shake the narrative. Like visiting Nadia in the hospital. Like that dream of Nick coming back to me, back to my bed, when he was actually already dead. Why revisit all three of my dear departed tonight? Just the unconscious mind's way of preparing me for my own departure?

I meant to shock the ghoul in the rain slicker and shake myself from the dream's grasp: "I'm not falling for this! I warned my students to avoid this dream-into-reality crap in their scenes."

"You're all wet, Ray."

My hair really was saturated, rain seeping down my forelocks into my eyes. My T-shirt clung drenched and cold to my skin. I seized my branch spear, meaning to improvise some menacing strike, but the ghoul approached me calmly, his strong hand clutching my raised wrist.

In a flash of lightning, I swore I could read the ball cap's lettering. NEW CARLSBAD: AMERICA'S PROVING GROUND. I dropped my weapon and surrendered to a more alluring subchapter of the nightmare. I met Larry's lips with mine.

The power went out while Larry toweled my hair, so we lit a candle. Though we'd already been naked together in that Confusion Range pool, celibate now, revirginal, I was glad for the cover of my sopping shorts. Larry sprawled beside me on the bed in his jeans and chambray button-down, Felicia snuggled against his side on the opposite edge. Margarita prowled along the pillows. She imitated Larry's toweling by nuzzling his crew cut with the side of her head.

Grateful for the dim, flickering light, I felt skinny and exposed, like a shorn sheep left too long in the rain. He slid the towel down my back, then without warning, slipped off my rain-soaked boxers. He folded the towel, laughing, to blot my butt, then dried me clear down to my toes.

I turned over, pulled the blanket up to my chest, then sat up against the pillow. "You're pretty good with a towel. For a ghost."

"I still don't understand why everyone jumped to the conclusion I had to die in the fuel tank explosion. Even the damn coroner!" He moved closer, shoulder-to-shoulder, and clasped my hand. "I mean, I'm glad they did, but I've jumped out of hundreds of planes just to earn my place in line at the Navy's test-pilot slop trough. I haven't forgotten how to open a parachute."

In the dim, flickering glow, he told me the whole story. Halfway to Salt Lake, he'd realized there was a malfunction in his fuel line. Past dinky Eureka, the Cessna started trailing smoke, a faint mist gradually darkening to ugly billows. Sure the line was about to ignite, he radioed his distress and made plans to evacuate the plane. He set a course slightly west from his original route, aiming away from population centers around Provo and hoping to aim the plane into salt flats or some gully in the Oquirrh Mountains before he jumped. "Just my luck, though," Larry said, "I made it to the Oquirrhs, but my poor Cessna dove like a moth to flame" toward the Desert Chemical Depot. It wouldn't do for an environmental peace activist to unleash a toxic conflagration of chemical weapons, so Larry forced the plane westward just before he bailed out. The Cessna ended up torching only the facility's propane storage tanks, leaving the chemical stores untouched.

He himself chuted a safe descent onto a ridgetop above Ophir, a mountain ghost town, where he watched the rural emergency workers' tortured arrival over back roads. Perched above, he witnessed the Salt Lake media's glitzy splashdown in LiveNews, FirstNews, and YourNews choppers. Watching the media convene with such expensive velocity, Larry figured he was more useful as a dead proselytizing science writer than alive.

In a small fanny pack, he'd stashed a water bottle, the tapes, and his camera.

After the videocams and choppers thwacked away, he hiked to the state highway and hitched a ride to Tooele with a laborer—"who literally worked in a salt mine"—where he was able to phone contacts in Salt Lake City.

He laid low in the city for days, monitoring the coverage of his death. Verona, the Guided Missile waitress, supplied Larry with a videotape of his New Carlsbad memorial after she learned through "contacts" that he was alive.

"That was a total Tom Sawyer moment," Larry said, smiling. "How marvelous to hear from Kurt and Patrick what a hero I was,

how much I'd helped them understand the limits of genetic manipulation, how inspiring my work had been to the entire staff of
the Mamie Doud and the Dominex executives. I hope they find it
just as inspiring when we establish a link to Dominex and whoever
screwed with my Cessna's last safety inspection."

After that, Larry hopscotched between more "contacts" in Vernal, Utah, and Steamboat Springs, Colorado, until he'd arrived in
Denver weeks ago, where he devoted his time to keeping a watch-
ful eye on Lottie and me.

"You couldn't have e-mailed, called, or left a note in my mail
slot? You had to slink around in that Volvo, making me think I was
gonna die any second? Grieving for you, alone, while I got
smashed like a bug on Kurt's windshield?"

"Contact was too risky. I'm not leaving any electronic or paper
trail. My death turned out to be great for publicizing our cause. So
I have to remain a ghost, managing media inquiries through safe
contacts. And we've all made sure you and Lottie were safe from
danger."

"Contacts? We? All?"

"We're not alone in this, Ray. Our League may not have the
numbers or resources of Dominex, but we're slowly coming together. You've met a few of our contacts. Verona's one of us. So's
the principal you met at the airfield. The League's got legal activists and subversive sympathizers planted all over the country."

"Then this can't be the same as Lottie's League."

"Well, Lottie's chapter here in Denver was a little sketchy."

"It was just her and Nick!"

"They never had the support they needed. Nick was just get-
ting things started before his death. But Brandy's abduction was
Lottie's own wild idea. Anyway, we're planning to expand our
Denver presence."

"What about a white Toyota watching over Lottie?"

"Yeah, did you enjoy the fall pageant at Globeville Elementary? I hear you went as a good-lookin' young teacher."

"Yeah." I turned on my side, my head on his chest. "I got an emergency makeover."

Larry let go of my hand. "I've been looking forward to an emergency makeout." He scooted Felicia off the bed, then reached under the covers to caress my side. His hand reached my hind quarters.

I wasn't sure I would be celibate much longer. Enjoying his touch, I said, "I've been looking forward to your expanding your presence here."

Larry shoved the covers off me. I fumbled with his buttons, loosening his shirt open, exploring his blond fur as we dove back into that desert pool to recover our embrace.

I woke beside Larry, who'd kicked the sheet off his bare body in his sleep. The candle had burned out, so, propped on my arm, I studied him in the deep blackout dark. My hand traced his smooth back, my imagination supplying the details I couldn't quite detect: the white butt, the strong, golden legs.

I fingered his styleless butch cut, so stubby it felt fresh from a basic training shearing. The Navy tags that had dangled from his neck on a steel chain during our lovemaking tangled backward now, along his upper spine. How funny, I thought. A forty-year-old peacemaker who still treasured these military relics. But I sure welcomed them as fantasy props. What could be better than this—a pilot fallen naked from the sky into my arms?

I kissed the back of Larry's neck, then calmed Margarita, who circled back into her curled-up purring between the pillows. I slipped my feet from under Felicia, who sprawled across the base of the bed, and slid out.

From my front window I could see that, though the storm had calmed to driving rain, the power was still out. Candles wobbled in windows up and down my narrow street, provisional but celebratory, as if a long war had ended in a sudden, all-is-forgiven armistice. I stood there, breathing with deliberation, aware how long fear had plundered my consciousness, liberated at last.

Of course, the same threat still lurked out there, no prettier despite random candles lit against a power failure. But whether it was renewed faith in mine and Lottie's subversive scheme or the promise of Larry's presence, I felt like we had a chance. In the kitchen, the wall clock kept celebrating, too, the frozen, approximate time of Larry's resurrection in my life. I fumbled in a cabinet for the bottle and, touching the ribbon that had been wrapped around its neck for ten months, carried it and two snifters back to the bedroom.

I didn't need light to know what was written on the little holiday card tied to the ribbon:

> My Ray,
> This is for some special moment in the New Year ahead.
> Just, whenever it is and whatever you're toasting, remember an
> old dame who loves you.
> Feliz ano nuevo,
>
> Nadia

Larry was awake, dangling Margarita over his chest, so I lit another candle and set the bottle down. I made an offer: "I can make you coffee or tea, but this is serious cognac."

He answered by reaching for the snifter.

I sat up on the pillows beside him. When we swirled, then clinked our snifters, I offered silent tribute to Nadia. "So, Larry," I said, "I have to ask you something. Lottie won't disclose any of your secrets, you know. But what went on between you and Kurt before he left the Proving Ground?"

"What are you implying, sir?"

"I know for a fact that whatever you might say about him, Kurt's very seductive."

"For a fact, huh? I can only imagine what facts excited Kurt when he first saw you."

"He just wanted to exert control. Throw me off. It was like the big dog humping the little dog's leg, that's all."

"Well, I wish I'd been that clear headed. Our worst moment, Kurt's and mine, actually came after he'd left the Proving Ground. He'd already joined Dominex at the Mamie Doud, and I was help-ing to shut down the Desert Ecology Project. Of course, I didn't realize he'd been responsible for its closure. Kurt came to the project without Lottie, in the guise of a friendly visit, offering to help pack the equipment and samples and ship off the livestock, but I figured something was up. We hadn't really been close for a long time, and he'd long graduated from heavy lifting or grunt work." But, as Larry explained, the work gave Kurt an excuse to stay at the project rather than down in the swankier digs at the Proving Ground. He proceeded to suggest that they take their friendship to a deeper level, the physicality they'd missed out on as students.

"I was surprised he didn't try the old strip poker or back rub strategies. But I'll be honest, Ray, I had to excuse myself for a cold shower more than once that weekend. I'd been fantasizing about this man for years, and he knew it."

"But?"

"But there was the problem of betraying Lottie, along with the problem of my suspicions. I wasn't just on the verge of sleep-ing with my old friend, who was married to my new friend. Kurt was the colleague with whom I'd learned everything in tandem. As researchers, we were like brothers. We'd shared breakthrough after breakthrough. But I was just starting my work on the animal experiments. Just enough to spur my distrust in Kurt's integrity. Without that, maybe I would have given in."

"It does seem like he slipped off some edge," I said, "once he decided genetics could be twisted into the ultimate weapon." I swirled the cognac, staring into the amber as it wavered in the candleglow. "Even if it meant destroying the people close to him."

"But not with his own bloody hands. He merely allowed people to be destroyed. And always, for the greater good, mind you. Through preemptive weapons development, he's only trying to protect his fellow citizens. Is that arrogant? Or, by his own rationale, heroic? No, Kurt would never bloody his own hands."

"Still, when he 'allowed' for your crash—Kurt shot over the cliff and straight into hell. He must figure he has nothing left to lose."

"Or everything." The power came on, but no electric light, since none had been on in the first place. Instead, Coltrane saxed the darkness in mid-note. The suddenly juiced boom box was playing the "Pursuance" segment of *A Love Supreme*.

Larry shut his eyes, as if following a blue note, then opened them, taking my hand. "But I do think that weekend was the turning point, Ray. Kurt meant to seduce me, then persuade me not to publish my first findings. Since the sexual connection didn't work, he tried sharing power, offering me a new research position with Dominex. When he realized none of that, the easy stuff, was going to stop me, I think he knew he had to resort to less pleasant forms of persuasion."

I squeezed his hand. "So, what now?"

"Now?" He kissed my ear and whispered, "How would you like to be my date, tomorrow evening, at the university ballroom? I'd like to attend the International Genetics Research Awards."

* * *

Kurt Weiss looked as handsome as ever, though when I walked up to him at the pre-Awards reception, his tanned brow grew knotted. "Ray . . .?"

"Yes, Dr. Weiss, Ray O'Brien." I took his hand, though he didn't really offer it. "Lottie's friend, you remember? We've spent quality time together in various hot pools, you and I."

"Yes. Good to see you, Ray," Kurt said, recovering his equilibrium. "I didn't know you were involved with the I.G.A."

"Independent Grocers of America?" I asked. "I love 'em."

"International Genetics Association," Patrick said, approaching behind Kurt. He also had a gorgeous tan, a desert glow, as if still burnished from his long runs across the Wah Wah Valley. Like Kurt, he had the well-toned build that men's formal wear flattered. "So, what brings you here, Ray?"

"You really haven't noticed?" I pushed out the small, baby-pinned oval, cut from a snapshot, on my rented tux's left lapel. "It's not such a great picture, 'cause she's got that too-wide smile that made her eyes all squinty. And see how her cheeks are so plump and robust? Easter brunch at my little duplex. Just this past April? We were planning to climb Mount Massive on her fifty-ninth birthday in July. Which we never did, since she died. Rapid neural system failure. You know, in May. Nadia Sanchez. You remember her, Patrick? Practically your mother-in-law."

"Ray," Kurt said, sipping from a martini glass, "do you have the credentials to be—"

"Yes, I'm the guest of a distinguished honoree. Please, don't worry. No one's going to make a scene and throw me out and embarrass you. Now, on my right lapel, you might have noticed a little oval picture of Nicholas Sanchez? Nadia's son? Dashing son of a bitch, huh? Killer smile."

"You think this is funny, Ray?" Patrick asked. He copied Kurt, sipping his martini studiously before he went on. "Mocking the deceased? People we all loved and honored?"

"Just as I love and honor your arch mock sincerity, gentlemen. As a drama instructor, I have felt obligated to spend this whole day practicing your tone, your delivery, your elevated vocabulary. That intense way you gaze into the eyes of whoever has to ingest your prevarications. How am I doing?"

Kurt gazed steadily into my eyes, unfazed. "We have security here, Ray."

"We have Fox's lovely Kaneesha Klein-Anderson, here on a tip about telegenic awards recipients. Including an attractive surprise. We have stringers from the *High Country News* and the *Nation*, a contact from *Mother Jones*, and even that reporter from the *Rocky Mountain News* who gets to write about science stuff every fourth Friday. Our legal department can't be here tonight, though. They're investigating the shop that rebuilt the brakes on Nick's roadster. Plus, that guy in Utah who passed a routine safety check on a fairly new Cessna. But we're all in touch via the miracle of wireless transmission." I fingered my lapels, propping the portraits again. "Anyhow, I wanted to make sure Nadia and Nick got to attend this gala, even if they could only be here in spirit. Hey! Hi, Lottie!"

There, squeezed into the little red dress, the silver scarf spread under her shoulders, Lottie faced forward as the crowd around her passed into the auditorium. She stared at me, bearing an empty goblet of wine. Finally, she smiled quizzically, then mouthed, "Holy God, Ray."

I excused myself from the huddle formed by Kurt and Patrick's broad shoulders and slinked around to Lottie. As we turned to join the general progress into the auditorium, I clasped her arm, and, pecking her cheek, whispered in her ear, "Don't worry about a thing, Lottie. We've got a plan. A senior member initiated me last night. Yes, ma'am. I've joined the League."

"Imagine the honor of sharing this podium with my colleagues at the Eleanor Roosevelt Institute," Kurt said, though he spoke alone at the podium. The Roosevelt's recipients still sat in a panel above the dais as Kurt prepared to accept the award on behalf of his Dominex research team. "Without the Institute's painstaking mapping of the human genome, our search at the Mamie Doud for peaceful applications of genetics defenses would be impossible."

Kurt paused as if he expected applause for his generosity to the rival team. None came.

The audience's reluctance to respond might have been inspired by the image that rose behind Kurt. Above the podium, a huge black-and-white poster rose, a blown-up photograph of Dr. Larry Lucas caught in mid-laugh, his eyes searching sidelong as if to include the viewer in some vast amusement. Nearly an icon now, that photograph graced bookstore windows, magazine covers, and antiweapons Web pages, and served as a backdrop for TV news coverage of Larry's posthumous message about genetics weapons development.

Undaunted, Kurt launched into a set speech. It was unworthy of his intellect and wit, full of the usual empty appeals to "freedom" and that Orwellian trope where violence is "liberty" and coercion is "justice" and warfare is "peace." He driveled on about our reduced and dangerous lives, now, in the Age of Terror.

I trembled in my just-polished best black loafers to think of the .000000000000012754 percent chance that I might die in an attack by foreign religious fanatics. Even scarier was the .000294 percent chance that frozen donuts from a careless airliner would smash my roof while I watched a *Simpsons* rerun. But Kurt didn't mention that threat. Nor did he include the 100 percent chance that religious fanatics in Colorado Springs would seek to deprive me of my civil rights. Blah, blah, blah, the usually baroque and well-spoken Kurt went on and on in tired old Scary Foreigners mode, shameless as a low-level Dominex contractor pitching a body-armor franchise overseas.

Lottie shifted uncomfortably beside me. Next to her, Patrick stared forward with unusual grimness, refusing even to meet my faux-friendly glances.

I scanned the auditorium. Lots of gray heads and bald pates, often paired with well-coiffed spousely 'dos. Socialites, hangers-on, the mayor, and the inevitable ex-senator claiming a squirt of Cheyenne or Arapaho blood. Real scientists, too, men and women in ill-fitting formal wear, stringy hair, and funky eye-glasses. A fraught mood over all, a cough-scattered, pent-up silence. As if we all struggled to reconcile Kurt's sermon of Eter-nal Terror under the rebuke of Larry's gigantic, laughing pose. At the railing above the last row, Kaneesha Klein-Anderson shoved her jaw into her fists, no doubt wondering what the hell she was going to say about this geeky snooze fest on Fox First-News at 5 freaking A.M.

Kurt wound up with a paean to the memory of Larry Lucas, "in whose memory I accept this award. Without Larry, I say with-out false humility, in the spirit of simple, empirical fact, I would not be standing here tonight. He discovered the foundations of animal and human genetics that not only enriched our work, but launched it." Finished, Kurt raised his award plaque to Larry's photograph and finally inspired applause.

From stage right, as the clapping climaxed, Larry appeared. For a moment, the applause intensified as he joined Kurt at the podium, smiling and enclosing Kurt's shoulders in a manly hug.

Then the applause died as the empirical fact sunk in across the auditorium. Kurt, for once, lost his cool. He grew visibly upset, pallid and anxious to extricate himself from the dead man's grip.

Lottie's hand tightened in mine. She vocalized a passionate and heartfelt "Oh my God!" heard throughout the silenced audience. Then, after clapping her hands in spontaneous delight, she pressed her head into my shoulder, laughed, and kissed my ear. "Welcome," she whispered, "to the League. Of course, you've been one of us all along."

Larry stepped forward to the microphone as Kurt, reeling, surrendered the podium and disappeared behind the Eleanor Roosevelt team. Dr. Lucas smiled kindly and raised his arms briefly, as if allowing all to inspect his being-in-reality. "I want to assure you all that I'm not a ghost, a ghoul, a goblin, or any other dead thing that starts with a 'g.' Many of you are trained empiricists and logicians. So please don't look to the paranormal. Look, instead, to the parachute."

Encouraged by scattered laughter, Larry offered an overview of his survival story. He apologized for not coming forward sooner and offered a rationale for his weeks of hiding and deception. "I was waiting for tonight. For this moment. First let me say, though, while the cameras are rolling, if any harm comes to me or my colleagues Ray O'Brien, Charlotte Vjiovinovic Weiss, or Brandy McConnaughty, your first suspect must be the corporate contractor at the Mamie Doud labs, Dominex. Even if I show up somewhere with a bad shaving mishap, check first with Dr. Kurt Weiss. Because this man, who once truly was my partner in seeking the truth, who once truly was my friend and colleague, clearly wants me silenced. He was happy to eulogize me, on behalf of Dominex, when he believed I was dead. Let me tell you, Dominex definitely wants me to stay dead."

Larry went on to refute much of Kurt's vision of an Age of

Terror and called for an "Age of Re-Enlightenment." As a modest volley in that direction, he offered to organize a press conference the next day, featuring, among other luminaries, his aforementioned colleagues. Larry gestured in our direction, asking Lottie and me to stand, asking the assembly to have a good look at us, asking the audience to look for us tomorrow at the press conference.

Lottie and I stood, awkward and shaky as if to acknowledge how far we were from Enlightenment, not to mention Re-Enlightenment.

"So tomorrow, we'll take any and all questions," Larry said, "and give you answers that just might tremble your neural pathways."

The audience finally broke into heartfelt cheers and applause. Laughing, Larry leaned sideways at the podium to match his enormous image overhead.

Under the spell of some ironclad yet breezy sense of security—freedom—Larry, Lottie, and I strolled into the warm evening from the university ballroom down to the Cherry Creek greenway. A pathway followed the creek, flowing between the campus and downtown. Domed lights lit our way below the sports arena and performing arts center, old railyards, creekside loft balconies, and the amusement park.

After a stroll we reached the point where Cherry Creek joined the South Platte River, feeble October flows spiked by last night's storm. In our formal finery, we plopped ourselves on a grassy hill overlooking Denver's birthplace, this confluence of two streams. "We ought to feel inspired by the pioneers," Lottie said, seated, legs crossed, between Larry and me. She flung back Nick's silver scarf with mock grandeur. "It took vision to see that this flyswat mining-supply camp would survive, let alone become a metropolis."

Larry sat, spreading his legs and loosening his bow tie. "But the visionaries were just gold-fever wannabes and smelly old prospectors."

"All right," Lottie said. "But there was nothing wrong with prospectors. They broke rock to see what was underneath. They panned for precious metals, crouching in cold streams for days on end, existing on hope."

As Lottie locked her arms in mine and Larry's, I remembered her at the Great Divide. Straddling a Wyoming stream, teaching Brandy where her spit would go, Pacific or Atlantic.

I thought of Nick, who'd paid no heed to the fate of Denver's waterways, who'd regarded them as barriers to crosstown speed, his life hounded to its halt in Cherry Creek's rapids. Below us, trapped in the kayak chute's artificial barriers, the muddy river's rowdy wave trails spewed like those caught in the wheels of Nick's doomed Austin-Healey.

Pressing each of our legs, Lottie heaved herself up. "It's so wonderful to breathe free again, isn't it, guys?" Turning back to Larry and me with a smile, she wandered alone toward the concrete embankment at the river's edge. Outlined against the water's reflected glow, she raised the scarf between both hands, then clutched it close as she cocked her head, watching the river flow.

I knew Nick surged through her thoughts, too. Our shock and grief had connected us and driven our whole absurd "rescue" operation. But looking at Lottie's solitary, silhouetted form, I realized she had attempted to rescue more than one clueless wonder. She had cast me from my post-Nick semicoma, the shiftless role I'd assigned myself, understudy to my own self-cancelled life. She'd thought that I was better than I was, inspiring me to perform my supporting but indispensable role.

Larry took my hand. It hit me that the League was so shadowy because it was just playful code for a loose association of all those existing on hope, allies who believe humane action really can heal the insane injuries we've inflicted on earth and each other. I had supposedly been inducted into the League last night, but in reality, anyone could join at any moment, anywhere.

I pressed Larry's fingers into mine and studied city lights whirling in a side pool. The South Platte River took its own absurd, clueless quest north into Nebraska to reach the Gulf of Mexico, south by southeast. I imagined a drop of water, born in summit snowmelt, pulsing through high-country meadows and wildcat canyons, roiling across the Plains until it gushed into the Mississippi. Always surging forward, that solitary drop would join the deep leagues of the all-accepting, open sea.

Tugging me back to land, Larry shuffled closer. He whispered, "Where do we go from here?" as Lottie turned away from the river and hurried toward us, the silver scarf stretched over her head. She crouched in front of us, laughing as she looped it around our necks. The scarf bound Larry and I even closer, lassoed into a kiss.